GRANTED

John David Anderson

WALDEN POND PRESS
An Imprint of HarperCollins*Publishers*

Walden Pond Press is an imprint of HarperCollins Publishers.
Walden Pond Press and the skipping stone logo are trademarks and
registered trademarks of Walden Media, LLC.

Granted

Library of Congress Control Number: 2017939011
ISBN 978-0-06-264386-5

18 19 20 21 22   CG/LSCH   10 9 8 7 6 5 4 3 2 1

First Edition

To those who made it home. And those who haven't yet.

The last time you blew out your birthday candles, what did you wish for?

Did you blow them all out on the first breath? It doesn't count otherwise. Also, do not let your brother or sister help you; at best they will waste your wish. At worst they will steal it for themselves.

Same for dandelions—the one-breath rule—or else the wish won't fly. It's harder than you think, getting all those seeds off in one huff. Harder than candles on a cake. If you can't manage it, though, don't worry. There are a dozen more ways to make a wish. A quarter flipped into a fountain. A penny dropped down a well. Some might tell you that bigger coins make stronger wishes, but that's simply not true. A silver dollar or even a gold doubloon doesn't increase the chances you'll get what you want. Your dollar is better spent on gumballs or ice cream; use a nickel instead. Wishes aren't for sale to the highest bidder.

A shooting star (or maybe just an airplane passing overhead—it's hard to tell), what was that wish for? You needn't wait for one to streak by. The truth is, any star will do, so long as it's the first one you spot. Just don't sing the song, you know the one—it grates on the nerves after a while.

Maybe you keep a wishing stone in your jacket pocket, rubbed smooth by time and worry, the circle of your thumb going round and round as you shut your eyes and hope. Don't. You're better off skipping that stone across a lake. Wishes are temporary things. You can't just keep them in your coat and ask for them whenever you please. That would be unfair— and the wish-granting process is nothing if not fair.

Wishes are made in moments of wonder and desperation. Wishes are prayers without a salutation and minus an *amen*.

Did you know that you can wish on a horse? But it has to be all white or all black, no patches or spots. A pony will do in a pinch. And contrary to popular opinion, you do not have to see its tail.

Or wait until Thanksgiving, and dig through the picked-clean carcass of that cooked bird to find the bone, shaped nothing like a wish (for wishes have no shape except the one you give them). Looking more like a pair of tweezers, or a *U* that's trying very hard to become a *V*. The bigger half is the one that counts, of course, and no fair breaking it all by yourself. Wishing is competitive. There's only so much magic to go around.

And less and less as time goes by, it seems.

Feathers, yawns, and falling leaves. Acorns and necklace clasps. Four-leaf clovers (yes, they can be wished on, but no, they aren't good luck—neither are rabbit's feet, at least not for the rabbit).

Eyelashes? Yes. But only if they fall out on their own and you happen to catch them on your fingertip. Plucked lashes are instantly disqualified.

The first rainbow of spring, spotted through the window of your moving car. You point it out and your mother tells you to make a wish on it. Go ahead. But keep it to yourself. Telling ruins it. And it makes Mom feel bad if she knows it will never come true.

Though she can't possibly know. Not for certain. Even though the odds are against you.

Some wishes do get granted, just not near as many as before. Perhaps you are partly to blame for that. Or maybe it's some fault in the system.

Or maybe that's just how-it-has-to-be.

The last time you blew out your candles, what did you wish for?

And did you get it?

1

The lottery was in less than an hour, and Ophelia still hadn't waxed her wings.

Her hair—as cobalt blue as the flower she was born from and just as delicate and fine—was brushed, of course, her bangs pinned back. Her uniform pressed, buttons polished, collar cinched so tight it was hard to swallow. Her boots showed little sign of wear—all the scuffs carefully buffed away—but her wings she simply hadn't gotten to yet.

Probably not an issue. There were no long-distance flights in her future, after all. But if anything could be said of Ophelia Delphinium Fidgets, it would be that she was always prepared, that she worried over every minor detail.

Some fairies called her fussy. She preferred the word *meticulous*.

When she was born—pulled from the dense cluster of dew-dropped flowers in Mrs. Haverstack's back garden—she looked at her Founder and immediately brushed the pollen grains off his shoulder. They bothered her, sitting there, impertinent and messy.

Tidy. That's how she liked things.

At the age of nearly nothing she was all about the particulars. Nothing out of place for this fairy. Never. That's how she'd risen in the ranks so quickly, the youngest ever to graduate from the Academy. Top marks. A certified field agent at the age of four.

A Granter.

Which is why it was a little bothersome to her that she wasn't ready for work yet. Normally she would be sitting in her chair by now, on her third bowl of honeyed oats, staring at the clock, waiting for Charlie to pick her up so they could commute to work. Not that she needed the company. He was the one who insisted; Ophelia's cottage in the Tree Tops was on his way.

Ophelia didn't mind being alone, at least most days. Granters almost always flew solo. Sometimes it's best if you have to count only on yourself, even if it means you will have only yourself to blame.

She reached into her cabinet and pulled out her jar of liquid beeswax and the bit of cotton that she used to spread it, cautious not to get the stuff on her fingers. It was nearly impossible to wash off completely and made your skin slicker than snot. For the rest of the morning she would fumble at door handles and have things slip out of her hands if she wasn't careful.

On wings, though, it did wonders. Especially if you were traveling in bad weather. Not that she would know. It had been nearly a year since she'd graduated, and in that time she'd made only brief forays outside the Haven—training exercises mostly, some cleanup detail, but no actual missions. Not the thing she had trained for.

Ophelia Delphinium Fidgets was a Granter, yes. But she still hadn't made her first wish come true.

2

She was Delphinium first. Fidgets second. Ophelia third.

When fairies are born (North American fairies, at least), they are given their names in stages, not all at once. The middle is always the first—fairy ritual is seldom logical—and is simply the name of the flower, bush, or tree they are born from. For fairies, as everyone knows, are creatures of nature in the most intimate sense, sprung from magic and beauty and wisdom—and even more specifically sprouted from lilacs, pine trees, and mulberry bushes (though there were several fairies, Ophelia thought, who must have sprung from tree stumps or boulders for all the sense they had). A leaf unfurls, a flower's petals part, and there, uncurling alongside and stretching his or her sun-blessed limbs, is a fairy in the flesh.

Perhaps you've seen it happen, though you wouldn't know it. Fairies are nothing if not stealthy. Stealthy and quick-witted.

And a touch mischievous.

The flower or tree a fairy springs from undoubtedly says something about her, contributes to her personality. Fairies emerge from redwood trees a little stouter than those stemming from phlox. Pansy-plucked fairies have a more delicate disposition than those born from bamboo.

Certain plants are more likely to harbor fairies in them as well. There are probably more fairies with the middle name of Rose than any other (Ophelia could count six in her department alone). Several with the middle name of Lily. Lots of Tulips and Violets and Daffodils. Quite a few Oaks and Maples and Birches.

Delphinium was a rare middle name for a fairy, which suited Ophelia just fine.

A fairy's *last* name is given by his or her Founder, the fairy who came to the outside world and brought the newborn sprite back to the Haven before she could be eaten by a goshawk or snatched by a fox or—worst of all—spotted by a prying human. The Founders are responsible for overseeing the care of new fairies, at least until they were able to care for themselves (which isn't that long, as fairies are naturally precocious and grow up quickly). As such, Founders are the first to see a new fairy's personality surface, to pick up on her quirks and ticks, her penchants and predilections. Often that's where a last name comes from.

Ophelia's Founder immediately noticed her messing with

his buttons and baubles, tugging on the loose threads of his uniform, wriggling and writhing in his arms. She couldn't be still—even as a newborn—and so it didn't take him long to figure what her last name should be. "Fidgety little worm, this one," he said when he returned to the Haven, bringing her home.

And so she was: Delphinium Fidgets.

As for her *first* name—that was simply a matter of luck. A fairy's first name was drawn out of a hat. Though not a literal hat. That's just to say that it was chosen completely at random.

More and more things are like that in the Haven, much to some fairies' dismay.

Ophelia felt fortunate to have her name. She liked the way the *f* sounds crashed together, like a hard rain. She liked the mouthfulness of it—a name so long you almost had to take a breath in between. Better than May Rose Crier, the fairy who ran the switchboards and was prone to sobbing jags. And much better than Argus Fothergilla Gaspasser. His Founder must have been sensitive to smells to have given Argus such an unfortunate moniker, though Ophelia could affirm from experience that his last name was well earned. Gus Gaspasser could clear a room faster than you could wish for a breath of fresh air.

Then there was Billy Lily Shrill, who you could hear from a mile away.

Sometimes a name could tell you most everything you

needed to know about a fairy. Sometimes it just gave you a hint.

Like Charlie.

Charlie Rhododendron Whistler. It was also a bit of a mouthful, Ophelia admitted, though it didn't have quite the same ring as her own.

He was a bit of a *hand*ful.

That's sort of why she liked him.

3

H e was late, as usual.

She could hear him outside the door. Fairies have exceptional hearing, like many small creatures of nature—bats and rats and owls and cats. Their ears pointed slightly at the tips, arced forward, sticking out like birch tree leaves. Ophelia's ears were especially large for her head—maybe too much, taking away from the otherwise perfect symmetry of her face. She frankly didn't care for them.

"Are you ready?" Charlie called out as he knocked. "The lottery starts in less than a tock."

Ophelia looked at the maple-wood clock on her mantel, at the little tocker hand so close to the eight already, the longer, faster ticker marching reliably along. "*You're* the reason we're late," she shouted, putting down her empty bowl. Every morning he insisted on picking her up. Every morning she shouted that he was responsible for their tardiness. Every morning they had to fly extra fast to make it to work on time. But she didn't mind that part; she liked flying fast.

Ophelia opened the door and found her colleague and friend—perhaps her only *real* friend—disheveled as usual, his bright pink hair in ruffled tufts, his acorn-hewed skin chafed rosy from the wind. She licked two fingers and reached up to try to smooth out a particularly ornery cowlick in front, but it wouldn't lie flat. Nothing about Charlie was easily tamed.

"Would you please just leave it alone," he told her, batting her hands away. "You aren't my Founder."

"If I was I would have named you Charlie Rhododendron Scruffrat." She looked him over. Uniform wrinkled and untucked. Stain on his pants. Even his wings looked ragged. "When's the last time you bothered to polish those boots?"

"When's the last time you spent the day in your pajamas sitting on your porch, drinking wine, burping out loud, and watching the clouds slink by?" he asked back.

"Never."

"Exactly. And you don't know what you're missing."

"And *you* don't know what a hairbrush is for," Ophelia chided.

"I know what it's *for*. I just don't happen to own one, is all." He was mocking her, she knew. It was like this every time he showed up at her door. She would make some weak attempt to straighten him out, and he would poke fun at her

12

dustless bookshelves and trimmed eyebrows. "I like what you've done with the place," he said, eyeing her mostly empty cottage, the clean, bare walls, the carefully polished wood furniture. "What's this hard stuff beneath my feet again?"

"It's called the floor," Ophelia quipped. "You have one at your house, too, underneath all the junk. Come on."

Ophelia stepped outside and looked at the sky. Just below the Tree Tops it was cloudy, a little overcast, but above it was bright and blue and warm. A perfect day for flying. All around her the other fairies of the Haven were taking wing, all dressed in the uniform of their respective guild. Builders and Growers. Gatherers and Harvesters. Teachers and Bakers and Menders and Makers. Founders and Whisperers and Alchemists, but only a few Granters. In fact, Ophelia and Charlie were the only two in this part of the Tops. The thought gave her a shiver of pride, as it always did. To be a Granter was the greatest thing a fairy could aspire to. Every other fairy relied on the Granters to keep the magic flowing and, in turn, to keep the Haven safe. It was the most noble of occupations.

Provided you ever got around to doing your job.

Ophelia closed and locked her door. Nobody in the Haven ever stole anything, of course; it was just one more thing for her to be fastidious about. There was little to fret over in the Haven, really. Whatever Mother Nature couldn't provide, the industrious fay folk produced for themselves and then shared without question. Locking her door was simply a matter of

13

habit, part of her morning ritual. Fairies were fond of rituals.

She took a deep breath, picking out the sweet tang of sugar maple trees tinged with a whiff of cinnamon that must be coming from the Baker the next branch over. Nowhere else smelled quite like the Haven either (though admittedly Charlie's cottage had its own peculiar aroma). Despite what she told Charlie, there *were* some days when she thought she could just sit on her porch for hours, breathing it in.

Ophelia's fellow Granter reached into the rugged canvas bag he had slung over his shoulder and removed a pair of goggles that he'd fashioned out of some scavenged glass and a smelted paper clip. Very little in the Haven was 100 percent fairy-made anymore. Those clever humans threw too much good stuff away not to take advantage of it. The goggles made Charlie's pink eyes loom almost twice as large as before. Rose-colored glasses, Ophelia called them. As if he needed to look goofier.

"It feels like a good day," he said. "A lucky day. I think we're going to grant at least fifty wishes today. What do you think?"

Ophelia shrugged. That part wasn't up to her; the Tree would decide, as it always did. She'd be happy to grant just one. She gave her wings a ruffle and then did some stretches, cracking her neck and knuckles. "Bet you can't beat me there."

"Bet you're right," he answered.

Ophelia rolled her eyes, then opened her wings to full bloom, letting the sun warm them for just one moment before launching into the sky. There were only a few sounds she liked better than the sudden stream of wind blasting past her ears on takeoff.

Behind her she could hear the steady hum of Charlie's wings, just barely audible beneath the sprightful, high-pitched melody of his whistling.

4

The sun-blessed, sloping green of the Glade was nearly full by the time they arrived, and Charlie and Ophelia had to squeeze their way through the throng of fairies to get to the front. Every fairy of the Haven was expected to attend the lottery if their responsibilities allowed. For most it was a stand-wherever-you-can affair, but the Granters always took their place at the head of the crowd. It was part of the ceremony, the pomp and circumstance meant to give the proceedings the proper sense of authority and grandeur.

It *was* a grand event, certainly. And Ophelia didn't mind showing off a little (she'd polished her boots, after all), knowing that when the leaves fell and the fortunate few were chosen, *her* guild would be the one to carry out the Great Tree's wishes. Everything in the Haven depended on it. Depended on her.

Okay, so not her *specifically*. But it at least depended on fairies *like* her, and that was something to be proud of.

Ophelia tucked in behind Charlie and took her place at the front. Another advantage of being a Granter: she had an excellent view. She could see the leaders of all the guilds lined up, sitting close together on their wood stump chairs. The crooked stone podium where the Chief would give his remarks.

And the Tree itself.

It was the only truly magical tree in the Haven, though Ophelia's teachers would remind her that all trees were magical in their own way, blessed with patience and beauty and unerring memory. But those others weren't magical in the way the Great Tree was, with its golden-yellow branches so thick with leaves that you could crawl into them and disappear forever. Every morning on first glance Ophelia had to stop and catch her breath—you could actually see the enchanted dust glittering around it, like a million fireflies circling its boughs. A large woven basket sat beside it, to collect the wishes as they fell.

"All right, everyone, settle down, fold your wings in tight, let's try to make space for the latecomers."

Mortimer Magnolia Pouts tapped his gavel to get everyone's attention. His frost-white hair was slicked back and his ghostly silver eyes never seemed to blink as he surveyed the crowd. He had been Chief Founder for nearly forty seasons now—long before Ophelia was born—but you could tell by

17

the pinched lines in his broad forehead and the even deeper trenches at the corners of his mouth that his cycle was coming to its close. Fairies weren't immortal. They were lucky to see two hundred seasons sometimes, and Pouts had seen twice that number. He'd been around to watch the steady decline of magic. To see the number of wishes the fairies granted each day dwindle from hundreds to dozens. But, like the Haven, he endured.

"Before we get started I have a few announcements. First off, there have been more reports of human hikers straying from the trails and stumbling close to the border recently. I'm assured by the Head of Security that our barriers remain strong and that the Haven is safe. However, I ask that you all be on your guard when venturing near the edge. We all recall what happened the last time one of us was spotted."

Ophelia remembered. Just last year a human had gotten lost, roamed too far out into the wilderness. He made it through the mountains and somehow stumbled past the magical protections along the Haven's outer ring. Normally when a human got that close they would suddenly feel a festering dread warning them to turn around and go the other way. There were no posted signs. Not a *Beware* or a *Keep Out*. Just a rustling of leaves, and maybe a glimpse of something slinking through the underbrush and then that sinking sense that one more step in this direction could be your last. And yet this foolish human had ignored the pit in his stomach and kept going, straight through the magic barrier. The Haven had to dispatch a containment team to knock the poor fellow unconscious and drag him twenty miles to the nearest hint of civilization, depositing him outside a bar. When he woke he remembered nothing—not even how the empty bottle had gotten into his hand. Those kinds of close calls were typical for Granters, of course, but only when they were on assignment, where human contact was often unavoidable and other precautions were taken. It wasn't supposed to happen so close to home.

"Also," Pouts continued, "the South American contingent has asked for our assistance with their rainforest problem. Apparently they are short staffed and are having trouble keeping up with their tree-whispering responsibilities; they're simply being chopped down faster than our brothers and sisters can grow them. We are accepting volunteers who are willing to temporarily relocate. Training will be provided."

Charlie leaned over and whispered, "South America? Forget it. You know there are spiders down there big enough to eat guys like us?"

Ophelia shushed him, though she did crack a smile at the thought of Charlie being chased by a giant spider.

"And snakes. Poisonous snakes. Thick as a tree root, some of them," he added.

"Would you stop?" Ophelia hissed, and elbowed him in the ribs for emphasis. "This is important."

"And finally," Pouts said, "just a reminder that the Forty-Eighth Annual Nut Festival is less than five days away."

All right, maybe not *that* important.

"All Haveners are encouraged to donate as many nuts as possible to make sure it's a success. I'm told we are particularly lacking in—cashews, is it?" Pouts looked at one of the other fairies standing to his left, a young girl with bright yellow hair and a nose like a cupboard knob.

"Pistachios," she confirmed. Pouts nodded gravely, as if a shortage of pistachios meant the end of the world.

"Plenty of nuts around here, if you ask me," Charlie quipped. Ophelia elbowed him again. A little harder this time, to make sure it hurt.

Pouts frowned at the crowd. "Pistachios it is. Very well. I will now turn the proceedings over to Mr. Squint."

A hush descended as Barnabus Oleander Squint stepped to the podium. He was the tallest of the fairies in the front—taller than a ripe ear of corn—and he carried himself much differently than Pouts did—angular and proud, shoulders back, chin up. Everything about him seemed to loom large, save for his eyes, which were narrow slits. Always. The running joke was that Squint couldn't see two feet in front of him and yet still always knew what everyone was up to. Anyone who knew him knew his squinting stemmed as much from suspicion as habit. He was cautious and calculating. A strategist. That's what made him good at his job.

Ophelia would know. He was her boss.

Squint squinted down at a piece of paper that had been handed to him and cleared his throat. This was the real reason everyone had been summoned—it had very little to do with cashews or pistachios—and the gravity of the moment wasn't lost on the head of the Granters Guild.

"Yesterday, in the North American territory, an estimated six million wishes were made," he said in a resonant voice that carried over the Glade. Ophelia twitched in her pressed uniform. A murmur coursed through the crowd, but Squint pressed on. "Of those, approximately two hundred thousand were disqualified due to improper procedures, and another four hundred thousand were found unlawful."

Unlawful. Meaning someone somewhere wished for something bad to happen. Ophelia could guess what some of them were. A kid hoping their teacher would come down with the flu on the day of a test. Wishing that their pestering parents would just disappear or that a meteorite would crash into their school. Or, if it was an adult doing the wishing, substitute *ex-husband* for *parents* and *office* for *school*. Most wishes were made by children, but full-grown humans weren't above sometimes spending a penny on the fleeting hope that someone out there might be listening. The first rule of wish granting was the same as it had been for thousands of years, however: honor no wish that would lead to misery, misfortune, or malefaction. The fay were in the business of making the world a better place, after all.

That is, when they weren't so worried about keeping safe their own place within it.

Squint reached up and scratched at his chin. "That still leaves precisely five million, three hundred and ninety-four thousand, two hundred and thirty-four legally honorable wishes, of which, it appears, we are able to grant . . ."

Squint paused; he appeared to scan the page he was reading, double-checking the figures. She wasn't sure, but Ophelia thought she saw the fairy's broad shoulders slump slightly. "Twelve," he finished.

The swarm of fairies was suddenly abuzz, thrumming like a hive of bees.

"That's it? Twelve?" Charlie whispered under his breath, adding a low whistle. "Yesterday it was thirty." Ophelia hushed him again, though she kept her elbows to herself this time. Twelve was low. *Really* low. The number of grantings had gone down steadily over the years—since Ophelia had been born, certainly, and *long* before then—but she could never remember there being so few. It could only mean that the supply of magic had ebbed even further.

So much for Charlie's feel-good kind of day.

"Please, please—settle down," Squint requested, waiting for the humming to subside. "We still have a job to do, so let's do it." He nodded to another fairy—the young one with the golden hair who knew about nut shortages—who took her place in front of the huge tree with its yellow leaves, standing proudly in the center of the Glade.

Twelve, Ophelia thought to herself. Out of so many. Who would even notice twelve wishes being granted? Who would even care? Except she knew the answer. Those twelve people would care—even if they had no idea just how lucky they were, or were *about* to be.

And her own kind would care of course. Every fairy gasping and murmuring in this glade cared deeply. Hence the gasping and murmuring.

"Let the lottery commence," Squint commanded.

The golden-haired fairy spread her wings and threw up her arms. Always the same ritual. The same motions. Ophelia felt one of Charlie's stubby-fingered hands grab hers as every fairy in the Haven watched with waiting breaths.

The Great Tree shuddered. It could grow and shrink as needed, blossom and shed in a heartbeat. Its leaves never changed color or shape, but they increased or decreased in number with each passing day, with every dropped coin, every shooting star. Every earnestly whispered want was up there somewhere.

Today it had exactly 5,394,234 leaves. And it was about to lose twelve of them.

As Ophelia watched, the first leaf drifted down, gently rocking back and forth before landing in the fairy's cupped hands. She read out the name. "Micah Walters."

"Micah Walters," the crowd chanted after her. The first of the fortunate ones. Ophelia recited the name along with the others. She knew nothing else about him. Everything the Granters would need to know was inscribed on that leaf, written in its tiny striations to be translated by the Recorders back at the office. Micah's age. His wish. His location. It would all be read and submitted to the guild and then, eventually, when Micah's wish was granted, entered into the logbooks—another dream fulfilled.

For now, all that mattered was the name.

"Shanaya Everett."

"Shanaya Everett," nearly a thousand fairies repeated.

The leaves fell, one after another, dropping from the impossibly large tree into the young fairy's waiting hands. She read the names and waited for the echo; then she dropped the leaf into a basket with its brothers and sisters. Ophelia counted each leaf as it fell. Fifty years ago, it would have been impossible to keep track. Back when hundreds of wishes were granted each day. It had never been more than that—not since the system had been put in place—but it was still more than a fairy had fingers and toes for.

Still, you make do with what you've got. Twelve wishes were better than none.

The last leaf dropped. The girl caught it and read the name she found there.

"Kasarah Quinn."

"Kasarah Quinn," Ophelia echoed. She liked the name. She hoped Kasarah had wished for something good. Something better than a new car or something smarmy like for some sweaty boy with skater bangs and pouty lips to kiss her. What a waste of a perfectly good wish *that* was. If you wanted a boy to kiss you, Ophelia guessed, all you had to do was ask him.

She was suddenly self-conscious of Charlie's clammy hand

in hers and pulled it free, crossing her arms in front of her.

The girl placed Kasarah's wish with the others, then took the basket over to Squint, who counted them again, just to be sure. He nodded his approval.

Twelve wishes. Twelve assignments. Twelve Granters who would be given permission to go out into the field and make those twelve dreams come true. No way would she be one of them. There were way too many fairies with seniority over her. Charlie had been a Granter for three years before she even joined the guild, and he never got assignments either.

Which meant another day in the office, filing paperwork, studying maps, brushing up on her humanity, biting her nails (what was left of them). She would go work out, maybe. Fly a few laps around the Tree Tops. Maybe get in some self-defense training—though her instructor said she didn't need any more the last time she pinned him to the floor.

Or maybe she would just take the afternoon off and go home and binge on cocoa beans before dusting her walls for the seventeenth time that week.

"Twelve," Charlie said again, not needing to whisper this time as the whole crowd was chattering about the same thing. "Just hope to Haven none of them wished for world peace again."

"That's the spirit," Ophelia remarked, but she knew what he meant. Another example of a wasted wish—though still better than a sloppy kiss. The problem with world peace was that it never lasted. Yes, if you wished for it and your wish was chosen, the Granters would make it happen, but for a fleeting moment only, and then the world went back to its usual routine. The last time that particular wish was granted it lasted for all of forty heartbeats (and fairy heartbeats at that, which are considerably faster). Less than a minute with no war, no bloodshed, no beating or bullying. Nobody really noticed.

That was the thing about humans, Ophelia knew. They spent their whole lives *wanting*. And that wanting caused them to do terrible things to one another. It was a shame. It would be so much easier, she thought, if we could just grant *every* wish. Then, maybe, the people who made them wouldn't fight so much.

But it wasn't possible to grant every wish.

It was getting harder and harder to grant any at all.

5

The Great Tree was the center of the Haven and the pillar upon which the whole fairy way of life rested. It had loomed over the Glade since long before Ophelia's Founding Day. It was older than most of the fairies who lived in the Haven, in fact.

But it hadn't been there from the beginning.

The history books told of a time when the fairies themselves, and not the Great Tree, decided which wishes to grant, based on their own whims and heart-whispers. Back then, the fay folk roamed the countryside freely, hiding from humans but still gleefully meddling in their affairs. It was a time when there were still plenty of places *to* hide and the Haven was little more than a gathering ground, a secluded spot for Ophelia's ancestors to come and make music and revel in shared tales of mischief and wonder, swapping stories of dreams fulfilled and narrow escapes.

That was centuries ago, however. So many seasons had passed since. So much had changed. *Humans* had changed. They expanded, exploded, built vast cities connected by seemingly infinite stretches of road, crossing and curving like the veins on a leaf. They spread like moss on a wet rock, replacing forests with foundries, wildflowers with wheat stalks, wooded trails with iron rails. They created machines and factories that ate fire and belched smoke. They took to the mountains, the oceans, the skies.

And they became more and more dangerous. With their flashing cameras and their printed papers and their insatiable need to know *everything*, uncover every secret, catalog every creature, explain every mystery.

The fay folk felt it, this sea swell, this shift. Magic and wonder began to drain from the world. The amount of dust produced by the fairy springs started to diminish. Before long, it seemed as if their entire way of life was in danger, foretelling a world where there was no such thing as their kind.

So they retreated, holed up in their beautiful Havens, securing their borders with enchantments designed to keep humans out. A system was put into place to carefully regulate the use of what magic remained, to make certain that enough wishes were granted to produce the magic dust needed to preserve the Haven and protect the fairies who lived there. Enough wishes granted today to ensure that more could be tomorrow.

And a guild of Granters specially trained to make those wishes come true.

But which wishes? Because in a world of waning wonder, there was no way to grant them all, or half, or even a *hundred-thousandth*. In the time it took to argue over which dreams should come true and which shouldn't, the magic could simply dry up, leaving them with no dust at all. And so, generations ago, the most talented Whisperers among the fay sang their sweet songs and the Great Trees were born across the world, shooting from seedlings to saplings to giants in less than a day. The Trees had their roots buried deep into the lines of magic that ran along the forests and into the mountains beneath them, tapping into every dream and desire. And a leaf dropped from a Great Tree's boughs constituted a promise to the one who wished it there.

There was no debate. The Trees were impartial. The leaves fell at random. It was, most agreed, the *fairest* way.

There were some who grumbled—often under their breath and only with those who they knew shared their opinions— that wishes should not be granted based on the luck of the draw. But even the naysayers couldn't deny that the system worked. It kept them safe for a hundred years. It preserved their way of life. Whether they were right or wrong, wishes could be argued over afterward, over cups of tea and cookies, enjoyed in a Haven made possible by the fact that any wishes were granted at all.

6

Ophelia was still mulling over the problem with world peace as she and Charlie meandered back through the Tree Tops, listening to the morning song of the vireos and stopping by the bakery for one of Seldana Snowbell Shiver's delicious cranberry scones before heading to work. As they entered the Tower, Ophelia stopped to brush the cranberry crumbles off the front of Charlie's uniform.

Grant Tower was the tallest tree in the Haven (if not the most exalted), with a girth the size of a small pond and a seemingly endless ladder of branches marching clear up to the clouds. It was the third-biggest tree in all the northern hemisphere, in fact, though none of the humans who studied such things even knew it existed, clumped as it was in a dense forest at the top of a mountain. Nor did they know that it was almost completely hollow, or that a tribe of fairies used it as their primary base of covert wish-granting operations. The Whisperers had been encouraging the old oak's growth for hundreds of years, and it was still adding new floors. The Builders had recently installed a café on the 147th. They served mocha lattes. Ophelia was a frequent visitor.

When she and Charlie arrived at the Tower, there was already a cluster of Granters in the office, standing in between desks, discussing the results of the morning's lottery. The general mood seemed glum, especially for a huddle of fairies.

Adelia Helleborus Brash was doing most of the talking, which came as no surprise.

"Nuts to that! Even during the *last* Great Magical Depression we were still granting a hundred wishes a day. Now it's twelve? *Twelve?* This is unheard-of. Since when has there been only enough magic to grant twelve wishes? I think the Great Tree is off its roots."

"Don't go knocking the Tree. We all know the reason. There's simply no imagination anymore," Tabbie Birch Smiley said with no trace of a smile at all. "No imagination, no wonder. No wonder, no magic. Simple as that. The humans have only themselves to blame."

Nothing was as simple as that, Ophelia knew, but Tabbie had a point. Magic was self-sustaining. The more people believed in it, the more there was to go around. Of course, it worked the other way, too. And it had been working *that* way for a while.

"I blame the internet," Gandry Geranium Gurgles said,

which also didn't come as a surprise. Ever since he'd heard about it, Gandry had blamed the internet for everything, even the mysterious rash under his right wing joint. Ophelia was fairly certain he didn't have the foggiest idea what the internet even did. She wasn't too sure herself, but it probably didn't cause fairy rashes. Odds are he'd brushed up against some poison oak again.

"But don't you think if people truly stopped imagining, they'd also stop making wishes?" Benjamin P. Query asked. The *P* was for Peony, though Benjamin didn't like to be called by his full name. Apparently somebody made a joke once that his middle name was actually Pee-on-me, and Ben hadn't forgotten.

"Of course they'll keep wishing—because it doesn't cost them anything. But they don't really think they'll come true, most of them," Tabbie replied. "*That's* the problem. They don't *believe*."

Actually, Ophelia knew, nobody was exactly sure *what* the problem was, why the amount of magic in the world had dwindled so, only that it *was* a problem. Every department was strapped for dust. It was a matter of supply and demand. Wishes required magic to grant, and regulating the number of wishes that came true was the only way they knew how to keep things in balance, to keep the whole system up and running.

"What do you think, Ophelia?" Benjamin said, pulling her and Charlie into the circle, but before she had a chance to answer, Rebecca Willow Whiner, the top agent in their section, burst through the door on the other side of the trunk, waving a sheet of paper.

"Just got my assignment," she huffed. She must have come straight from Squint's office. She didn't look pleased, though in all honesty, Ophelia couldn't remember the last time she'd seen Whiner look happy about anything.

"Brandon Orten. Age thirteen. Wants a frothing PlayStation. Can you believe it?" Rebecca rattled her paper in everybody's face, her own pudgy face growing pinker by the second. "Probably a blue million kids out there hoping that their parents get back together or that their grandmother gets out of the hospital or that somebody would save the everloving whales for Haven's sake, and I get a spoiled little twerp jonesing for a PlayStation. I mean—why couldn't it have at least been a kitten? Who doesn't like kittens?"

Tabbie raised her hand. She'd been bitten by a cat once.

"What's a play station?" Ophelia asked before Benjamin could get around to it. It was part of her job to keep current on human culture, she knew, but frankly there was just too much. Only yesterday she'd learned that a Super Bowl was not a fancy serving dish.

"It's a stupid toy," Rebecca said with a pout. "One of their fancy electromagizzers with the buttons and batteries and such."

"They're actually kind of fun," Charlie whispered to Ophelia. "I tinkered around with one once."

She flashed him a reproachful look. It was completely against regulations—messing with human things—unless you were a Scavenger. Or it was an emergency. "When was this?"

"Before your time," Charlie answered. "The house was empty. I'd already found the wishbone and performed the granting, so I decided to look around. It helps to know what the kids are into these days."

"You're impossible," she said.

"I'm thorough," he countered.

"Thoroughly impossible."

Rebecca was still griping about her assignment. She had reached a fevered pitch. "I'm not going," she concluded. "Forget it. Squint can take this wish and shove it back up into the Tree for all I care. It's not worth the effort, and it's *certainly* not worth the magic. It's not even the kid's birthday!"

"I'll go," Ophelia said.

The other fairies looked at her, including Charlie. She could practically *feel* their eyes appraising her. The youngest of the bunch. The rookie. Talented but untested. Not a single granting to her name. She stood up straighter.

"What? I'm just saying, if she doesn't want to, I'll do it. What difference does it make? A wish is a wish." *Whatever it takes to finally get out there*, she thought. To get out there and *do* something.

Rebecca rolled her eyes and sighed dramatically. "Forget it, Fidgets. It's fine. I'll go. I'm not sure you could handle it."

Ophelia felt her cheeks flush. Before she could come to her

own defense, Charlie piped in. "At least she wouldn't moan about it the whole time."

"What's it to you, Whistler?" Rebecca shot back. "I'm just saying what we're all thinking. This whole lottery thing isn't working. It's not good for us. It's not good for them. I just don't see why we can't be a little more selective."

"Because that's not how the system works," a deep voice called out.

Ophelia turned with the rest of the fairies to see Squint standing in the doorway, tall enough that he had to hunch over to fit. He'd overheard them, obviously, or been spying on them perhaps. Sound carries easily in a giant hollow tree, even to his office two floors up.

"There's no way we could all agree on whose wishes get granted and whose do not," he continued. "The Tree's selections are calibrated to use a precise amount of magic and produce a precise amount of magic. It is that very magic that protects the Haven from ruin, need I remind you. And we can't jeopardize our safety, our very livelihood, with a potential misuse or waste of it. If you have a problem with your assignment, Agent Whiner, I'm sure I can find another Granter who would be willing to fulfill it." Squint's voice *sounded* pleasant enough, but it barely masked the threat underneath. Even with his namesake expression, Ophelia could tell he was staring straight at Rebecca.

The fairy carefully folded her paper and shook her head. "No, sir. No problem. I was just going to prep right now."

Rebecca dug her chin into her chest. Squint stared down the rest of the Granters until they dispersed as well, getting back to work. Ophelia started for her desk when she heard her name called.

"Fidgets," Squint said, his tone none too friendly. "I'd like to see you in my office. Now."

"Yes, sir," Ophelia said, nodding as Squint turned to go.

"What's that about?" Charlie whispered to her.

Ophelia shook her head. She didn't know, but she felt a seed of excitement planted in her gut. A tiny seed buried deep under a huge mountain of worry.

"It's okay. It's not like he's going to *fire* you. You haven't done anything," Charlie assured her.

"Exactly," she said.

That was the problem.

7

As acting Chief of the Granters Guild, Barnabus Squint had almost an entire floor of the Tower to himself, set along one of its heftiest branches. Ophelia had been in his office for group meetings, debriefings, general procedural talk, but had never been summoned there by herself. He motioned for her to sit down as she stepped through the carved archway.

The engraving just above it read, *Expect Nothing, Anticipate Everything.* Ophelia wasn't sure what to *expect* from this meeting with Squint, but she was *anticipating* the worst.

The office was spacious and clean, the polar opposite of Charlie's cubicle downstairs. All of Squint's furniture was made of polished cedar or pine. Several Builders had transitioned to work more in metals, especially with the increased loads of scrap brought in from the outside world by the

Scavengers. Some had even started branching out and using the newfangled materials that the Alchemists had cooked up, but Squint obviously preferred old-style, all-wood craftsmanship. As such, the chair Ophelia sat in was ornately carved, exquisitely beautiful, and butt-numbingly uncomfortable.

"I'd like to know where you stand, Miss Fidgets," Squint said.

Ophelia looked down at her feet, tucked between the legs of her chair. Hadn't he asked her to sit? And weren't they supposed to make small talk first? Discuss the pistachio shortage, perhaps? Leave it to Squint to cut straight to the core. "Excuse me, sir?"

"Rebecca's assignment. The lottery selection. Brandon Orten's wish. Do you agree that it's a waste, giving this boy a toy? That the magic would be better used on someone else?"

It felt like a trick question. Was Squint testing her? Probably. She would have to be careful. She took a deep breath and spoke hesitantly. "I'm not sure it matters what I think, sir. It's not my wish to grant."

Squint frowned at her. "Yes, but I want to know. Is it a waste of our time, our resources, to get some kid who has probably not had a single care in his life something he really doesn't need when there are so many other wishes out there worthy of our attention?"

Ophelia squirmed in her seat, trying to keep her wings from fluttering. Squint was shrewd. As smart as any fairy Ophelia had ever met. Like her, he'd graduated top of his class, oh so many seasons ago. Maybe that's why she assumed he was also a stickler like her. A rule follower. But maybe not. Maybe he was hinting at something.

Squint waited for an answer, tapping his fingers on the highly buffed desk, which offered a distorted reflection of Ophelia's pinched face and pursed lips. *Did* she think it was a waste? Imagine the look on that kid's face when he opens his door and finds his playthingamabob waiting for him. It would make him happy—there was no question. And that was what they were in business for, wasn't it? That was their mission. To bring a little bit of wonder and awe back into a world that was steadily losing it.

Then again, maybe Brandon Orten would be plenty happy enough without it. She didn't know anything about the kid— except that he was lucky to have been chosen in the first place. Exceptionally lucky.

"I think . . ." Ophelia said, trying to look anywhere but across the desk. "I think it's wonderful when any wish gets granted. Besides," she added, swallowing thickly, "it's not my call. That's how the leaves fall. I just do my job."

It was a generic answer, she knew, but it seemed to satisfy Squint, who leaned back in his own even more uncomfortable-looking chair. "Exactly," he said. "That's how the leaves fall. Fidgets, I've been acting Chief of the Granters Guild for twelve years now—almost fifty seasons. Much longer than you've been alive. And in that time, do you know how many wishes this guild has failed to grant?"

Ophelia knew the answer. Everyone knew the answer. It was posted on a huge sign the moment you walked into the first floor of Grant Tower. "Zero, sir."

Squint made a goose egg with one hand. "That's right. *Zero.* Not a single missed wish. And do you know how we've managed such a feat?"

Ophelia figured it probably had to do with there being so few wishes granted anymore. After all, it's easier to get twelve right than a hundred or two hundred. The more wishes you grant, the greater your chance of having something go wrong. And there were so many things that *could* go wrong. But she guessed this wasn't the right answer either, so she kept quiet and waited for him to tell her.

"It's because I follow the code and do exactly what's asked of me. We have rules for a reason, Fidgets. Something goes wrong out there, at the very least it's a waste of perfectly good magic. *Rare* magic that we can ill afford to lose. At the worst. Well—you don't need me telling you what the worst-case scenario is."

She didn't. But of course he told her anyway.

"Magic is a tenuous and temperamental thing, its effects far-reaching and unpredictable. We have not failed to grant a single wish because doing so would constitute more than a broken promise—though that would be bad enough. It could result in a complete breakdown of the system we've created. A system put in place specifically to protect what little bit of the world we fairies have left to live upon. There's no room for error here."

40

"I understand, sir." She knew the Granter's Code of Conduct better than anyone. She'd studied it over and over. She could recite it word for word. Which made her wonder why she was sitting here, getting an earful from Squint, when she hadn't even been given the chance to *follow* the rules, let alone break them.

"Tell me, Fidgets, how long has it been since you've been beyond the border?"

The last time Ophelia had ventured outside the Haven was a full season ago, a training exercise that lasted less than a day. She was on a team practicing covert operations, how to blend in so the humans couldn't spot you in case your camo ran out. It mostly involved hiding under bushes or, in moments of desperation, inside mailboxes. "It's been a while, sir," she admitted.

"And the last time you went out solo?"

Ophelia didn't need to answer that. Squint was the head of the guild. He was the one who assigned every mission. Her silence made his point for him.

"It's a dangerous place." Squint sighed. "I mean, it's always been dangerous for our kind, but it's only gotten worse. Everything moves so fast. Cars. Planes. Helicopters. Have you ever seen a helicopter, Fidgets?"

"Only in the Archives," she admitted. The guild kept hundreds of books about the human world for fairies to study, to learn more about their behavior and environment before they ventured out to face it. The ones with lots of pictures were

41

best. She remembered seeing a photo of a helicopter in mid-flight; it reminded her of a deformed hummingbird with a swollen head and a funky tail. Hardly dangerous, but that was just a picture on a page.

"Well, I hope you never get close to one," Squint huffed. "We had a Granter nearly get sucked into the blades once. Barely escaped with his life. And that's hardly the greatest threat. Fairies who go beyond the border regularly know that things aren't as clear-cut as they seem here in the Haven. You have to make choices out there. Deal with things you never could have predicted. It takes a certain kind of fairy to be a Granter. A certain disposition. Let's face it, Fidgets, most of our kind are content to stay here, safely tucked behind the barrier, away from the chaotic outside world. They think of humans the same way humans think of us—as stories. Myths. Larger than life. They don't know what it's really like. Not every fairy can handle it. Most can't." Squint paused, frowning at her.

"What are you saying, sir?" Ophelia asked, suddenly feeling her stomach tighten. Was she actually being fired? Or demoted? Transferred to another guild? She couldn't think of any others she'd be happy with. She wasn't really the building type. She didn't want to teach. She absolutely *sucked* at baking. She'd once nearly set her house on fire, not to mention the tree it sat on top of and all the other houses and trees along with it just trying to make a cupcake for Charlie's Founding Day. She'd never pictured herself anywhere but here.

Squint wove his fingers together and leaned in. "I'm saying that there comes a time when every fairy is tested, forced to show her true mettle. We try to put it off for a while, hoping the initiate absorbs some of the wisdom and knowledge of her fellow fairies without being sent beyond the border. But at some point every Granter eventually gets her wish."

Suddenly it hit her. Ophelia sat very still, determined to control herself, to look professional. Squint opened his top drawer and removed a piece of paper, sliding it across the desk. There was a name at the top, next to the word *Wishmaker.*

The name was *Kasarah Quinn.*

And below that, another name, next to the word *Granter.*

Ophelia Delphinium Fidgets.

She stared at it for a moment, biting her lip, then looked back up at Squint. She couldn't help it.

She squeaked.

A high-pitched, fist-clinched, tremble-bodied squeak. A little *meep!* like a startled mouse might make. Then she quickly regained her composure, straightening herself in her seat. She cleared her throat. "Thank you, sir."

"Congratulations on your first assignment," the head of the Granters Guild said. "Now don't screw it up."

8

It was easier said than done.

The not-screwing-up.

If her training at the Academy had taught Ophelia anything, it was that being a Granter was not just the most important job in all of faydom; it was also the hardest. And not because of the cars and the helicopters and the cameras. Not *just* because of them, anyways.

It was the candles that were tricky.

The candles and the turkey bones. The clovers and the coins.

On the one wing, wish granting was a simple process. The magic itself—gathered in the form of dust from the fairy springs in the Glade and carefully apportioned—did most of the work. *How* a pinch of fairy dust somehow turned a coin or a candle into a first kiss or a diamond ring was quite beyond Ophelia's comprehension. If there was a reasonable explanation, after all, it wouldn't be called magic.

No. The difficulty came in *activating* the magic, triggering its ancient and mysterious and increasingly precious power by performing the Ritual. Or as Charlie called it, "the prickly part." Because activating the magic required access to the *source* of the wish.

And *that* required a fairy brave enough to go out and find it.

Of course there were exceptions. If the wish was made on something fleeting or celestial, say a shooting star or a rainbow, it only required the fairy to go to the wishing *spot*—the place where the Wishmaker stood when they saw said object—and then perform the ritual there. After all, even fairies have learned that shooting stars are just meteors crashing through the Earth's atmosphere and burning to a cinder. And good luck grabbing hold of a rainbow long enough to perform a magic ritual with it; anyone who has chased after one knows how hard they are to pin down.

More complicated were the everyday objects. The coins. The candles. The acorns. The wishbones (though only the bigger halves). These tokens and tidbits were required—*in hand*—to make the wish come true. The bones were especially messy, often requiring a fairy to dig through piles of garbage, shoving their hands into mounds of cold mashed potatoes, congealed gravy, and smeared cranberry jelly. Any Granter with a lick of sense will pack a pair of gloves before heading out the day after Thanksgiving.

As bad as wishbones were, though, they had nothing on

eyelashes. Ever looked for a needle in a haystack? Try searching for an eyelash in a Starbucks. Impossible—or, it would be, except for the fact that a fairy can trace the chosen wish. It speaks to her. Literally, she can hear it being chanted over and over again so long as she listens in just the right way. If she's close enough, she can even see it glow. Fairies are most amazing creatures, after all.

Once you found the source (and maybe cleaned the stuffing off it), *then* it was simply a matter of sprinkling the allotted fairy dust over it and saying the four words that made it so.

Your wish is granted.

Not *So be it*. Not *I hereby do solemnly confer upon you the manifestation of your deepest desires*. Not *Here comes your stupid PlayStation, kid*. Just those four words. The same four words that had been spoken by fairies for hundreds and hundreds of years.

Then, *boom*. The magic happens. Inexplicable, wonderful, and strange.

And *bam*. A new car. Or a kitten. Or approximately five seconds of world peace.

Of course there were a hundred things that could potentially go wrong *between* the moment a wish was chosen and the moment a fairy said those four magic words. Which could explain Squint's parting advice as Ophelia exited his office.

But in *that* moment, all she could do was stare at her name at the top of the sheet and think, *My turn.*

9

"Bicycle," Ophelia exclaimed as she came back to the office, finding Charlie sitting at her desk (probably because his was way too messy and there was nowhere to put up his feet).

"What?"

"Kasarah Quinn," Ophelia explained. "Age thirteen. She wants a new bicycle. Actually, she probably wants a whole mess of things. But she *wished* for a new bicycle." She handed the paper with the assignment—*her* assignment—over to him. He loosed a high, shrill whistle.

"Wow. You actually *got* one? You're going out there? Where is it?"

"Somewhere in Ohio. A little over three hundred miles north." The sheet she'd been handed told her the essentials.

47

Who wished and what for and where from and on what. It even told her why.

"Four tocks flying time," Charlie calculated.

"Closer to three," Ophelia corrected. She was faster than him, after all.

Charlie read over the sheet; Ophelia had already memorized the whole thing on her way down. "The Town Center Mall?"

Ophelia shrugged. "Some outdoor shopping area. They've got a fountain, and the girl had a nickel. Apparently her last bike got stolen. That's all that was in the wish. Oh, and she wants it to be purple."

Ophelia knew this because the Great Tree knew this. Because when Kasarah Quinn, the thirteen-year-old girl from Kettering, Ohio, made her wish, she gave specifics. Most people would just say, *I wish I had a new bike*. Not *I wish I had a new bike because some jerkface stole my last one. And make it purple.* Kasarah wasn't against adding details.

Ophelia pushed Charlie's feet off her desk, then sat in the empty space. She noted the slight droop of his wing, the gray clouds in his eyes. "Well, don't look so excited," she said. There were plenty of fairies Ophelia suspected wouldn't be thrilled for her, either because it wasn't in their nature (Gordon Scowls) or because they'd be jealous of the opportunity. But she expected Charlie, of all fairies, to support her.

"No. Yeah. No. I am," he said, fumble-tongued. "It's just . . ."

Ophelia gave him a long, hard look. "It's because it's lame, isn't it? A boring old bicycle."

48

"It's not that," Charlie said. "It has nothing to do with the wish. The wish is . . ." He chewed his lip for a moment, considering. "It is what it is. We can't change it even if we wanted to." Ophelia's fellow Granter and best friend scratched at his crown of pink hair and took a long, deep breath. "It's just you've never been out there," he spit out finally.

"I've been out there plenty of times," Ophelia said quickly. "I was born out there, remember? Just like you."

"But you've never been *out there* out there. Not like this," Charlie said. "Not on assignment. Not on your own. You don't know what you're getting into."

That seemed pretty bold coming from a fairy who'd been stationed at a cubicle for as long as Ophelia had known him. Yes, she knew he'd been on assignment before—he'd shared stories of his grand adventures in the terror-filled wilds of human civilization—but it had been several seasons since Charlie Whistler had granted a wish. He spent most of his days pushing papers and making jokes and trying to cajole her into taking extra-long coffee breaks. Obviously he was worried for her, but she was plenty nervous enough without his anxious face in hers. "Are you talking about the helicopters? Because Squint already warned me about them."

Charlie looked confused. "*Helicopters?* Who said anything about helicopters? I'm talking about little kids with baseball bats trying to take a thwack at you. I'm talking about semitrucks with windshields as big as your house barreling at you at seventy miles an hour. I'm talking about grizzly bears,

Phee. Griz-a-lee bears." He pounded four times on the desk for emphasis, accidentally moving a pencil that she had perfectly placed next to her coffee cup.

She put it back where it belonged.

"I'm pretty sure they don't have grizzly bears in Ohio," she said. Actually, she didn't know this for sure. They had plenty of black bears around the Haven. You could sometimes hear them barking to each other all the way up in the Tree Tops. They didn't pose a threat to her kind; fairies would serve as little more than an appetizer for them. Foxes were much more dangerous.

"Alligators, then," Charlie countered.

"Florida," Ophelia said, recalling her zoology.

"Siberian tigers."

"I'm going to go out on a limb and say 'Siberia.'"

"Fine. Wombats!" he said, snapping his fingers.

"Australia, I think," Ophelia said after a hesitation. "And I'm *fairly* certain they're vegetarian."

"But you don't know that for sure," Charlie countered. "That's just what you *read*. Have you ever *met* one? Wombats are probably a lot more dangerous than you realize. Just listen to the name. Wom. Bat. They probably ram into you, like *wom*, knocking you out of the sky, and then swoop down to suck your blood."

It was clear that Charlie had never even seen a picture of a wombat. He'd probably slept through his zoology class. And anyway, Ophelia knew Charlie wasn't really worried about wombats. He was trying to fluster her, for some reason, but Ophelia refused to be flustered, at least not by the possibility of bloodsucking marsupials. "What's the big deal? I fly out. Track the wish to this fountain. Find the coin. Say the magic words and *presto*! Kasarah Quinn's got a new set of wheels and I'm back here in the Haven before bedtime."

"You make it sound so easy."

"That's because it *is* so easy."

"It's not." Charlie sighed. "Trust me. It's not. Things get . . . messy out there."

Squint had said pretty much the same thing. Ophelia didn't know Charlie and Squint to agree on a whole lot. This wasn't the Charlie she was used to, the fairy who couldn't take anything seriously, suddenly so solemn. Ophelia tried to remember how many times he said he'd gone out. How many wishes he'd granted. A few dozen, maybe more? He was ten seasons older than her, but he hadn't stepped foot outside the Haven in all the time she'd known him.

Maybe *that* was what had him spooked. It had been too long. He felt out of practice, didn't know what to expect either. Ophelia reached over and tried to tuck a disobedient tuft of pink hair back behind his pointy ear.

"You know me. I don't do 'messy,'" she assured him. "And it's sweet, you worrying about me all of a sudden. But you're starting to annoy me."

"Sorry," he said. "I just wish I could come with you. Be your wingman."

Ophelia pointed to the top of the paper still in his hands. "Except I don't see Charlie Rhododendron Whistler's name anywhere on that sheet of paper. Besides, this is my first assignment. A chance to prove myself to Squint and the rest of the guild, to the rest of the Haven. You know how long I've been waiting for this."

Charlie pouted at her. She arched one blue eyebrow back at him.

"But you *can* help me pick out what to wear."

10

Of the 170 floors of Grant Tower (it's a *very* large tree), the vast majority were devoted to record keeping and general wish management, the basic bureaucracy of fairy life. Filled with clerical fairies who sat in spherical chambers with their wings spread, or hunched over mahogany file cabinets double-checking to make sure the Granters did their business by the books. At least a dozen of *those* floors were filled with actual logbooks stacked one upon another, tracing hundreds of years of wish granting—from the moment a human first thought to make one.

That very first wish was recorded down there somewhere: a man lost in a forest, aching to find his way back home, pulling up a stem of clover and hoping for a miracle before settling down to rest beneath a tree. Little did he know he was in the presence of a magical creature, one of Ophelia's ancestors from eons ago, who took pity on the poor soul. The man woke to find a set of tracks leading him straight out of the forest to salvation. He kept the clover in his pocket, and fairies developed a reputation—some might even call it an addiction—for meddling in human affairs.

Most of the Tower was devoted to such history. Only the top thirty floors were dedicated to the actual tracking and granting of a given day's pick of wishes, including the guild head's office (with its uncomfortable wooden chairs), the solar control room, and the operations center at the very top. Ophelia had been in most of them at one time or another. They held very little in the way of secrets anymore.

Floors 140 to 145 were the exception.

Those floors were home to the Modders—a name they had given themselves. The most eclectic wrangle of fairy folk you could hope to find in the Haven. A mixture of talented Builders and Makers and Alchemists, they were responsible for the creation, maintenance, and repair of the gadgets and gear that every Granter took with her into the field. Everything from wish-intensification goggles to underwater survival suits to wolf repellent—because wolves, unlike bears, were not above having a fairy for breakfast if they could catch one.

They were geniuses (the Modders, not the wolves)—though you wouldn't know it by walking past their office, seeing them compete for who could sit on a spinning acorn top the longest without throwing up or who could stuff the most blueberries into their mouth (six—which is impressive given the size of a fairy's cheeks). Still, when they stopped flitting around and put their minds to their work, the results were just short of magical.

Some of it, in fact, *was* magical. If only a touch.

Most of the tech was borrowed from humans, of course, running on stolen watch batteries or tiny solar-power arrays, adapted for fay purposes, a great deal of it shrunk down, miniaturized to easily fit into fairy hands and clip onto fairy belts. The homing devices that each Granter carried into the field, for example, were mostly electronic in nature, built from discarded cell phone parts, tinkered together with whatever scraps the Salvagers brought back from their weekly forays into the outer world, and then given a bit of flair to make them "fay friendly." The Modders were experts at melding the natural and artificial, taking the human addiction to plastic, silicon, and steel and merging it with the fairy's love for wood and woven hemp. The results were often impractical or sometimes dangerous, but they were always unique. And some of it was essential to any fairy heading out beyond the border.

They were still just contraptions, though. Even with their growing technical know-how, the Modders knew there was no beating fairy dust when it came to getting things done. One pinch of the good stuff could get an agent out of a bad scrape better than three hundred electro-confabulated doo-hickeys. Unfortunately, the Modders were allocated only a scant amount of dust to use. Just enough to give the Granters who went beyond the Haven's borders the necessary tools to do their jobs. To keep the system running. To keep the Haven safe.

Arnold Amaryllis Rolleye met Ophelia by the door wearing a pair of sunglasses that he'd obviously constructed himself. A fashion statement, he called them, but Ophelia guessed he wore them to keep his left eye from being too much of a distraction. It never stopped moving, like water circling a drain.

Today he also wore patched-together denim shorts and corkboard sandals. The writing on his homespun T-shirt warned, *Don't Tinker with My Bells.* Ophelia had no idea what it meant, but she guessed Arnold's friends probably found it hilarious.

"Ophelia Fidgets," he said, welcoming her inside the workshop where he and his fellow geniuses spent most of their waking hours and even some of their non-waking ones. "I figured I'd see you down here soon. Squint sent us the assignment sheet; you're number twelve on the list. This is your first time, right?"

Ophelia's smile faded. Arnold offered much the same look Charlie had given her moments before, equal parts doubt and concern. Why was everyone looking at her that way? It's not as if she hadn't been training for this moment for most of her life. No one looked worried when Rebecca came down to the office complaining about *her* assignment—unless they were worried that she'd never stop talking about it.

"The first of many," Ophelia said. She realized she was messing with one of the polished brass buttons of her shirt and tucked her hands under her arms. Hard to exude confidence when your fingers are fiddling with your uniform.

"Sure. Sure. Just. You know. First time. Can be a little nerve-racking. Am I right?"

"It's the alligators," Charlie muttered from behind her. Ophelia turned and scowled before remembering she was the one who asked him to come along.

"Alligators. Pish posh. We've got them covered," Arnold said with a wave. "Don't worry your pretty blue head over it. We'll get you prepped and ready to fly in no time. Have you given any thought to your loadout?"

Ophelia nodded. How many nights had she spent lying in her hammock, looking up at the stars, imagining what she would bring with her if she ever got an assignment? She had a list for every environment, every conceivable situation, whether she was granting the wish of an Eskimo in the snowbound arctic tundra or that of a man dying of thirst in the parched wasteland of Death Valley.

Kettering, Ohio, was neither of those, of course. It probably wasn't too different from Gatlinburg, the city in which they did most of their training (on account, Charlie said, of it being full of oddities already, so who's going to notice a fairy). That didn't mean she couldn't be prepared. It was spring, the first season, but the air still held a considerable chill, and she was traveling north, where it could be even colder. "I'll need a flight suit," she said. "Thermal. With decent-size pockets."

She'd also need a locator, of course, and a med kit. Some lip

57

balm to prevent chapping. And some granola or peanuts just in case she got hungry during flight. Some twine—always handy—and a roll of the stuff the Modders called Super Silver Sticky Strips, a miraculous substance they pilfered directly from the humans and cut down to fairy size. Probably some goggles to keep the bugs out of her eyes in flight. Charlie would let her borrow his, of course, but she doubted they would fit and they were already filmed with grime.

Oh, and an extra pair of socks. There was a chance for rain mid-flight, and there was nothing Ophelia hated more than the sickening squish of walking around in soaked socks. She rattled off her list to Arnold, who nodded after every item.

"Uh-huh. Extra socks. Gotcha. And what about self-defense?"

"Self-defense?" Ophelia repeated. "Well, I planned on taking a knife. And I'll have camo, of course."

The use of camouflage was standard operating procedure for all fairies leaving the safety of the Haven and was the only magical protection the guild provided. It played tricks on the eyes and boggled the brain. A human could look dead on at a fairy using camo and think she was seeing a dragonfly or a small bird, something natural and beautiful, but certainly not *enchanted*. It was how fairies had stayed virtually undetected for the past hundred years in a world where there were more and more people and fewer places to hide.

Humans feared what they didn't understand, Ophelia knew.

Everything had to be studied, picked apart, dissected and classified and explained—at least that's how Squint put it when he delivered his little speeches about the importance of being secretive and stealthy. Get caught and the whole fairy world might come crashing down. So no matter how much the supply of fairy dust dwindled, Squint still insisted on camouflaging his agents.

Arnold nodded. "Well, sure. Camo will help with the humans, but it's not going to do a thing if you get caught by an owl or attacked by a cheetah. They'll eat you no matter what you look like. It's just in their nature."

"I don't think there are any cheetahs in Ohio," Ophelia said, though she was starting to doubt her knowledge of Midwestern ecology.

"I'm only saying that a human looks at you with your camo on and sees a butterfly or a hummingbird, but there are some creatures that are going to look at you and just see food. They don't care what shape it takes."

"Told ya," Charlie seconded. Charlie and Arnold exchanged looks. Ophelia groaned.

"Fine. Give me some cheetah repellent then."

"Yeah. We don't carry that," Arnold told her with a scratch of his scruffy chin. "But we do have this."

Arnold fluttered to one of a dozen shelves along the wall and came back with a little metal cylinder—like one of those things humans used to store their lip paint—except it had a hole near the top and a little wooden button.

He handed it over and Ophelia immediately started shaking it.

"Whoa! What are you doing?" Arnold shouted, snatching it back and suddenly speaking a whole new language. "Are you serious? That's fully weaponized fairy dust extract, chemically restructured in aerosol form and contained in a high-pressured dispersal unit capable of firing an accurate blast of somnolence-inducing compound at a full twenty feet!"

Ophelia cocked an eyebrow.

"Did *you* catch any of that?" she asked Charlie.

"I got 'feet,'" he said.

"Okay. Basically it's knockout gas," Arnold explained. "One shot of this stuff and it's sweet dreams for anything under a hundred and fifty pounds. More than that might take a couple of hits, but it will still do the job. A real noggin-boggler."

Ophelia studied the canister, careful not to shake it this time. "You mean it puts them to sleep? Does it hurt?" She realized it was a stupid question as soon as she said it. When had fairy dust ever hurt anyone? Then again, she'd never heard of it being weaponized before.

Arnold shook his head. "Naw. Renders them unconscious is all. I mean, I guess if you sprayed somebody while they were standing on the edge of a cliff, it could be dangerous. I'll set you up with two cans. Just, you know, don't use it unless you have to. Consider it a weapon of last resort. We only get a pinch of dust for R-and-D purposes anymore, and I hate to waste it."

Ophelia considered telling him not to bother, to save it for a fairy who might need it. Then she remembered the inscription above Squint's office door. *Anticipate everything.* Maybe a little sleepy spray wouldn't hurt.

"Of course if it *is* a cheetah, it will probably pounce on you and gobble you up before you even get your finger on the button," Arnold mused. "Now let's get you fitted for that flight suit. Got a color in mind?"

Ophelia was distracted, picturing herself getting mauled by a wild animal in the middle of Kettering, Ohio. "What? Oh yes. Color." She was hardly ever out of uniform—the nut-brown tunic and pressed pants with the bloodred stripe running along the leg—but nearly everything else she owned that wasn't the brown and scarlet of the Granters Guild was blue to match her hair and eyes. Blue sweaters and coats and dresses. Blue shoes and socks. Even her jewelry—what little of it she owned—was set with sapphires. The color reminded her of the day she was found.

Except Ophelia's Founding Day was over four years ago now. Today was a different kind of first. It called for a change, something remarkable to mark the occasion. Ophelia looked at Charlie, and he smiled back, his hair still flaring out in every direction.

"Maybe pink," she said.

"Pink?" Arnold questioned. "Not exactly subtle. The birds especially are going to notice you. Even with the camo on you'll look like a fat flying worm."

"You sure do know how to compliment a girl," Ophelia told him.

"I'm just saying. Birds are nasty creatures, the whole lot of 'em. Back me up here, Whistler."

"It's true. A bird ate my grandmother," Charlie said. It was a joke, of course. Fairies didn't have grandmothers. Or mothers. Or fathers or brothers or sisters or cousins. They had Founders who helped to bring them into the world, and after that they had each other.

Ophelia shook her head. She wasn't worried. "If a bird wants to eat me, it's going to have to catch me first," she said.

And good luck with that.

11

Ophelia had a full tock until dustoff, and she wanted to squeeze in a little research before squeezing into her new pink suit. She promised she'd catch up with Charlie before she left.

She blamed him, actually. All this talk of bears and alligators had her spooked.

She fluttered down to the Archives on her beeswaxed wings (not a waste after all, it seemed). Ophelia actually liked it down here. All this information at her fingertips, knowledge collected and compiled over centuries. She liked the musty smell of the paper, even if she scoffed at the layers of dust lining some of the shelves. Ophelia made her way to the section labeled "Known Predators." Here were books about everything that might kill you, sorted by region, complete with recommended precautions, self-defense measures, and relative threat levels. Some also came with graphic pictures that prickled the hairs on your neck.

She sat down with a heavy tome on the native fauna of the Midwestern United States and flipped through the crisp pages. She was right: there were no wild alligators in Ohio. There were rattlesnakes, however. And several species of raptor, including owls and eagles and peregrine falcons, which could clock in at over two hundred miles per hour. Maybe there was some cause to worry. She continued to flip through, making a mental catalog of potential threats: coyotes, copperheads, brown recluse spiders. Who knew Ohio could be such a dangerous place? She had paused on a picture of a bobcat with a dead rabbit dangling from its jaws when a raspy voice called over her shoulder.

"Finding everything you need?"

Ophelia startled, leaping halfway out of her seat. She turned to find Silas Sequoia Snorer hunched beside her, wheezing and leaning on his wooden crutch. Just about everyone knew Silas, an esteemed Archivist and one of the oldest fairies in the Haven. Of course it would be hard *not* to recognize a fairy with only one ear—the other having been chewed off by a red fox when he was young (Ophelia had heard the story three times already). He could still hear fairly well out of the other one, though, provided he remembered to dig out the wax.

"Oh. Yes, sir," Ophelia said. "I was just looking up common predators of the Midwest. Do you happen to know if bobcats pose a significant danger to our kind?"

"Bobcats?" he said. "Bobcats?" The old fairy often repeated things twice, sometimes to make sure he heard correctly, but mostly because he'd forgotten he said it the first time. "Can't say as I ever met one. Met a wind-chime maker named Bob once, though. Least I think his name was Bob. Might have been Frank. Not so good with names anymore, I'm afraid."

Ophelia nodded politely. Talking with Silas was a little bit like flying into a stiff breeze—takes a lot longer to get somewhere and you're usually exhausted by the effort.

"Are you thinking about making a wind chime?" he asked.

"Um . . . no," Ophelia replied. "Actually I'm headed out to grant a wish. It's my first assignment."

"Ah!" Silas Snorer said, his face brightening, hands clasped. "A first granting, how marvelous! And what an honor!"

"Thank you, sir. I'm very excited." She rubbed her own hands together.

"Used to be a Granter myself, you know, back in the day. Long before your time." Ophelia didn't doubt it; judging by the wrinkles congregating in every corner and fold of his old fairy face, it was *way* way back in the day. "A good amount of magic back then," Snorer continued. "Hundreds of wishes, every day. More than enough to keep things running at full steam. Not like today, eh?"

"I suppose not," Ophelia said, though if the Great Tree had dropped only one wish she would still have been

65

satisfied—provided she was the one sent out after it.

"What's the wish for, if you don't mind me asking, Agent . . ."

"Fidgets," Ophelia answered.

"Agent Fizzjets," he repeated.

"Fidgets."

"Fejits."

Close enough. "The girl wished for a bicycle," she said. *And make it purple*, Ophelia reminded herself.

Silas Snorer shrugged. "Bicycle. Hmph. Well, there are worse things, I suppose," he said. "Once did a granting for a little boy who swallowed a quarter on a dare. He wished he had the quarter back, naturally." The old fairy winked a sly wink. "So he got it back. *Naturally.*"

That was a tad too much information. Ophelia closed her book with its bloody-mouthed bobcat as a sign that she was finished with her work and ready to leave, but Silas jabbered on.

"Feels like there should be a better way, though, doesn't it? So many good wishes. And then some nincompoop comes along and swallows a quarter, and *his* is the one that gets granted. Still. Best to let the Tree do its job and we do ours, I suppose. Don't fix what isn't broken."

Ophelia felt like she'd just had this same conversation with Squint. She felt like she'd had it with quite a few fairies lately. "A bicycle's not such a bad wish," she said. "Her last one was stolen."

"Ah, well. That *is* a shame," Silas mumbled, shaking his head. "In that case, I hope you make her happy. I know how it feels to lose something dear to you. Thought I had my teeth stolen once. Turns out I was just sitting on them." Silas Snorer smiled, showing off his wooden dentures. "The problem with old age. You stick around long enough and *something's* liable to come along and bite you in the butt. Say . . . did I ever tell you how I lost this ear of mine?"

Ophelia stood abruptly. If she stuck around any longer, the old fairy might talk both of *her* ears right off. "I'm sorry. You'll have to excuse me. I have to finish prepping for my mission. But thanks for your help," she said, though he hadn't really been much help at all.

"Nothing of it. Nothing of it," Silas repeated, patting her on the shoulder and escorting her to the door. "All for a good cause."

As she was just about to leave, the old fairy snapped his fingers.

"Felix!"

"Sorry?" Ophelia asked.

"The wind chime maker. His name was Felix. Made the prettiest chimes you ever heard. Sounded like a nest full of nightingales. If you're half as good at granting as old Felix was at making wind chimes, you'll be just fine, Agent Finjits. Don't you worry."

"It's Fidgets," Ophelia corrected. She thanked Silas again

for his help, then told him he shouldn't worry either.

After all, she had no intention of being half as good as anybody.

Ophelia left the Archives hastily. Her conversation with Silas had delayed her slightly, but she still had time to make one last stop. It would take only a moment.

About halfway down Grant Tower, nestled between floors of bustling offices, sat one quiet, mostly hollow ring. A circular chamber with polished oak walls and a marble slab floor that had been a pain to install but was cool as crisp snow on bare feet—and Ophelia always took her boots off before entering, afraid that even her footfalls might make too much noise. No one dared to speak in here, not above a whisper at least. A single glowworm-powered lantern cast the room in a somber light. It was the only tranquil space in the otherwise bustling tree.

The Femoriae.

The Hall of Memories.

Ophelia came here often, just to sit and be still, to shove her hands in her lap and stop fussing for a moment. Magic might be hard to come by, even in the Haven, but this particular room held its own kind of magic. It cast a solemn spell, chanted from the writing on the walls.

Names. Hundreds of names. Carefully carved by a fairy whose only job was to maintain this room and the records it held. Records of great fairies who had given their lives in service to the Wish.

The Femoriae was their memorial.

Ophelia circled the chamber, grazing her fingers over the carved letters, feeling the scars in the wood, letting her heart ache just a little over each one. Fairies who had accidentally been stranded in a storm, struck by lightning, or drowned at sea. Fairies, like Silas, who had been caught by a sneaky fox or cornered by a house cat while digging for a birthday candle but who, unlike Silas, hadn't managed to escape. Fairies who never came home. Ophelia had heard plenty of stories. One fairy mistaken for a quail, her camo working all too well, shot out of the sky by a hunter. Another who had been momentarily blinded by twin bright beams in the night and struck by a car.

It was rare to lose an agent in the field—it hadn't happened since Ophelia had joined the guild—but the names on the walls of the Femoriae were testament to the myriad dangers that awaited her. Most fairies merely drifted away when their course was run, their essence leaving as quietly as it had come and returning to nature, to rain and sun and soil, only to be reborn again in the petals of a primrose or among the needles of a sappy pine. But Granters weren't always destined for a peaceful passing. To be a Granter was to risk life and limb in pursuit of . . .

Of what, exactly?

It was the one question she asked herself, every time she came. And the only time she ever asked it. Why risk your life—as all these fairies did—granting somebody else's wish?

Some *human's* wish? Kasarah Quinn was no fairy. She wasn't born from a bellflower or a cherry blossom. She might be a darling girl, a tribute to her kind—but that was hardly a reason to stick one's neck out. Ophelia didn't owe Kasarah Quinn anything, so why bother?

The answer, of course, was magic. The magic willed it. That's what it was there for. Even as the number of wishes they could grant spiraled ever downward, as long as the Tree's allotted wishes were granted, the magic would persist. And as long as the magic endured, the Haven would endure.

And there was also that *other* thing—that feeling she had yet to experience but that her fellow Granters spoke of. That sense of pure wonder and joy that you supposedly got when you fulfilled the promise made by the Great Tree. The fairies had a word for it, that sudden rush. They called it *amaratio*. The satisfaction of a wish granted. Charlie had tried to describe it for her once—a feeling of wholeness, he'd said—and Ophelia longed to experience it for herself. To say the magic words. To make a wish come true.

But not for some girl.

Or not *only* for the girl, at least. And not just for that feeling either. Or for the guild. Or to protect the Haven—though all those reasons weighed on her heart. She wanted to prove that she could. That she had what it took to be a Granter. One of the best Granters. Better than Adelia Brash. Maybe even better than Squint. She wouldn't end up like these poor souls. No one would come to the Femoriae and find her name carved on the wall.

Ophelia heard a shuffling step and turned to find Charlie standing in the archway, staring at her. "Thought I might find you here being all morbid and mopey."

"I'm being *thoughtful*," Ophelia corrected, hoping her whisper would remind him not to be so loud. "You should try it sometime."

"Thinking's overrated," Charlie whispered back. "I prefer eating puff pastries and taking long naps in the sun. Are you ready?"

Was she ready? Ophelia took one last sweep of the room, the hundreds of fairies who'd probably asked themselves that same question and thought they'd known the answer. Who had had just as much training as she did and probably more experience, yet who didn't return.

Maybe Charlie was right. Maybe it was better not to think too hard about such things. Ophelia slipped her boots back on and tied each with a triple knot. "I'm ready," she said.

It was time to get to work.

12

When Ophelia first emerged, the fairy who found her—who lifted her from the petals of the delphinium flower she was wrapped in and cradled her in his arms—that fairy hummed to her. All the way back into the Haven.

His name was Paolo. Paolo Hydrangea Speechless. Like all fairy last names, Paolo's was befitting his personality. Most fairies learn to speak fluently at a startlingly young age—before their first season has passed—but Paolo was unusually quiet as a young fairy and grew up to be just as soft-spoken as an adult, seldom uttering more than a sentence, and that only when necessary.

He would hum, however, often making up new melodies on the spot, his voice bright as birdsong. When he drew Ophelia out of the delicate flower folds and into the wide new world, he was humming a tune that had been stuck in his head the whole long journey from the Haven. It was simple and cheerful, and she smiled at the bouncy refrain. Paolo's humming was the only thing about her Founding Day that Ophelia remembered clearly. That, and that his hair was blue like hers, but lighter. Like the sky.

Ophelia hummed that same tune nervously to herself as she stood in the ready room. Charlie whistled in harmony alongside her, smiling broadly though she could tell he was just as nervous as she was. She mentally marched through her checklist as she buttoned up her pink flight suit. Not quite the glaring fuchsia of Charlie's eyes, but a nice flamingo color at least. She really would look like a fat pink worm flying through the air. She thought of the peregrine falcon's top speed again and fumbled with her belt.

"You have everything?" Charlie asked, interrupting her in the middle of her list.

She shushed him. *Knife, check. Twine, check. Goggles, check.*

"And you've got the route memorized?"

She gave him a look, hoping that would do for an answer. *Bandages, check. Ointment, check. Sticky strips, check.*

"And you packed a snack?"

Ophelia whirled around. "Bless the Havens, do you *ever* shut up? Yes, I packed a snack," she told him, then double-checked to make sure the yellow M&M—a gift from Charlie, in fact, on her last Founding Day—was still in her pack. It was a nice satchel, roomy canvas with reinforced straps and plenty of small pockets on the outside to hide trinkets and tools. It had been a gift from Speechless on his passing. They hadn't been that close—Founders were known to nurture hundreds of fairies in their lifetimes, and when you have that many charges it's hard to get attached to any one for too long. But before his spirit returned to nature he did see fit to give Ophelia something—his bag, which he'd used for twenty seasons. He also told her how proud he was of the fine fairy she'd become. It was more words than he'd spoken to her in a year.

She checked the bag now to make sure it had everything else she needed. A reed whistle for startling wild animals. A fishhook, corked to prevent it from jabbing her in the leg mid-flight. The bag was bulging. Charlie must have noticed her straining to lift it.

"Maybe you overpacked?"

"Or maybe I'm just being thorough," she teased.

Charlie helped her with the back of the thermal flight suit—too tricky to get it buttoned around the wings by yourself. If she only had real feathers or fur to help keep her warm. "It looks good on you," he said. "Pink is definitely your color."

She smirked at him and slung the satchel across her shoulder, tying it again to her waist with extra twine so it wouldn't dangle while she flew. Charlie noticed her fingers fumbling with the knot. "It will be all right," he said.

Ophelia snorted. "A tock ago you were telling me that the world outside was a giant fairy death trap. Now you're telling me not to worry?" She clipped the two canisters of Arnold Rolleye's magic knockout spray to her belt. "Make up your mind. Am I coming back alive or not?"

Charlie's face went white. "Don't say that. Don't even think it."

He looked so serious all of a sudden. It surprised her. "I'm kidding," she said, smirking. "Seriously, Chuck. Lighten up."

"And please don't call me that."

"Okay, *Charles*. You don't need to pretend to be worried," she said. "I know you're just mad that it's me and not you."

"I'm not jealous. It *should* be you," Charlie said. "You deserve it. You're the brightest, quickest, most resourceful fairy I know. There's a reason Squint chose you over me." He paused, glancing down at his untied boots. "Probably more than one."

Now she felt bad for bringing it up—hinting at how long it had been since he'd stepped foot outside the Haven. "You'll get back out there someday," Ophelia assured him.

"Yeah, I wouldn't bet on that," he muttered.

He followed her through the ready room onto the platforms at the top of Grant Tower, where the guild's launch operations spread out beneath the bright late-morning sun. Most everyone up there was a Techie, the newest guild in the Haven: fairies trained to operate the increasingly complex contraptions the boys downstairs rigged up. Several fairies sat on a nearby branch surrounded by equipment hacked and mashed together from bits and pieces brought back by the Scavengers. Cracked screens. Long metal antennas nearly bent in half. Wires running this way and that, some of them snaking their way to a bank of solar panels soaking up nature's number-one source of free energy. Several fairies sat on wooden stools with headphones made of walnut husks, monitoring radio signals. It wasn't the most high-tech operation, Ophelia knew—supposedly some of the fairies over in Europe were on the verge of hijacking a satellite—but you start relying too much on gadgets and gizmos and you lose sight of the magic.

Maybe that was part of the problem.

Squint was standing at the launch platform, pacing. He took one look at her and frowned. "Pink?" He glared at Charlie—or glared as much as was possible through those narrow slits of his.

"All her idea," Charlie said, pointing.

"Just so long as you don't get caught, shot, or eaten, I suppose it makes no difference."

That was Squint for you, Ophelia thought, a fountain of cheer. The head of the Granters Guild handed her a baby green acorn no bigger than her thumb. At least it looked like an acorn. Ophelia knew better. She could see where the geeks downstairs had carved out the insides and replaced them with all kinds of wiry metal bits. The acorn top had been replaced with a wooden button. She knew exactly what it was for.

This was her locator. Her SOS. Her just-in-case device.

"If you should get into trouble—and I mean a real dust kicker, not just some minor inconvenience," Squint instructed, "click that button. It will activate the distress signal, and hopefully we will be able to pinpoint your location. Though keep in mind it will take a while to get a rescue team out to you."

"It won't be necessary," Ophelia insisted. She had no intention of having to be rescued. Then again, who *plans* on getting rescued?

"Don't eat that," Charlie told her. "The wires'll get stuck in your teeth." Ophelia groaned and tucked the acorn into the only empty pocket left in her satchel. She wondered if Charlie had ever had to press the button. His last mission hadn't gone well, though he never gave her the details, no matter how hard she pressed. She knew only that the wish had been granted.

Because no wish had ever gone ungranted under Squint's watch.

"And here's this."

Ophelia watched Squint remove a small glass vial from his pocket, attached to a length of triple-braided twine. Ophelia took the diamond-shaped vial gingerly and held it between two fingers, letting the light catch it. She could see the iridescent motes of pure fairy magic swirling inside, like miniature starlight. She sensed the promise it contained, made by the Great Tree, waiting to be fulfilled. This wasn't her first encounter with fairy dust. But it was the first time she'd ever been entrusted with it.

"You understand what happens if you should lose this?" Squint's expression was as serious as a cemetery.

Ophelia nodded. One hundred percent pure fairy dust was not to be trifled with. Even the little bit she was given. Lose this vial and it was mission failure. Instant abort. That's why it didn't go into her bag or her pocket. She handed it to Charlie, who tied it around her neck. She gave the twine a firm tug, just to be sure, then tucked the vial inside her suit and even under the collar of her uniform so that it lay right against her heart. She wanted to feel it there at all times.

"All right. Time for the camo." Squint stood back and two Techies, both with striking orange hair, approached and stood on either side of her. They each held glass flasks with bulbous sprayers at the top, much like the spritzers Celia Sniffs—one of Ophelia's neighbors—bottled her noxious flowery perfumes in. The liquid inside the flasks was completely clear, which was funny only when you considered what it was about to do to her.

"Soak her good, boys," Squint said. Ophelia raised her arms and shut her eyes tight.

The two orange-haired fairies proceeded to douse Ophelia in a fine mist, coating every inch of her, from feet to hands to face. They sprayed everywhere, making her purse her lips and hold her breath, though the residue still lingered. The camo wormed all the way through the fabric and seeped into her skin, making it tingle. This wasn't the first time she'd been camouflaged—her training exercises at the Academy had taken her outside the Haven before—but she forgot how bitter it tasted until she unwittingly licked her lips.

"Rolleye should work on adding some peppermint to this," she spat.

"It's not designed to taste good, Fidgets," Squint told her. "It's designed to keep you alive. That's enough camo to last until the close of the day. Which gives you about twelve tocks to complete your mission. After that it's going to wear off and humans will see you for who you really are."

"And *nobody* wants that," Charlie said.

Ophelia ignored him. She wasn't concerned about the time. She wouldn't need until the end of the day. Three tocks there. One tock max to locate and grant the wish. Three tocks back. She'd be home in time to celebrate with a late-evening meal of candied apples and corncakes and the bottle of dandelion wine that she'd been saving for a special occasion.

For this exact occasion.

She could feel the camo warming behind her ears. It was fairy dust again—heavily diluted, but she could still feel the magic working, making her sweat. Or maybe that was just nerves.

One of the fairies came up to Squint to deliver a weather report. "Scouts say it's a little cloudy between here and Kettering, sir, but no rain in sight."

No rain. Smooth flying. Nothing at all to be nervous about.

Squint put his hands on Ophelia's shoulders, his face close enough that she could actually make out the color of his eyes between the narrows. She expected them to be pink, like an oleander, the flower he was found in, but instead they were silver to match his hair.

"The wish is active, so it should be easy to track. I don't have to remind you what's at stake. Find the coin and do what you've been trained to do, and by tomorrow at this time, you will have preserved the Haven for yet another day, and Kasarah Quinn will be riding a shiny new purple bicycle up and down her block."

Kasarah. Right. Ophelia had momentarily forgotten about her. How odd. She was so focused on the flight and the ritual, anticipating everything that could possibly go wrong, that she momentarily blanked on who the wish was for. She tried to picture it: the thirteen-year-old girl standing by the fountain, reaching into her pocket almost absentmindedly and finding a nickel there. Plunking it into the water with a shrug, because why not? What could it hurt? *And make it purple.*

Ophelia would make it perfect.

"I won't let you down, sir."

Squint nodded, satisfied, and turned to consult the Techies on the other upcoming launches. There were eleven other wishes being granted, after all. Charlie grabbed Ophelia by her elbow and pulled her gently aside.

"So listen, whatever happens out there, don't do anything foolish. Stay focused. Stick to your training. Remember what this is all about."

"Are we back to this?" she asked. "You keep giving me that sad-sap look and I'm going to start nervously messing with your hair again." She reached out and tugged on a pink tuft until he batted her hand away.

"I'm not kidding, Phee. Not everything out there is cataloged in the Archives. There are things that can get you sidetracked, make you doubt yourself. Make you doubt what you're doing. Humans are . . ." He struggled to come up with the word.

"Dangerous?" she offered. "Unpredictable? Totally insane?" Maybe all of the above?

"Complicated," he concluded. "Some wishes are harder to grant than others. It's better—just easier on everybody—if you stick to the plan." He glanced over her shoulder, where the launch deck opened into the beauty of the Haven and the human world beyond. "Don't lose sight of what's important."

He reached out and shifted the strap of her bag, making it slightly off-kilter. She reached up and put it right back. Before she could say anything Squint had returned and was ushering her to her launchpad, little more than a woven reed mat secured to the end of the branch.

"Ophelia Delphinium Fidgets, ready takeoff," one of the headphoned fairies said.

Ophelia pulled down her goggles and gave her wings a test flutter, just to make sure they weren't at all restricted by the suit or the bag slung across her shoulder. They hummed eagerly. They felt good. She felt good.

"Come back to us in one piece," Charlie called out.

"And make the Haven proud," Barnabus Squint added.

Ophelia popped her neck and cracked her knuckles. In her head she was already flying back home. She gave everyone on the top floor of the Tower a thumbs-up. *Your wish is granted,* Ophelia thought to herself.

And then she was gone.

13

It's hard to believe (as so many things are), but Ophelia Fidgets wasn't the first fairy to ever grant a wish in Kettering, Ohio. Some twenty years ago a man suddenly found himself with a change of heart, having been inexplicably (which is to say *magically*) bumped to the top of the transplant list. He still lives in Kettering to this day with someone else's ticker beating time in his chest. His family called it a miracle, which is one name for it.

Ophelia didn't mind not being the first. She didn't have to be the first in *every*thing.

Just *most* things.

She *had* been first in her class at the Founders Academy. Top marks in Fay and Human History, in Natural Studies and Environmental Protection. The best in her class at close-quarters combat and Fayitsu—the highest form of fairy martial arts. She didn't fare as well in shop classes, earning only passable grades in Alchemy and Woodworking and barely squeaking through Basic Blacksmithing. She would never fashion her own furniture or sew her own garments or learn how to put weaponized fairy dust extract into a twenty-foot blast-a-majigger, but nobody questioned her tenacity or talent in all other fields.

Especially flying.

Her instructor, Jennia Hawthorn Everything (so named because that's what she was always getting into as a foundling), called Ophelia one of the most natural, gifted, graceful flyers she'd ever seen. It helped being short, which Ophelia was for a fairy—barely tall enough to look over the top of a pumpkin (the squat kind, no less). Her compact frame was easy for her wide, sloping wings to carry. But she also had a knack for it. There was something transcendent about being up there in the clouds, the sun on your wings, feeling the strain of the muscles in your back as you fought to pick up speed and then glided and dipped and twisted, riding the currents, letting the cold air sting your nostrils and prickle your lungs. She loved it as much as Everything—maybe more.

The flying part of this mission she could handle. Three tocks? She'd been up for much longer. She'd once challenged the strongest fairy in her class, Stilton Sweetgum Hiccups, to a flyathon to see who could stay airborne the longest. Even when he folded—after seven hours of circling the Tree Tops—Ophelia felt she could fly more.

I could fly a little faster now *if I went up higher and got out of this crosswind*, she thought. Recommended cruising altitude according to guild policy was between five and ten thousand feet, but Ophelia's lungs were strong. She lived at the top of a mountain for Haven's sake. And it was only a recommendation, after all.

Ophelia catapulted herself upward, breaking through some clouds and finding a current of warmer air to glide on. The world below her was just a patchwork of yellows and greens. As she flew she thought about Kasarah Quinn and wondered about all the other wishes being granted today. She knew about Rebecca's assignment, of course, but not the rest. What other promises had the Tree made? Were they all pretty much the same? Had any little boys swallowed quarters yesterday? Was someone out there about to fall in love? She thought about what Tabbie Smiley had said back at the office: *Of course they'll keep wishing—because it doesn't cost them anything. But they don't really think they'll come true, most of them.* Ophelia wondered about that, too. Did Kasarah have any real hope of getting a new bike, or had she just flipped that nickel on a whim? Did she even remember doing it?

Well, Kasarah Quinn, you're a double-lucky girl. Lucky to be chosen, and extra lucky to have Ophelia Delphinium Fidgets assigned to your wish.

This was the thought coursing through her brain when she heard a low rumble in the distance, almost like a growl, though she couldn't imagine what kind of animal could growl *and* hover twenty thousand feet aboveground. Did peregrine falcons growl? She thought not. A flying bear perhaps? Only Charlie could imagine such a thing. Ophelia was peering through her misty goggles at the line of clouds before her when she spotted the source.

No, not a falcon or a winged bear, just an airplane. A small one. Barely a speck on the horizon. She'd seen them a hundred times before in the Archives. It was headed west while she was headed north, and she could just make out the purr of its engines over the vibrato hum of her own wings. She watched it slice through the clouds. It *was* sort of remarkable, she had to admit, seeing one in real life. Like an oversize metal insect. How did it go so fast without ever once flapping?

You couldn't wish upon an airplane, she knew—it didn't count. But you could make a wish while you were *on* one, she supposed. If you were traveling at night and looked out the window and saw a star, for instance. Good luck to the fairy who had to grant *that* wish. Ophelia had it easy; Kasarah Quinn's coin was just waiting for her in the bottom of a fountain. It wasn't going anywhere.

The small plane crossed in front of her, and Ophelia frowned at the white tendril it left behind, like a comet's tail. She'd read about that, too. The plumes of smoke belched out by these human contraptions. There were some places in the world fairies refused to go because the air was too thick with the fog of mechanical flatulence. Kettering, Ohio, probably wasn't one of them, thankfully. Still, Ophelia was glad not to be following in the flying machine's wake.

The plane stayed its course, moving steadily away from her, though oddly the rumble of its engines didn't grow softer.

It should have, but if anything the growling actually got *louder*.

Much louder.

Until it became like a thousand flying grizzly bears growling in her ears all at once.

Ophelia looked behind her and screamed.

14

ENORMOUS FLYING WHITE TUBE OF DEATH!

If she'd been able to form actual words, those might have been the ones, as she glanced back at the jet—easily ten times the size of the plane that just passed by—coming in fast on her booted heels. It filled her vision. Pointed nose. One long narrow black eye stretched across its face. Hulking body. A mechanical beast hundreds of feet long, aiming to crash into her, turn her into nothing more than a splotch on its chin. Its roaring engines deafened her; she could feel the currents of air getting sucked into them, threatening to pull her backward and chop her to bits.

For a second she thought she could outrun it, and she dug her chin into her chest and clenched every muscle, willing her wings to beat even faster, but it was no use. The jet was gaining. She looked again—she could almost see the faces of the pilots behind the glass. She was three seconds away from becoming fairy goo.

Ophelia lowered her head and kicked out with her legs, folding her wings in tight as she dove, hoping to shoot down far enough fast enough that the plane would miss her. She could hear it above, its grumble becoming a bone-rattling roar. She felt the sheer force of it passing overhead, blocking out the sun, casting her in its immense shadow. Then her ears popped and she was sent spinning out of control, caught in the jet wash, the mini cyclones of air left in the huge plane's wake.

Trapped in a vortex, twisting and tumbling, head over feet, no sense of up or down, she gasped for air, fought to stay conscious. She spread her wings again and tried to stabilize, but the force of the current overpowered her. Everything swirled. One of the straps securing her satchel to her waist broke and the bag came free, whipping around as Ophelia somersaulted through the sky. She saw the top flap open and watched helplessly as Charlie's old M&M tumbled free. The med kit, the whistle, and her spare socks followed suit, scattered in the wind, lost forever.

Then, to her horror, the baby green acorn with the little wooden button began to jiggle from its pocket.

Oh no you don't!

Ophelia contorted, gaining some measure of control, and snatched her satchel to her chest, one hand cupped over the locator, protecting it. Then she strained against the force of the wind to straighten herself out. She was no longer caught up in the wake of the jet, but she was falling. Way too fast. She could feel the pressure in her head. Black spots started to cloud her vision.

Get control of yourself, Fidgets. Pull up. Fly, you stupid fairy, fly!

Ophelia arched her back and straightened her wings, making them as rigid as possible, trying to find the right angle to slow her descent without snapping them in two. Fairy wings were strong—as strong as anything on earth, practically—but they were still paper-thin to keep them pliable. Moreover they were *attached to her*, and she could feel the muscles in her back straining at the effort. Suddenly the wind shifted, another current swooping up from underneath her, and she caught it, coming out of her spin and arcing upward, gritting her teeth and fluttering like mad to even out.

At last she came to a hovering stop in midair.

Three choking breaths, her heart fluttering faster than her wings, Ophelia tried to recover her wits. She wasn't a splotch. Everything was all right. True, she had absolutely no idea what direction she was facing, but at least it was no longer straight down. She glided for a moment, letting the wind cradle her as she secured her bag, now a great deal lighter at least, and felt her pockets to make sure she'd lost nothing else. The two canisters of weaponized fairy dust remained clipped to her belt, as did her knife. She had most of her supplies still, though nothing in the way of food. She pressed her hand to her chest, not to feel her heart, which raced like a hummingbird's, but to make sure the vial was still there, that it hadn't somehow snapped off while she was performing her unplanned aerial acrobatics.

It's okay. Calm down, Fidgets. You still have everything you need to grant your wish. It was a minor setback; she was bound to have one. And now, at least, she had a story she could tell Charlie when she returned. The important thing was that the mission was still a go.

If she only knew which way *she* should go. She was completely turned around.

Ophelia spotted the jet that had almost quashed her, high above her now, about to disappear into the clouds. It had been headed the same direction as her before.

She just hoped it still was.

15

M ost wishes *can* come true. If you're lucky. But there are limits to everything.

Some wishes are flat-out impossible—well beyond the limits of a fairy's meddling. Life and death, for example, are stronger forces than all the fairy magic combined. Once nature had reclaimed a spirit, no Granter, Scout, or Scavenger could track it down and no amount of dust could bring it back. And even if it could, fairies don't believe in making zombies.

Some wishes were not *impossible* so much as *unsustainable*. The fay folk had learned this from experience. World peace, of course, but also ending hunger, eliminating poverty, and ridding the world of injustice. Noble sentiments—and worth fighting for—but ultimately outside the limits of what fairies could accomplish. Some problems required much more than a pinch of dust and a shooting star to solve.

Sometimes—not often—the wish takes care of itself. Like the four-year-old birthday boy who blew out his candles too soon, wishing everybody would shut up and stop singing so he could eat his cake. That wish was granted before the fairies even knew it was made. Sometimes a wish will backfire and lead to unintended consequences. Like the boy who wanted to be invisible, only to be struck by a car. Or the woman who wished that she could eat as much chocolate as she wanted without gaining any weight but still developed diabetes.

Then there are wishes that get tedious after a while, like a song overplayed on the radio. Wishes to be famous. To be popular. All the wishes for money, be it gold coins or paper stacks. Technically grantable—the fairies of the Haven had been known to fiddle with the Powerball from time to time— but tiresome. And, frankly, overrated.

Keep your wishes simple. That's what most fairies will tell you. Keep them simple and earnest.

And don't ever count on them coming true.

Because the Great Tree doesn't discriminate.

And the odds are most definitely *not* in your favor.

16

Ophelia wanted a map.

She was pondering wishes and which one she would make if she saw a horse or a rainbow. Impossible, of course, as fairies weren't allowed to make wishes, but that didn't stop her from thinking about it. Once she got past an initial craving for a giant peanut butter milk shake with seven cherries on top, she settled on having a map. And maybe a compass. Anything to help her pin down her location.

She knew that when she got close enough the magic would begin calling to her, she'd be able to hear the wish whispered in the girl's own singsong voice. Then she would see the coin sparkling, only a dot at first, but growing brighter the closer she came. But so far, no voices. No sparkles. No nothing.

She obviously wasn't that close.

Or maybe she'd gotten off course.

The jet—that roaring monster that had tried to murder her—quickly vanished into the horizon, never to be seen again, but Ophelia flew after it for another full tock at least. Judging by the sun and the time of day, she was positive she was headed north*ish*. If it were nighttime, she could easily use the stars to help her navigate—any fairy worth her wings could—but it was only midday still. She should be getting close, she thought, the muscles in her shoulders aching. She *should* be almost there.

She was also getting hungry, her exertions taking their toll. Too bad her chocolatey provisions had tumbled out of her bag in the jet stream. Ophelia hovered for a moment, looking around at the long stretches of flat land beneath her, trying to get her bearings. She couldn't keep flying blindly. An emergency pit stop was in order. Find some water, maybe wrangle up some berries if there were any to be had, and then stop and ask for directions.

After all, Ophelia was one of nature's children. Surely *something* down there would help her.

She broke through a thin carpet of clouds and took in the painted green landscape—glorious blossoming trees and rolling grass meadows. It wasn't the majestic fir-studded and snow-dusted mountains of home, but it still gave her comfort. She could trace the squiggly paths of a few dirt roads lined with human habitats of various shapes and shades, though nothing suggesting a city close by.

She caught sight of patch of blue beneath her. A pond, or a

lake, rimmed with white dots. Birds. Geese, or maybe heron. Ophelia was too far to tell for certain, but she hoped they were heron. She'd never personally met either species, but everything she'd read had said that geese were not to be trifled with. Relatively smart, but ornery—Charlie told her a goose had tried to chew his arm off once, though it would have taken some time, seeing as how they had no teeth. Regardless, Ophelia didn't think she could put up with anyone's attitude right now. At least not until she'd given her wings a rest and had something to drink.

She touched down gently at the edge of the pond on the empty side and let herself collapse, her wings folding back, sighing in relief. She didn't let herself rest for more than a tick, however, before sitting upright and inspecting everything again—pockets patted, bag checked, dust accounted for. Then she tore off her goggles and bent over the water to get a good look at herself, careful not to get too close. Like most fairies, Ophelia was a terrible swimmer; it was a superfluous skill for one with wings, which is why she kept her feet firmly planted on the bank, taking in her reflection in the glassy surface of the water.

The camo worked only on humans whose brains and imaginations it was specifically designed for, so Ophelia could see the ragged state that she was in. Her hair was a knotted blue bird's nest (not necessarily a bluebird's nest, but maybe), tangled and wind-whipped. Dark red rings circled her eyes from where her goggles pressed too tight. Her cheeks were pink and raw, and she had a split in her bottom lip. She must have bitten it while she was trying to regain control during the flight.

So much for this being the easy part.

Squint had warned her. The world moves fast. Charlie had warned her, too. But it was all right. Nothing she couldn't handle. Ophelia splashed her face, then drank down four handfuls, relishing in the coolness winding down her wind-parched throat. Somewhat recovered, she took a moment to assess her surroundings. Namely, the geese on the other side of the pond.

They were definitely geese—at least if the pictures she'd studied in Zoology were any indication. Ophelia tried to remember everything she'd read about them. Approach slowly. Don't be loud. Try calling them by their first name. Except she didn't know any of their first names. There were at least a dozen of them, nuzzling the grass, scrounging about for something to eat. Bugs probably. Disgusting.

Ophelia straightened herself up and advanced on foot, afraid the beating of her wings might startle them. All she wanted was a little conversation.

Fairies were nature's most ephemeral creatures, but they were still bound to the woods and fields and to every living thing, big and small. The best of Ophelia's kind—the Whisperers—could talk a blade of grass into bending or a flower into budding, could even convince a tree to blossom early. There were very few things—plant or animal—that a fairy couldn't commune with, and even with those exceptions it was hardly the fairy's fault that communication broke down. Woodpeckers, for example, were notoriously hard to talk to. And howler monkeys. Cats for the most part just ignored everything you said. There were probably a dozen others, but most animals were open to talking to a fairy.

Most.

Ophelia approached cautiously, but it was no use. The first goose to spot her started honking instantly. *Honk! Honk! Honk!*

Ophelia understood his words: "Our lake. Our lake. Trespasser. Trespasser. Go away!"

The other geese started to honk as well, creating a chorus of hooting and hollering. "Trespasser," they cried. "Trespasser. *Sors d'ici. Vous n'êtes pas les bienvenus.* Get out of here!"

Canadian geese, Ophelia thought to herself. *Figures.* She slowed her approach, wondering what they made of her—this bizarre creature with a human form and folded insect wings and strange coverings from head to toe—if they'd ever seen one of her kind. She hoped they found her too big to eat. She thought of Charlie and his arm. Though these beasts were all larger than she was, they also looked fat and uncoordinated. They'd never be able to catch her. Still, Ophelia thought it best to bow before she spoke.

"Greetings, feathered ones. My name is Ophelia Delphinium Fidgets—*Special Agent* Fidgets. Daughter of the Fay and Granter of Wishes," she began, using her full title, hoping it impressed. "What's your name?" She was nearly nose to beak with the first goose now, the one who'd started the ruckus. He straightened himself up to his full height, stretching out his neck so that he was twice as tall as her.

"I am Olivier. And *you*," he added haughtily, "are an intruder. This is our territory. We have claimed it in the name of our gaggle. And we request that you vacate the premises *immédiatement*."

Ophelia rolled her eyes. Some animals could be so pompous. This wasn't going to be easy.

"Olivier," she said, straining to keep her tone polite. "That's a noble-sounding name for a noble-looking bird. And that's a handsome bit of plumage you've got." She pointed at the goose's backside, a tuft of white feathers poking out in every direction. It reminded her a little of Charlie.

Her flattery was lost on the bird. Olivier puffed out his chest and bobbed his head up and down for a moment before he resumed his squawking. "Maybe you didn't hear me, *petit insecte*. Must I honk louder?" The head goose began to strut, giving his wings a shake. "Perhaps I should buffet you once or twice about the head. I could crush you beneath my webbed feet, you know, *vous malodorant ravageuse!*"

I'd like to see you try, Ophelia thought. She glanced down at her belt. No point wasting any of Rolleye's precious spray on this foul-tempered waterfowl. One little poke from her knife and he'd fly away fast enough. But that wouldn't help her find out which way to go. She took a measured breath. "Look, Olivier. I just need some directions and then I'll be out of your feathers. Can you tell me where I am?"

Olivier turned to the other geese and honked. "It wants to know where it is. Brainless creature. *Sa tête est remplie de pierres.*" The other geese honked heartily, laughing at her.

Ophelia crossed her arms defiantly. Did this strutting peacock just call *her* stupid? A fairy who scored a perfect hundred on her Granter's Entrance Exam? "My head is *not* full of rocks," she shouted, putting a quick end to the gaggle's giggles. "I just need to know if I'm anywhere near Kettering, Ohio." Surely she was in the right state at least. Hadn't she crossed a big, winding river a ways back? "I mean, you *migrate* for Haven's sake. Surely you must know your way around."

Olivier snorted at her, ruffling his wings. "Of course I know my way around, you frilly little bug-person. I know that there are ponds and there are lakes and there are trees and mountains and giant towers of glass and stone and there are stars in the sky and insignificant *imbéciles* like you who ask stupid questions. Now go away before I give the order to peck you to death."

She might have taken offense, or at least been more on her guard, but Ophelia's attention had snagged on something

Olivier said: towers of glass and stone. Buildings. Big ones. High-rises. A city. It could be the one she was looking for.

"How far to those towers?"

"How far? We passed them only this morning." Olivier craned his neck behind him. "That way. Though such places are not suited for a *moucheron* such as yourself. You would be squashed like a cockroach. That's provided you even make it out of *here* alive, which I am starting to doubt." He honked his loudest honk and the geese behind him followed his lead, creating another volley of unbearable bleating. They started to move forward en masse.

It was clearly time to leave.

"Thank you for your help," Ophelia said begrudgingly as the mob closed in, waddling and hissing and flapping, trying to surround her. Maybe they'd decided they would try to eat her after all.

Ophelia unfolded her own gossamer wings, much more elegant than Olivier's, and the geese paused at the sight of them, the wings' rainbow pattern reflecting the sunlight, capturing it almost like stained glass. It had been only a short rest, but she couldn't let that stop her. She lifted into the sky, away from the pond and its gang of graceless geese too lazy to pursue.

"*Bon débarras!* Good riddance!" she heard Olivier call after her, the rest of his brethren taking up the chant.

That was the last time she'd ever bother asking directions from a goose, she decided.

Ophelia gained some altitude, then pointed herself in the direction Olivier told her. Toward the towers of glass and stone and what she hoped was the city she was looking for. Home to a fountain and a coin.

And a girl without a bike.

17

wish.

Ophelia's ears perked.

At first she was certain it was just her mind playing tricks, making up words to accompany the wind music that whistled in her ears, but the farther she flew, the clearer it became. A steadily building incantation. She had to concentrate in order to home in on it, but when she closed her eyes she could almost see the thread of magic dangling in front of her, ready to be tugged, and she could hear young Kasarah's voice.

I wish. Jerkface. Purple.

That was definitely her wish. Which meant Ophelia wasn't lost at all.

Thank you, Olivier. That ill-mannered goose had actually pointed her in the right direction. Of course it had taken her longer than three tocks to get here, she guessed, but what mattered is that she'd found her way.

Ophelia shrouded herself in clouds, low enough to avoid any more brushes with giant killer metal flying machines but high enough to avoid the swarms of birds that seemed to wander aimlessly from rooftop to rooftop of the houses below. Because there were houses now, hundreds of them. She had come upon the outskirts of a city, with its mazelike neighborhoods stretching beneath her, patches of fenced-in green and roads like gray capillaries branching between them. She took note of the metal boxes crawling along, looking like brightly painted steel tortoises. Automobiles. Probably just as dangerous as airplanes if you got caught with one behind you, except she didn't plan to be on the ground that long. Just long enough to snag a coin, release the contents of the vial around her neck, and seal the deal. Then she could get back to the Haven. Back to rolling mountains and crisp-scented Fraser firs. Back to her little cottage and the stack of wool blankets she kept carefully folded by her bed to snuggle under.

This was a different world than she was used to. Amid the Tree Tops of home, there was a perpetual thrum: the rustle of leaves, the buzzing of insects, the sounds of nature like the heartbeat of the world, but it was still peaceful in its way. The city she approached was much louder. Grittier. Cars everywhere. Lights flashing. A cacophony of mechanical noises. Beeping. Grinding. Growling. The thunder of machines, building and breaking and rebuilding. Crowded parking lots and flashes of neon, the giant signs posted every fifty feet along the side of the road, the brown bins overflowing with waste, the long stretches of asphalt and metal and plastic punctuated only occasionally by a lonely tree or straggling line of bushes. These overcrowded monoliths of brick and steel—all signs of an advanced civilization. Something to be proud of. But it only reinforced what Ophelia already knew.

This world was no place for fairies. Not anymore.

And yet there were pockets of beauty in between the buildings and the billboards. As she flew Ophelia picked up the high trill of children's laughter. She watched as two smiling men walked hand in hand in a park. She saw a woman with a can dutifully watering her pots full of flowers, perhaps one of them nursing a fairy that would be found someday. There was happiness. There was wonder.

There was a wish.

She let the whisper guide her, followed it the way a bat follows its own bouncing voice, over the housetops and the flower beds that reminded her of her own founding. It had been in the backyard of a house very much like the ones below her that Ophelia was born, barely the size of a date, curled up on that delphinium bud, eager to stretch her limbs and take her first real breath. Paolo told her he'd had to dodge a curious squirrel and fend off a pollen-hungry worker bee to get to her, but such was the way of things—nothing beautiful was easy to come by.

I wish.

Up over a row of bigger houses with bigger fences, along

a road clogged with even more automobiles, occasionally honking like temperamental geese. Past towers with blinking lights, as if giant fireflies had alit upon them.

And something else—a white glow, like a distant star. She recognized it the moment she saw it.

Kasarah's coin. Guiding her. Beckoning to her from the bottom of a fountain, glittering with the promise of magic-to-be. Right where the dark gray of the parking lot merged with the sun-bleached stone walkway. The entrance of the Town Center Mall.

Ophelia slowed the beating of her wings, hovering a full tree's length above it. There were bushes on the outskirts and grass that looked almost too green to be real. Rows of flowers lined the path leading to the front doors: bright white lilies and, Ophelia noted with a smile, bright pink azaleas the same color as her suit.

There were also people. Not many, but enough to be worrisome, walking quickly along the path past the fountain, leading in and out of the mall. No one sat on the stone benches or stood idly by the entrance, but the fairly steady stream of bodies coming in and out could prove problematic. Somebody would surely see Ophelia smuggling a nickel out of the fountain's pool. They wouldn't see a *fairy*, of course. They would see a bluebird or a chickadee or whatever else the camo triggered in their easily distracted brains, but even that was a risk. If *she* were a human and saw a bird diving into the water after a nickel, she'd be curious. She'd keep watching.

She might even try to get a picture of it. And that *would* be a catastrophe.

She couldn't just barge right in and take what she wanted, as much as the burning white glow of Kasarah's wish demanded it. This would require stealth and cunning. Luckily, next to flying, fidgeting, and giving Charlie Whistler a hard time, stealth and cunning were the things Ophelia was best at.

She eyed the bushes closest to the fountain. They were thick boxwood shrubs. Perfect cover for a fairy on a covert op. Ophelia put her hand to her beating heart one last time, just to make sure the magic was still safely contained. Then, to herself—because there was no one else to listen—she whispered, "This is Agent Fidgets, in position. Target acquired.

"I'm going in."

18

It started with wells—this business of watery wishes—though it wasn't always coins that were thrown in them.

Rocks and leaves. Rose petals. Rings of lost loves. Brass buttons and plucked feathers and weapons of your slain enemies still gory with blood. All these had been tossed into springs and bogs and fountains through the ages, often with a wish attached. But coins were the most common, stemming from the completely ludicrous idea that fairies actually took the money and *used* it for something—a tip, if you will, for services rendered.

Of course human coins were basically worthless, as far as fairies were concerned (unless you were one of those black market collectors who traded them for children's bloody-stumped teeth—a disgusting enterprise, to say the least, but a lucrative trade as human teeth contained many interesting alchemic properties). Ophelia tried to imagine the look on Verna Tulip Frazzle's face if she tried to exchange a moldy human penny for a bottle of Frazzle's Famous Honeysuckle Mead. *What am I supposed to do with this?* Verna would say, holding up the coin. *Make a wish, I guess,* Ophelia would reply, and they would both giggle at the thought.

No. Fairies weren't at all attracted by these circular metal bits with portraits of ugly dead humans scrawled on them. But coins were easy to come by, Ophelia supposed. And at least such a wish did, in fact, cost the maker *something.* Maybe having to pay for it—even this piddling amount—made them think a little harder about what they wanted before they tossed it into the water.

But probably not.

The fountain at the Town Center Mall was thick with copper and nickel. Either nobody had bothered to come and empty the fountain of its riches in years, or the people around here were desperate and had a lot of spare change. They blended into a kind of background roar. She could probably hear them all if she listened long enough—the murmur of a thousand bygone wishes, some quite faded with age—but it would be like picking one cricket's chirp out of a forestful. Besides, there was only one wish that mattered, and the sound of Kasarah's pining far overshadowed the rest, made louder by the magic of the Great Tree's promise.

Ophelia watched the crowd, waiting for a lull, a perfect opportunity to dart out and do her job. Except the water shooting from the top of the fountain was kind of mesmerizing—the way it frothed over, cascading down the sides, burbling into the bluish pool below. There *was* something magical about it, above and beyond the actual magic she knew to be there, and Ophelia could see why people passing by might pause and fish in their pockets or purses for a penny to throw. *Burble, gurgle, splash*, said the water.

I wish, said Kasarah's coin.

Ophelia shook her head. She needed to focus. She shifted inside her bush, trying not to rustle the leaves. A mother with two kids, both boys aged somewhere between two and ten (Ophelia was admittedly terrible at guessing human ages), handed them both a quarter and pointed at the fountain. The smaller one threw his coin in right away, probably adding the wish after the quarter had already sunk, which unfortunately didn't count. The other, older boy stood by the side, though, head cocked. You could see him working through the puzzle, weighing the possibilities. *What to wish for, what to wish for?* He took his time, and though she was impatient to get on with her mission, Ophelia found herself smiling as she watched this kid. He was a planner. Thoughtful and meticulous. She could appreciate that. Finally he dropped his quarter over the side with a satisfying plop.

Ophelia didn't try to discern his wish from the others, not over the sound of Kasarah's voice echoing in her head, but she knew that at this very moment, the Great Tree was sprouting another leaf with this boy's name on it. Part of her hoped his

110

leaf would fall, though she realized just how unlikely that was.

There was a time when a fairy could sneak out, pick up that boy's coin, sprinkle a little dust, and vanish back into the trees. When fairies roamed the valleys and glades and forests freely, granting any wish they pleased with little worry of running out of magic. But that was ancient history. Ophelia's world was different. There wasn't room for error. She had to do her duty. She had to do what was best for her kind.

The mother shooed the two boys toward the entrance and Ophelia scanned the area again. Perimeter temporarily secure. She carefully reached beneath her collar and removed the vial that had been nestled there, the glass warm in her hands. Enough magic for one wish only. Kasarah's nickel still shone bright amid the sea of shimmering coins.

Ophelia darted out of the bushes and flittered up to the edge of the stone fountain. The water was deep, nearly half as tall as her. No danger of drowning, but there was no way she was staying dry either, which meant an even colder journey home. It was too late to take her flight suit off. She was here; this was her moment. Grab the coin. Sprinkle the dust. Say the words.

She plugged her nose with one hand, closed her eyes, took a deep breath, and jumped off the stone edge.

But instead of hitting water, she was suddenly flying instead.

19

Ophelia's world somersaulted around her and she fought to catch her breath, her body stinging from the sudden blow. Something had knocked her, sent her soaring off the fountain and tumbling down to the cement walkway, where she landed in a heap.

Ophelia shook her head, then looked up to find the shadow of a man draped over her. He had a thick beard and much too heavy a coat for the late-spring sun. His cheeks sagged into his thick silver beard. His pants were torn and his toes threatened to poke through the tips of his thin-skinned sneakers. He had swiped at her almost absentmindedly, as if she were a wasp or a moth, sweeping her off the fountain in mid-jump. With her eyes shut, she hadn't seen him coming.

Ophelia's right hand clasped the vial as her left went straight to one of Rolleye's canisters, afraid this man would need a good spritzing, that he'd probably seen too much. Except he wasn't paying any attention to her. He sat on the edge of the fountain, leaning back, stretching out his legs, looking up at the clouds. Ophelia scurried backward on hands and knees, finding the bushes again and crawling underneath them, wings folded tight against her.

"Fiddlesticks!" she said, frustrated enough to use the f-word—or one of them, anyways. First the airplane, now this. Didn't these people realize she was a benevolent being of magic and light? Now she would have to wait for him to move before she could finish the job. That or knock him unconscious, though he looked like he had enough problems without some fairy blasting him with knockout gas. His eyes spoke of a sort of bone-deep weariness. Ophelia didn't want to add to his troubles, but she would do what she had to. She would give him a good solid tick or two, and if he was still in her way, he was getting sprayed.

She watched from behind her cover of leaves. The man pulled at his beard, glancing around the same way Ophelia had, then leaned back farther. One of his hands dipped into the water, trawling the bottom, drudging up whatever treasure he could find. Without opening his dripping wet fist he crammed his gatherings into the pocket of his coat and then went back for another haul. Ophelia could hear the coins scraping against the bottom of the fountain. She counted in her head.

He did this six times, three with each hand, before a boy—a

teenager, she guessed—paused on his way into the mall and stared. "Hey. What're you doing?" The boy's voice was laced with accusation.

The man with the coat full of coins startled, then stood up and stumbled off, the cuffs of his sleeves soaked through, fingers dripping. The teenage boy shook his head and went the opposite way.

Ophelia waited for them both to go, checked once more to make sure the area was clear, then quickly fluttered back up to the edge of the fountain.

"Oh bumblebutts," she muttered.

She turned and looked for the old man with the worn pants and shabby shoes, spying him in the parking lot. Six fistfuls of ungrantable wishes in his pockets.

Plus one.

The one she needed. That she'd been *this close* to grabbing.

Taken before it was granted.

20

When a fairy finishes her first four seasons, her Founder, along with a committee of other nosy fairies (which describes the vast majority), helps her choose her path. From that point on the young fairy trains to become part of the guild that will employ her for life.

Builders are trained to build. Bakers are trained to bake. Alchemists are trained to . . . Ophelia wasn't entirely sure exactly what Alchemists did. They alchemized. Which is to say they turned slightly useful junk into even more useful junk, or differently useful junk, like acorns into radio transmitters or fairy dust extract into camouflage spray. Though, in Ophelia's estimation, that was nothing compared to the wonderful things Bakers could turn cocoa beans into. Chocolate cake was its own special brand of alchemy.

There were well over two dozen major guilds in the Haven,

each with its own rules, its own bureaucracy, its own *way of doing things*. But the best job, by far, was that of Granter.

Granted, it took all kinds of fairies to make the Haven hum, to keep the enterprise running, to ensure that fairies had houses to live in, hot water to bathe in, charms to keep their home safe, wooden forks to eat delicious chocolate cake with. But none of it would be possible without magic. The magic served to keep the Haven safe. And magic wouldn't be possible without Granters—the best of the brightest, trained in the noble enterprise of making wishes come true.

To become a Granter took seasons of training. Tests and trials, both physical and mental. Untold tocks spent studying by moonlight (it does not pay to light *too* many fires in a forest). Ophelia estimated she spent six hundred days training for her position in the guild. The ritual and rigmarole involved in actually *granting* a wish took one. One whole day.

The remaining five hundred and ninety-nine were spent learning how not to get caught doing it.

In other words, Ophelia had spent over half her life preparing for situations just like this one—stalking an old man through the streets of a strange city, waiting for the most opportune time to knock him unconscious and steal his money. Putting it that way, Ophelia thought, it didn't sound like such a noble enterprise after all.

Of course it wasn't really *his* money to begin with, was it?

That's what she kept reminding herself as she darted and dodged, taking cover in bushes and treetops, under the shells of parked cars: not the thing about the money, but about her training. That she was the best of the brightest. That she could handle this.

Admittedly, her first instinct upon seeing the coin missing was to panic, but she quickly squelched it. It was all right to be *concerned*, maybe even a little *worried*, but she had absolutely no intention of getting worked into a tizzy fit. Only once, as the old man was crossing a busy street into a small crowd, did Ophelia even look down at her bag and the pocket with the baby acorn nestled inside. Then she thought of what Squint would say when she returned, having had to bail her out on her very first mission. She wouldn't get another one. She'd be relegated to paperwork for the rest of her career, filling out requisitions for more capable fairies. Or worse, she'd be transferred to the Gatherers Guild and forced to collect cashews for the stupid Nut Festival. Or was it pistachios? She didn't much care for either.

None of that mattered, because she was *not* going back to the Haven without granting this wish. Everything was under control. She still had the dust. She still had a half day's worth of camo. And she could still hear the girl's voice calling her through the pocket of the man's thick coat.

If only she could corner him. Get him alone. Then she could knock him out without fear of being seen. Unfortunately the streets were spotted with people, and it was all Ophelia could do not to draw attention to herself.

She wasn't always successful.

As she flitted from a hiding spot behind a bright blue box to the protective arms of a tree, a little boy who was walking close by pointed right at her and whispered something about a butterfly. Thankfully the adult he was with simply nodded without looking and pulled the boy along. Kids were danger- ous, Ophelia knew. They had big imaginations. They saw the wonder in the world. Luckily her camo held, and the butterfly the boy supposedly saw disappeared farther into the branches.

Ophelia looked around for the old man with the long coat and saw him enter the corner building: a long, white-bricked box with a lighted sign on the top that just said *INER* because its *D* had gone dark. Ophelia heard the clang of bells as the door opened and shut, leaving her crouched behind a tapestry of dogwood flowers just starting to blossom. At least he was no longer on the move.

She had no choice. She had to go in there after him. He had her coin. But simply slipping through the front door seemed too risky with this many people around. Five hundred and ninety-nine days of training had taught her that there was almost always another way in.

Ophelia fluttered across the street, staying high to keep out of view and scanning the outside of the building until she found a vent situated just under the roof. The Haven didn't have heating and air-conditioning—Ophelia made do with sunshine and blankets in the winter and cool breezes and refreshing waterfall baths in the summer—but she had stud- ied the basics. Enough to know that she'd found an alternative entrance, and a much stealthier one at that. She waited till nobody was watching and then darted up to the roofline.

The vent was made of metal, the slats much too narrow for her to squeeze through, but nuts to that. Fairies were disproportionately strong for their size. Not on the order of ants or dung beetles, but certainly stronger than humans, ounce for ounce. Ophelia could bench-press forty pounds—nearly twenty times her own weight. Far from the record held by Selma Redcedar Thick, but enough to earn her a round of applause from her fellow trainees at the Academy. And more than enough to bend the slats on the outside air vent, making a hole big enough to squeeze through.

Readjusting her bag and brushing off some cobwebs that had annoyingly clung to her uniform, Ophelia found herself in a warm, moist tunnel that led downward toward a puddle of faint light. She let herself flutter toward it, taking it slow, her wings brushing against the metal sides of the duct, and landed softly on the tips of her boots. To her left was a longer tunnel leading who knows where, but immediately in front of her was another vent looking out upon the diner's floor.

Ophelia peered through the slats, first at a collection of feet, then up at a number of people sitting around, talking and chewing, slurping and clanging. From where she crouched, she could not see the old man, but she knew he was in there. She could hear Kasarah's voice loud and clear.

She could also smell the food, a whiff of maple syrup followed by a tremendous waft of cinnamon that caused her lips to smack involuntarily. She knew what Charlie would say—*The wish will wait, get in there and find some way to stuff your gut!*—but Ophelia told both Charlie's voice and her own growling stomach to hush. There would be time to scrounge something to eat after her mission was complete.

Ophelia gently pried the slats open, just enough to stick her head through, hoping that she was low enough to the ground that nobody noticed. If they did they might mistake her for a hairless pink rat with her wings folded and tucked, and she could only imagine how well *that* would go over in a restaurant. She scanned the room, letting the whisper guide her until she found what she was looking for.

There he was, sitting at the counter. The old man's back was angled to her but she could see that he was spooning something steaming from a bowl, eating slowly, deliberately, clearly in no hurry to leave.

That meant she had time to make some kind of plan; but how to get to him? There were a dozen other humans in the room, and that was just what she could see from down here. She could hear someone else banging away in the kitchen, shouting orders over the sounds of a sizzling grill. Ophelia had only two canisters of sleepy spray. Certainly not enough to knock out the whole diner (and she could only imagine what Squint would have to say about *that*). Maybe it was best to sit tight. Keep her eye on the target. Wait for the old man to finish and then try to intercept him again outside. Besides, she figured it was better to be robbed with a full belly than an empty stomach.

As she crouched behind the vent cover, one eye fixed on the old man, Ophelia's ears tuned in to the voices chattering all around her. Not difficult for a fairy given their heightened senses, but Ophelia's hearing was especially sharp, perhaps owing to the disproportionate size of her ears. She was eavesdropping, of course (just as nosy as the rest of her kind), but Ophelia preferred to think of it as *surveillance*. At the very least she could get a sense of who was finishing their meal. If enough other people left, she might be able to make her move.

"You hardly ate anything. Is it not any good?"

It sounded like *someone* was almost done, at least. Ophelia shifted to get a better angle. A family of three, sitting at the table closest to her. Ophelia looked upward to see a boy staring gloomily at his plate. He wore a green jacket with lots of pockets. The girl sitting next to him was obviously younger—Ophelia could tell that much, at least—and wore her dark hair in pigtails with yellow ribbons to match her dress. Ophelia couldn't really see her face, though, only the boy's. Wavy bangs and chestnut eyes and a mouth creased with a frown.

"Just not hungry, I guess," he said, and poked at the plate with his fork.

"It's pancakes. You *like* pancakes. You eat them all the time. Did you think the pancakes were good, Anna?" The voice came from the other side of the table. The kids' mother, presumably.

"They were pretty good," the girl said.

"Not as good as Dad's," the boy cut in.

"No. Not *that* good," the girl conceded.

The mother let out a heavy sigh, the kind of sigh Ophelia was fond of giving Charlie. "Well, I'm sure when your father gets home he will make you all the pancakes you can eat. Until then, we make the best of what we've got. Okay?"

Ophelia saw the boy shrug, but the mother wasn't finished yet.

"C'mon, you two. It's a lovely Saturday afternoon. We're not going to waste the day moping. That doesn't do anybody any good. Instead we are going to finish our errands and go home and you two are going to find something fun to do . . . preferably together, and preferably outdoors. Affirmative?"

"Affirmative," the boy and girl said in unison with varied degrees of enthusiasm.

With that the mom gathered her bag, stood up, and headed toward the counter. The kids reluctantly stood up after her.

"He makes them with chocolate chips. That's why," the girl named Anna said.

"And whipped cream," the boy in the green jacket added. "In a smiley face." He turned and looked toward the windows at the front of the restaurant, and Ophelia saw the disappointment on his definitely-not-smiley face. Hard to blame him. Who in their right mind would choose a plain panned-cake over one with chips of chocolate and whipped cream? Of course it wasn't worth *crying* about either, and it looked as if the boy was about to do just that. That is, until a clanking sound coming from the tunnel behind Ophelia carried out

122

through the vent. The boy's head twisted around suddenly, those tear-sheened eyes darting downward.

Darting her way.

Ophelia scrunched low, her back pressed to the metal siding, slinking backward as quietly as she could. Had he seen her? And if so, *what* had he seen? He hadn't yelled "Rat!" yet. He hadn't yelled anything. She retreated farther back into the shadows, contemplated taking off, flying up the vent. She could just make out the boy's shoes—silver-and-white sneakers with the laces double-knotted—taking two steps closer. She readied her wings in anticipation of having to make a quick escape.

The mother's voice again, calling out across the diner. "Gabe? Are you coming?"

Ophelia held her breath, expecting to see his face bending down, spying her through the slats, but after a moment the shoes turned and retreated, the boy obeying his mother's command. She crept cautiously toward the vent cover and watched him follow his mother and sister out the door and into the busy street, the bells on the door clanging them a good-bye. Crisis averted.

So long, Anna and Gabe. Sorry about the pancakes. She glanced around the dining room. Three down, but still several potential hostiles scattered about. She focused her attention back on her target, the old man, who had put down his spoon and pushed his bowl aside. An apron-clad woman behind the counter came to take the bowl away. Ophelia strained to hear what she said.

"The coffee's on the house, hon, but you're going to have to pay for the food. Can't let the boss catch me again."

"It's all right," the man in the thick coat said. "I got it this time."

Ophelia watched the old man's hand dip into his pocket, counting out a handful of coins and sliding them across the counter. One was much, much shinier than the others.

"Keep the change," he said.

"Oh, I don't think so," Ophelia whispered to herself. She glanced at the other patrons at their tables, at the woman in the white apron, at the nickel that was about to get swept up and stuck somewhere no doubt *much* harder to get to. She balled her hands into little fairy fists and bit her lip in the same spot she'd bit it before.

Things were about to get dusty.

21

The old man was already headed toward the door, but that didn't matter. Kasarah's nickel sat in a pile of loose change by his empty cup, the waitress having been distracted momentarily by another customer.

She had to act. Like, *now.*

Ophelia wrenched the slats of the vent open with both arms, her wings snapping free, sending her airborne after three steps, hurling her toward the counter at a full-out charge. The coin's silver halo beckoned, but she was the only one who saw it.

Everyone else saw her, though. She made it impossible not to.

Several customers pointed up toward the ceiling where she hovered. An elderly-looking lady in a fur coat screamed. A little boy cried out, "Birdie!" Ophelia couldn't worry about what they saw—or thought they saw. So long as nobody shouted "Fairy!" or "Monster!" or "What *is* that thing?" she figured she was safe, protected by the camo. What mattered was the coin. Grabbing it and getting out of here as fast as she could. Ophelia shot down from the ceiling and landed on the counter, only a few inches away.

"Shoo!"

She saw the giant paw of straw sweeping toward her just in time to duck out of its way. *Swoosh*. The head of the broom passed overhead, swung by the same waitress who'd tended to the old man. Ophelia recovered and made a lunge for the nickel when the broom came down again, smacking the counter this time, *slam*, rattling forks on their plates and sending half the coins clattering to the floor. The other two humans sitting at the counter stood up and backed away. Another got up from his table and ran to the door, holding it open, shouting, "Sweep it outside!" Ophelia went airborne again.

"Max! There's a crazy bird in the dining room!" the waitress yelled behind her, taking another swipe at Ophelia, who had to shoot backward to avoid it. Ophelia gave the woman a dirty look, then spotted another man in blue jeans and a button-down striped shirt coming up behind her with a club of rolled-up newspaper in hand.

Fwoosh. Another near miss. Now she was dodging attacks from both sides, juking left and right, keeping one eye on the nickel and the other on whatever weapon was determined to knock her senseless, broom or newspaper, wielded by frantic, crazy humans shouting at one another.

126

"Get it out of here!"

"Don't hurt it!"

"Here, give me the broom!"

Ophelia rocketed back up to the ceiling, out of reach of the rolled-up paper, at least. She could still see the nickel on the counter, several feet away. It would take her half a tick to perform the ritual, but it would take only a heartbeat for her to be swatted out of the sky.

Time to go on the offensive.

Ophelia bolted downward, right into the nest of brunette curls on top of the waitress's head, hoping she couldn't thwack what she couldn't see. But the man with the newspaper could, and he gave a good swing, missing Ophelia, who darted upward again, but delivering a solid smack across the waitress's noggin.

"Hey. Watch it!"

"Sorry," the man said, reaching out for the waitress, only to have his own hand slapped away. In the moment of distraction, Ophelia went for the coin.

Suddenly a large man with a black beard and shrewd little eyes that reminded Ophelia of Barnabus Squint came bursting out of the kitchen with a strange, red contraption in his hands—like a skinny red elephant with a black trunk. The trunk was pointed her way.

This couldn't be good.

A blast of white foam shot from its one giant nostril, dousing her in something like soap but thicker. Whatever it was, it stung her skin. Some of it got into her eyes, burning them. Ophelia fluttered backward, away from the steady *foom* of white spray, rubbing at her eyes with her knuckles, clearing her vision just in time to see the broom again.

But not in time to get out of the way.

It smacked her head-on, sent her tumbling backward, head over heels, right out the door.

22

Humans, she thought, literally spitting flecks of white from her lips like some kind of rabid, half-crazed creature. *Humans are to blame. For everything.*

She sat in the dogwood tree and glared at the impenetrable fortress of INER, guarded by a cadre of humans with brooms and newspapers and nozzled foam-blasters. She couldn't go back in there. They were too well armed. Though part of her (the seething, cursing, nails-digging-in-palms part) considered barging in with her fingers on both canisters of knockout spray, just to teach them a lesson about how to treat all living things. Her eyes still burned, and the specks of foam that had stuck to her face and hands had started to itch. There was a tear in her flight suit and one button had come loose, dangling by a thread. She looked ruffled. Scruffy, even. She continued to curse everyone in the restaurant. Swatted and shot at. Chased out the door. The *behavior* of those humans—and they just thought she was a *bird*! No wonder pigeons took pleasure in pooping on all their stuff.

Humans. If it weren't for them—for their cities and their roads, for their cameras and their cars, for their insatiable need to explore *everything*—fairies wouldn't need to hole up in the Haven. They wouldn't need to carefully regulate their use of magic. They wouldn't need a Great Tree or a Granter's Code or even camouflage.

Of course if it weren't for them, there would be no wishes to begin with. It was a sticky situation. As sticky as the foam that clung to her once-pink flight suit.

Ophelia removed the acorn from its pocket and let her finger hover over the polished wooden button. *Now* should she press it?

The situation hadn't blown clear to the Tree Tops yet. The coin was still contained. It was somewhere in that restaurant. Perhaps she'd been a little rash—bolting out of the vent like that into a crowd of people. She'd seen the coin and panicked. What happened to being meticulous? What happened to thinking things through? She'd been distracted by the boy and his family, that look on his face. She'd let herself get sucked into their conversation. Hadn't Charlie warned her about that? About keeping her focus? *Don't lose sight of what's important*, he said.

The wish was what was important. It was the only thing that mattered. Ophelia needed to regroup, just rest here a moment and come up with a better plan.

And while she was resting, she might as well fix her button, which hung impertinently from one thread. She removed the spool of twine from her satchel and used her knife to fashion a makeshift needle from the stem of a dogwood leaf. It wasn't great—but she was no Arnold Rolleye. It would have to do. It was while she was sewing the loose button back on her uniform that she heard the bells on the diner's door ring out again and looked to see a man—the man in the denim pants and red-and-blue-striped shirt who'd taken a swipe at her with his rolled-paper club. Ophelia froze mid-stitch. She could hear Kasarah's voice calling to her from the man's pocket. Her wish was on the move again.

"Thank the Havens," Ophelia whispered; finally something swinging her way, *besides* brooms and newspapers. She stuffed the twine back in her satchel and stood up, forgetting to tie off her knot and letting the button come loose again as she took flight, quickly closing the distance between her and her target, keeping high and out of sight. Not that he would have noticed her. The man had his nose pressed to his little flashing electra-ma-jigger as he absentmindedly turned the corner and started down the street. Ophelia hovered above him, her eyes fixed on his balding crown (an inviting target for an unhappy bird, she thought), waiting for the right moment.

He crossed into a lot full of parked automobiles that appeared otherwise deserted. As good a place as any for an ambush. There would be nobody around to see. He paused in front of a beat-up box of a car that looked older than he was, complete with dents and patches of rust. He opened the door with a creak.

This was it. Ophelia unlatched a can of Rolleye's spray. She'd take her shot, spray him right in the face—maybe a *little* payback for his attempts to thwack her back in the diner. He'd wake up a few hours later expecting his wallet to be gone or his car stolen, so relieved that he would hardly miss the nickel from his pocket.

Ophelia swooped down as the man lowered into his seat, the door still open. She was less than twenty feet away. A perfect shot. She squinched one eye closed. *It's for a good cause*, she thought, repeating what Silas the old fairy had said to her before. She pressed the button.

Nothing happened. She pressed again, jamming her thumb into it. Still nothing. The canister was busted, its mechanism broken. Maybe it had gotten smacked too hard by the broom? Ophelia tossed the can aside with a hiss and tucked her body in tight, making herself into a dart, aimed at the door that was starting to shut way too fast—a fissure, then just a sliver, barely wide enough for her to slip through *maybe* . . .

Slam.

Ophelia pulled up at the last second, nearly crashing into the man's window. She watched as he craned his neck to look out, wondering what had nearly smashed into his car—perhaps the same lunatic bird that had gotten caught in the diner—but Ophelia quickly hovered to the roof.

The car growled to life after a spluttering of coughs, its back end belching dark clouds as it started to move. Ophelia circled above it, looking for another entry. She still had one can of sleepy spray left, provided *it* worked (she would make Arnold's other eye roll if it didn't), but all the windows were closed and there appeared to be no way to get to the man. She certainly wasn't about to crawl into the pipe that was hiccupping black smoke. Maybe her knife could cut a hole through the roof? But as soon as she thought it, she realized how foolish it was. The blade was strong—and Ophelia stronger—but it was barely the length of a rose thorn.

Forget it. If Ophelia couldn't get inside, she would have to get the man to come back out.

The rattling white car pulled into the street and sped up. Ophelia flew ahead, ten feet above, looking back over her shoulder to make sure it was right behind her. She knew she could at least get him to stop the car.

She twisted and dove, heading straight for it. Ramming speed.

Ophelia did a half flip and dropped, fanning out her wings as wide as they would go, creating enough drag to slow her down but also making herself appear as big as possible. It was a lesson she learned from studying gorillas and frilled lizards. The bigger, the scarier. She added a barbaric shout for effect. "Aieeyah!"

Apparently that wasn't scary enough.

There was no telling what the man saw with the camo,

but he didn't slam on the brakes as she'd hoped, and Ophelia smacked into the windshield, her face mashed, cheek to glass, one eye looking right at the man who was escaping with her wish. *Now*, at least, with her plastered to his car, the man would surely skid to a stop and scramble out the door screaming, loose change spilling out of his pockets and onto the street for any passing fairy to just pick up.

Instead the man in the striped shirt got a weird look on his face and pulled a lever.

Instantly a stream of burning blue liquid struck Ophelia, soaking her suit and stinging her nostrils. She shielded her eyes this time, having learned from her confrontation at the INER, but that only blinded her to the black metal arm that sprung from out of nowhere, thwacking her in the side, prying her loose from the glass.

Half blind and spitting from whatever noxious poison the wheeled white turtle had assaulted her with, Ophelia hovered for a moment, heart thumping, the world a teary-eyed blur. She tried to keep her focus on the car, knowing she had to give chase or risk losing the wish, which simply could *not* happen.

Which meant she didn't see the truck coming at her the other way.

23

In the Haven, when a fairy's body fails her or becomes too broken for even the gifted Menders to fix, her spirit takes to the sky, where it is sponged up by the clouds and mixed with rain that falls back to the earth, feeding the plants that would someday produce fairies of their own.

The Menders call it *recycling*.

Which sounds a lot better than *dying*.

Ophelia wasn't dead, though she felt like she was. Or felt like she should be. Everything hurt. It hurt to move, to breathe, to blink. It hurt even to think about how much it hurt to do these things.

The truck hadn't slowed, though Ophelia had reflexively tried to bolt out of the way when she finally looked behind her, so rather than becoming a permanent hood ornament she glanced off its edge, catching most of the blow on her left side.

The impact sent her soaring, landing amid a pile of trash bags that had been set along the curb.

It was a softer landing than the street, at least, and the black plastic that billowed up around her helped hide her from the outside world. She blinked (hurt) and wiggled her fingers and toes (hurt even more) and turned her head, a chorus of bells ringing inside. For a moment Ophelia forgot where she was—everything around her seemed so alien and unfamiliar—and then like a wind gust (or a big truck) it struck her.

The wish. She'd lost it. The man in the white car had taken it and now he—*it*—was gone. Ophelia closed her eyes again and listened, reaching out for Kasarah's voice. She could still catch the faint whisper of it—like a tuft of cottonwood floating in the breeze.

I wish.

She had to go after it while she could still track it. Ophelia gritted her teeth, took a deep breath.

Get up.

She tried, but a lightning bolt struck her from behind, a searing pain that blasted her between the shoulders and followed a course clear down her left arm. Ophelia chanced a look behind her and choked down a startled cry.

Her left wing was broken. Part of it was crushed and crumpled, a long tear working its way halfway down from the tip, looking like cracked glass. She tensed, bracing herself, and tried to give it a flutter, just one beat, but the pain immediately caused her to swallow another scream. Ophelia looked

136

up at the clouds, tears in her eyes. You can't chase down a car if you can't fly. And you can't fly with only one good wing.

"Look, I think that bird's been hurt."

Ophelia glanced up to see a little girl tugging on her mother's sleeve. Pigtails with yellow ribbons. Big, bright eyes. The girl from the restaurant, her brother shuffling several paces behind, watching his own feet.

"Hey, Ma, do you see it? I think its wing must be broke."

The mother stopped and looked, her forehead furrowing, mouth set in a pout. Then she and Anna started to walk toward the pile of trash. Figures. *Now* a human was going to try to be helpful.

Ophelia had to move.

Her wing felt like it was being ripped off as she forced herself up, scrambling to find purchase in the slick, lumpy surface of the trash bags, somehow rolling over and down one side, planting her feet back on pavement. With solid ground beneath her she stumbled away from the girl and her mother, toward the deserted alleyway in front of her. No doubt she looked like a wounded bird hobbling along.

"Poor thing," she heard Anna say. Ophelia looked behind to see the girl's mother pulling her away.

That's right. Move along. Nothing to see here but a crippled fairy completely tanking her very first mission.

Ophelia dragged herself behind a cardboard box big enough to be her bedroom and collapsed, careful not to move her broken wing too much. She didn't cry out. She refused. Fairies were unnaturally strong for their size, but that didn't mean they all handled injury the same. Rebecca, for one, was a wuss—complaining every time she got a splinter. Even Charlie couldn't handle much in the way of physical discomfort, and he squirmed at the sight of blood. But Ophelia could take it. She had a high tolerance for pain.

Failure? That was a different story.

There was no way around it anymore. In her current state, knowing the coin was getting farther from her, knowing she couldn't fly, there was nothing else she could do but call for backup. After all, the wish was what was important. Keep the magic flowing, maintain the system. At that moment, Ophelia couldn't care less about Kasarah's brand-new purple bike; but a promise was a promise. And if that meant Ophelia would have to choke down her pride and press the stupid button and call for help, then that's just what she would do. She'd press the fiddlesticking but—

Ophelia froze, hand on her satchel, staring at the empty pocket where the baby acorn used to be; her only direct contact with the Haven.

Gone.

It must have been knocked free when Ophelia got hit. She stood up slowly and retraced her steps, hobbling to the alley's entrance, scanning the sidewalk around the mound of trash bags and the street beyond. A discarded paper cup bounced and rolled as cars shot by. Loose gravel was kicked up under tires. But no sign of a green acorn with a button on top. Not that she could see.

Great. Just terrific.

Just absolutely gobsmacking, nutcracking, hornswoggling, peach-pie perfect.

Ophelia felt herself boiling, her anger frothing from deep inside, clawing its way up. She couldn't help it. It was too much to stomach. The airplane. The geese. The old man. The lady with the broom. The guy with the newspaper. The stupid truck. The broken wing. And now *this*?

"GYAH!" she screamed, stomping with one foot, ignoring the pain that shot up her leg. "Fornswaggled, filthridden, barkaddled, hurlygurts!"

She turned and started kicking the brick wall of the building beside her, despite the renewed burning it triggered in her back. She was too mad to care. Every curse she'd ever heard sprang from her lips in a volley of spit and fury.

"Flabforkin', fartfiddled, toejammed, spitwashed, lumpsucking, bonyheaded buttfish!"

She turned and found an empty soda can and kicked it over, then proceeded to jump up and down on top of it, crushing it flat beneath her feet, hoping to smash it to oblivion.

"If this isn't the biggest, boot-up-the-back-end piece of fistsucking, pig-nosed, turkey-flapped, snotwad, vomit-crusted, wart-eating, mother-punching, kitten-kicking pile of rotten, wrinkled monkey dung in the whole wide WORLD! Now

139

DIE . . . YOU . . . STUPID . . . CAN!"

She gave it one last teeth-gritting stomp. Then she stopped and looked down at the tin pancake underfoot, realizing, only now, what kind of spectacle she'd probably made.

She looked out into the street to see if anybody had heard or seen her, but no one stopped to watch the angry bird chirping violently and mashing a soda can. She was alone. Completely alone.

Exhausted and broken, Ophelia Fidgets stood in the middle of the alleyway and cried.

24

There are *legends* of humans who have mistakenly ventured into the realm of fairies. They usually don't end well.

Sometimes the humans are turned into reeds or pansies. Sometimes they are turned into smoke. Most of the time they are simply driven mad and sent back to their village or town to be locked away in a hospital or a sanitarium where men in white coats write down all their gibberish about little flying people and the beautiful music they play. They aren't true, these stories. Not most of them, anyways. They are whispers, carried by the wind, invented by the fairies themselves to prevent humans from venturing too close. A scare tactic that has worked for centuries.

Of course there are also stories—recent stories—of fairies who have stayed too long in the *human* world. Those *never* end well. And unfortunately most of them are true.

Ophelia might have stayed there forever—right in that exact spot by the flattened can—if it weren't for the loud bark that startled her and caused her to spin.

In the alley, only ten feet away, stood a mangy-looking, golden-haired mutt, who had somehow padded up without Ophelia noticing. She didn't know much about dogs—they weren't exactly roaming the wild beneath the Havens, unless you counted the coyotes she sometimes heard braying or the occasional red wolf on the prowl—and the Archives considered them a relatively low threat to fairies in general, on account of the fact that they could neither fly nor climb trees. She knew just enough about dogs to identify the slobbering beast in front of her as one. With its dolorous brown eyes and its tongue hanging limp out of one side of its mouth, the creature didn't look half as cunning or clever as either a wolf or coyote. But it knew how to talk. And because she was a fairy, Ophelia knew how to listen.

"Hello," the dog said cheerily. "I think I would like to eat you."

Oh, really? she thought. Ophelia's hand dropped to the curved wooden handle of her knife. She took three steps back, careful not to corner herself against the wall. "You try it and I swear I will carve my way right back out of you," she barked back. Maybe that was a little harsh. Technically all of nature's creatures were sacred and precious and whatnot, but this mound of matted fur had caught her at an extraordinarily bad time, and she wasn't messing around.

The mutt's dripping tongue retreated back into his mouth and he barked a little softer this time. "Okay. I will not eat you. Instead maybe I could chew on you some and then find a nice hole to put you in?" He said it like he was presenting a suitable counteroffer, hoping she might agree. He took a tentative step toward her but froze when she hissed at him.

"I am *not* kidding, dog. You have no idea the kind of day I'm having. You take one more step and I will totally split you in half."

Actually, Ophelia wasn't sure she could if she tried. She wasn't exactly in sparring shape. But it wasn't as if she could just fly away either. And she couldn't outrun him, not in her current condition. Her only choice was to stand her ground.

The dog cocked his head sideways but didn't come any closer. "You are very strange," he said, panting now. "You are not a bird. At first I thought you were a bird, but birds do not talk like you; they are squawky, and you are not squawky. Plus, your beak is too short and you don't have any feathers and you are pink and blue and I have never met a bird that is pink and blue before, so since I don't know what you are I am hoping to sniff your butt."

Ophelia choked. "Excuse me?"

"Oh, it's okay. I will let you sniff mine, too," the dog said encouragingly, looking behind him and wagging his tail to indicate where his was located, in case she didn't know.

Ophelia's face contorted in disgust. "No. *No.* Nobody is sniffing anybody's butt. If you could please just go away, I have some serious prob—"

"You are small," the dog interrupted.

Ophelia looked at him with raised eyebrows.

"There is a squirrel I used to chase by Master's house. She was bigger than you, but very fast. I do not think you would be as fast, but I think I would still like to chase you anyway," the dog added.

Ophelia put one hand up again in protest—the one not gripping the handle of her knife. "Okay, dog. Listen carefully. You're not eating me. You're not sniffing me. And you're certainly not chasing me. I'm not going anywhere. Not yet. I have to figure out which way—"

"Chase is my favorite game. It works like this. You go and I chase you. It is the best."

Ophelia slapped her forehead. What an *idiot*. He was worse than the goose. She didn't have time for this. She turned back toward the street and the cars passing by, concentrating again, listening for the wish. The dog's sudden intrusion had snapped her out of her funk, forced her to try to get ahold of herself. She wiped her cheeks with one torn sleeve. The mission wasn't over. She couldn't call for backup, and the wish was out of range, but there were still several tocks left in the day. If she could somehow pick up the trail of Kasarah's voice, locate the white car, maybe find a way to fix up her wing, at least temporarily, then maybe . . .

"Did you get kicked?"

Ophelia turned back to the mutt, who was still staring at her.

144

"What? No, I didn't get kicked. What makes you think I got kicked?"

"You said you had a terrible day," the dog explained.

Ophelia paused to take in this creature a little more closely. She could see some scratches along his ear now, and a swollen spot on his side. A mark on his snout looked like it had healed long ago, but it left a firm reminder.

"Okay. No. I didn't get kicked," she said softly. "Just nearly run over. And I've got this." She turned slightly so he could see her busted wing.

"Oh. You are broken," the dog said.

"Yeah. I guess so. It's not terrible, but I can't really fly, I don't think, so—"

"You are broken. I will lick you."

"What?" Ophelia panicked as the giant, panting beast came toward her. "No! Wait!" But it was too late. The dog's meaty, sticky tongue rolled out of its mouth like a fat pink carpet. She didn't even have time to draw her knife before she was slimed, a trail of saliva running down the front of her suit, which was already soaked in white foam and blue spritzy stuff. "Stop! Cut it out, all right? I don't need your stinking dog spit all over me!"

The dog scooted back a little, panting, clearly pleased with himself. "Don't you feel better?" he asked.

"No, I don't feel better! Now I'm broken *and* gross! What did you have to eat last? Your breath smells awful!"

"Oh. For breakfast I had thing-on-the-side-of-the-road,"

the dog said thoughtfully. "I think it might have been a possum. It was not very good."

Ophelia fought down the urge to retch. She did her best to wipe the dog spit from her face.

"You do not taste very good either," the dog admitted.

"Sorry to disappoint you," Ophelia snipped. She felt all-over disgusting now. She needed to get out of this flight suit. It wasn't doing her any good anyways; she obviously wasn't heading back home anytime soon. She began to undo the buttons—easier since one of them was broken already—and peeled off the slimy, foamy, dead-thing-on-the-side-of-the-road-smelling outer layer, being especially careful pulling it free from around her broken wing. She let the pink suit crumple into a pile at her feet. For a moment she considered burying it, hiding it, but any human who passed by would surely see only a scrap of dirty fabric. Maybe a bird would make it into nesting material. When she was done she felt a twinge better, like snakes must feel sloughing off an old skin. She touched her hand to the vial nestled above her heart. At least she hadn't lost that.

The dog was still panting next to her. He obviously didn't have anywhere pressing to be. "Do you have a name?" he asked. "Or do I just call you broken-thing-that-is-not-a-bird-and-doesn't-play-chase-and-doesn't-taste-very-good?"

"My name is Fidgets," she grunted. "Ophelia Delphinium Fidgets. I'm a fairy."

"Oh." He didn't seem too impressed. He'd probably never met a fairy before. Or even heard of them. "My name is Dog. Stupid Dog. I am a dog."

Ophelia squinted at him. "That can't be your name," she said, even though she'd called him pretty much the same thing only moments ago.

"Oh no, I have lots of names. You can pick the one you like best. You can call me Useless. Or Mangy Mutt. Or Worthless-Son-of-a—"

Ophelia put both hands up. "Okay. All right. I get it. Lots of names. How about I just call you . . ." She stopped to think. She was no Founder. She'd never had to name anything in her life. She looked around the alley and spotted an empty crate that once held something called *Samuel Adams Boston Lager.* "How about I just call you Sam."

Sam slapped his tail against the pavement. "Oh. I like that. I like that name very much."

"I'm glad. Now, listen, Sam, I'd love to stay and talk, but I'm on a very important mission. There's something I've got to try to track down."

At the word *track*, Sam's ears perked. "Oh yes. Oh yes. I can help you," he said. "Master says that is the *only* thing I am good at."

Ophelia didn't doubt it. Not the *only* thing part—he was obviously good at annoying people, and licking them when they didn't want it—but the other part. She'd read somewhere

147

that dogs were excellent trackers with a tremendous sense of smell. But that wouldn't help her. You can't sniff out a wish. "Maybe some things. But not this," she said.

"Is it a cat?"

"No. It's not a cat," Ophelia answered.

"Is it a bird?"

"It's not a bird either."

"Is it a cat?"

"What? I just told you it wasn't a cat. It's a wish, okay?"

"Oh! A wish. I can track a wish," Sam said emphatically.

"Do you even know what a wish is?" Ophelia asked.

"No. But it sounds delicious. Can you eat it?"

"No, you can't eat it." She supposed you could swallow the nickel if you wanted (easier than a quarter at least). Knowing what little she knew of Sam already, she guessed he might try. "Wishes aren't like other things. They don't have smells. You can't eat them or sniff them or lick them. You can only grant them. I lost one. And if I don't find it soon, there could be serious trouble."

Sam whimpered. "That's bad," he said.

"What's bad?"

"Being lost," he answered.

Ophelia forced a smile. She was starting to put his story together now. No tags. No collar. Abused and then abandoned, probably. Or maybe he ran away. If she was a Whisperer she might know what to say. If she was a Mender, maybe, she would take a look at the scratches and bruises and do

148

something to make them better. But she was a Granter. And even if dogs could make wishes—which they can't—Sam's wish wouldn't be hers to grant. What little magic she had wasn't meant for him.

"I'm sorry, Sam. I'd love to stay and chat," she lied, "but I really have to go."

She turned back toward the street, figuring she would head off in the direction she had seen the white car go, hoping to follow the thread of the whisper. It would take forever, walking instead of flying, but along the way she might think of something, a way to fix her wing, perhaps, or a way to travel faster. Until then she could do little more than put one foot in front of the other. There was still time. It wasn't *completely* hopeless. She still had the dust. Still had a canister of spray (provided this one worked). Still had her training to rely on. Still had that moist, rotten-smelling breath on the back of her neck . . .

Ophelia whirred around, coming nose to snout with the dog.

"What are you doing?" she growled.

Sam wagged his tail emphatically. "I am following you," he said. "It is like chase, but less fun because you are not going very fast at all."

"I know you're following me. *Why* are you following me?"

"Because you are broken and lost and I licked you, so now we are friends."

Ophelia groaned and shook her head. She considered

explaining that that's not how it worked. You don't just lick people and hope they will like you. In fact, probably just the opposite. "We aren't friends, Sam. I'm a fairy. You're a dog. We have absolutely nothing in common."

That wasn't true, of course. As soon as it came out of her mouth, she realized it. In fact, this dog and she probably had more in common than she wanted to admit. They were both obviously on their own. They'd both seen better days. They could both stand to eat something, preferably *not* lying dead on the side of the road. But the last thing she needed was something else to worry about, something else to distract her from her assignment. And this mutt was obviously a distraction.

"I am Sam and you are Ophelia. You are tracking a wish but you are broken. I am a good tracker. I will help you to track your wi . . . uh-oh . . . here it comes."

The dog dropped to his haunches, his back paw shooting up, desperately trying to reach a spot behind his right ear. As he clawed for it he growled and moaned at the same time, the same word, over and over. "Itchy itchy itchy itchy itchy."

Ophelia rolled her eyes. "You've got to be kidding me," she whispered to herself. "Okay, just bend down," she said.

To her surprise, Sam followed orders, his belly hitting the ground, his snout so close to her she could feel the warm air from his nostrils on her face. She circled around his muzzle, careful not to get too near the teeth. She'd never been this close to an animal before, unless you counted the kestrels and warblers who often confused fairies for their own kind and tried to get fresh with them back in the Tree Tops. If Sam suddenly decided that Ophelia would make a good snack or a chew toy, he could easily twist his head and have her in his jaws before she could react. But he lay still as she reached up with both hands, planting them in the thick tufts of blond fur behind his ears.

"Oh yes. Scratch scratch scratch itchy itchy scratch . . ." His back leg started to thump.

"I'm getting it, all right?" Ophelia huffed. She dug in with all ten fingers as he begged her for a minute more, then she wiped her hands on the front of her pants, trying to get the dog stink off. "There. I scratched your stupid ear. Now will you leave me alone?"

"Oh, I can't leave you alone *now*," Sam said. "Now you are *definitely* my friend."

Oh Havens, what had she done? Ophelia had friends, she wanted to tell him. A bunch of friends. Well, a few of them, at least, waiting for her back at the Haven. She didn't need another.

"You are my new best friend, and I will help you find your wish," Sam reiterated.

"Yeah, but see—I don't *want* your help," Ophelia said forcefully. "This is going to be hard enough for *me* to do without also having to drag you along and stop every time you see something you want to sniff or eat or talk to. I'm moving slow enough already. So this is it, okay? Good-bye."

Ophelia waved behind her and continued down the alley. She had almost reached the street when suddenly her feet left the pavement.

She was flying. Actually flying. Except her wings were still folded against her back, one of them half in tatters. She felt the tug of her uniform pulled taut in the back, the collar nearly choking her, then something wet in her hair and something fuzzy tickling the back of her neck.

"What are you doing?" she screamed.

"I wem warrying ewe in mwy mouf," Sam replied through clenched teeth.

"You're drooling all over me!" She could feel it dripping down her back. "Put me down!"

She dropped suddenly. It was only a few inches, but it took her by surprise and she collapsed to her knees. Sam looked at her with cocoa-colored eyes.

"Of all the wood-headed, dim-witted creatures I could have possibly run into . . ." she started to say, but she stopped herself.

It wasn't just the hurt look on Sam's face that gave her pause, though that was part of it. It was something else. An idea. A way to cover ground faster and maybe avoid being seen, or not be seen as much, at least.

It wasn't a *great* idea, and she was pretty sure the other fairies back at Grant Tower would frown on it, but hairy times sometimes called for hairy measures.

"All right, Sam. Do you really want to help me?" Ophelia asked.

"Oh yes, I do. I really do."

Ophelia sighed, still not sure what she was getting into.

"All right, then," she said. "Lie down. And whatever you do, do *not* lick me again."

25

Not all fairies have wings.

The fairies of the North American contingent are winged, of course, but there were many of Ophelia's kind who were born without all the flap and flutter. This doesn't mean that those fairies didn't fly. They just talk other creatures into doing the hard work for them.

Ophelia had seen pictures of her distant relatives on the backs of brown bats and brush finches. Fairies who harnessed turtledoves and took them for a dive. There was even a race of fairies known to ride on the backs of hawks, though Ophelia guessed them to be incredibly brave or incomparably stupid, for a hawk would sooner eat a fairy than let it hitch a ride. Legends even tell of giant fairies that rode on horseback, but you can't believe everything you hear.

Fairies on *dog*back, however—*that* was unusual. Ophelia

was fairly certain she was the first fairy to try it.

And just as certain that it was the smelliest mode of transport she could have picked.

The advantage to having thick, tufted fur was that it made it easier for Ophelia to bury herself in it, pressing flat against Sam's back as he trotted dutifully in whatever direction she whispered. It also gave her plenty to hold on to, though the dog would occasionally yip at her if she pulled too tight.

The disadvantage was that her new ride stank of damp garbage, and Ophelia had to lift her head every few seconds just to catch a fresh breath. Not to mention she had to suppress the urge to work out all the tangles in Sam's fur and pick out the burrs that had nested there for Haven knows how long. Never in her life had she seen an animal in as sore a need of a bath and a brush; even Charlie would surely shake his head.

At least the dog didn't have fleas. None that Ophelia could see. More important, he could trot much faster than she could walk in her current state.

Ophelia pressed herself close to Sam's warm skin and closed her eyes, listening carefully, past the *fwoosh* and *fwoom* of passing cars, past the steady drum of Sam's heartbeat, through the hissing, beeping, honking symphony of city life, picking up the thread of Kasarah's wish. She thought she could start to make it out, though it wasn't so much a heard sound as a hunch, and it wavered, sputtering in and out like a candle flame flickering in the wind.

"I think it's more left of here," Ophelia whispered, and Sam changed course. Thankfully the sidewalks weren't as busy as the streets; humans preferred to roll around in their big metal boxes rather than use the two good feet nature gave them. The few people they passed couldn't help but look at Sam as he went by, though. She wondered what they thought they saw—a bird hitching a ride on the back of a dog? Or did the camo make her appear to be a giant tuft of fur instead? At least if the camouflage *were* to fail, her brown uniform would blend with Sam's dirty fur better than the pink suit. She tried to stay as low as possible, and whenever Sam saw a person he changed direction slightly, putting some distance between them. Ophelia got the impression that he wanted to avoid human contact just as much as she did.

It became easier the farther they went, away from the mall where Ophelia had lost her wish and the INER where she'd met the business end of a broom, the streets getting narrower, the buildings more spread out. Grass soon replaced concrete, trees replaced lampposts, and Ophelia started to relax, just a little. When the streets were completely empty she sat up and took in a huge lungful of air. As she did she caught a hint of something in the wind.

Not the wish. She'd already told Sam that wishes carried no scent. No. This was something else entirely. Something almost as good. "Do you smell that?" she asked.

Sam stopped abruptly and lifted his snout to the sky. "Oh yes," he said. "That is a very good smell. What is it?"

"That," said Ophelia, snorting up another glorious whiff, "is doughnuts." She was almost certain of it.

"Oh," Sam said, clearly impressed. Ophelia wondered if he'd ever even had a doughnut before. Or how long it had been since he'd eaten anything that wasn't already decomposing. She hadn't eaten since the morning, and just the sugary-sweet smell made her light-headed.

She couldn't continue to track this wish on an empty stomach, she decided. "Follow your nose, Sam," Ophelia said. "It's time to fill up."

Fairies are born from rose petals and fern fronds. They are nurtured on nectar and dewdrops. They take what they need from Mother Nature in return for being her caretakers as well, making homes of her trees and feasts of her seeds, living on nectarines and wild onions and dates dipped in honey borrowed from bees. But even fairies have their cravings. Things they discover outside the natural world. Sumptuous treats and exotic delicacies brought back by the Scouts, whose mission it was to stay abreast of human activity and keep the Archives full. Things like caramels, and ice cream, and spiced Frappuccinos. Charlie was especially fond of those.

Almost all fairies had a bit of a sweet tooth, but Ophelia had a mouth full of them. Her true weakness was doughnuts. From the moment she first tasted one, the sugar glaze dissolving on her tongue, sending tremors racing up and down her whole body, she knew she was in love. There were so many things humans had invented that gave her pause. Their explosive weapons and their smog-belching factories. Their boxy gizmos always bleeping and buzzing. Their giant towers stretching clear to the clouds. And airplanes, newly added to the list. But doughnuts? Ophelia wondered why no human had ever wished for a never-ending supply of them. A selfish wish, but one she could get behind.

The source of the smell was only a block away, and Sam easily sniffed it out. A sign sat over a little pink-and-brown building with peeling paint: *Sweet Sally's Bakery.* The parking lot was practically empty. Sam shook his head. "I have never had a doughnut before," he said, confirming her suspicion. "Is it better than dead stuff?"

"On my wings, it's a million times better than dead stuff," Ophelia told him. "The question is, how do we get some?" She supposed they could just gallop in and rob the place, like the outlaws she'd seen in pictures down in the Archives, from a time when humans wore giant silly hats and scarves around their faces. She pictured herself on Sam's back, a can of knock-out spray in hand, hooting and hollering as they ransacked the bakery, leaving a trail of unconscious bodies in their wake.

Except that would be breaking at least thirty rules of fairy-human engagement. Wanting a doughnut probably didn't count as justifiable cause for going on a fairy-dust-spraying rampage. "We need a plan," she said. Ophelia and Sam sat and watched a man emerge from the bakery holding a bag. She could smell them from where they sat on the side of the road, at least fifty yards away.

"We could take *his* doughnuts," Sam suggested.

Ophelia shook her head. "That's not a good plan."

"But you said doughnuts were better than dead stuff," Sam reminded her.

"They are. They're wonderful. But you can't just take whatever you want when you want it. You have to pay for it, one way or another. There are rules. Everything comes at a price."

"Even doughnuts?"

"Even doughnuts," she replied.

Sam whimpered and dropped to his belly, resting his muzzle on his paws. He was watching the door, waiting. Then he licked his chops and sat up suddenly, nearly knocking Ophelia off.

"Trash," he barked.

"Trash? What about tra—" Ophelia started to say before nearly falling over backward and gripping a clump of fur as Sam took off, bounding across the street toward the bakery. "Sam, where are you going?" she shouted, but the dog ignored her, galumphing through the parking lot and skirting clear around the back of the building, his snout held high, taking big sniffs, the smell of sweet fried dough growing even more intense.

And then she saw it. The brown plastic bin. *Mike's Waste Management Services* printed in white along its side. The lid was open and there was a platoon of bees circling above it, occasionally plunging down into its belly before buzzing back up. Clearly there was something in there worth diving for.

"Trash," Sam repeated. Ophelia nodded in appreciation. Glorious, glorious trash.

26

Books can teach you only so much. Ophelia had been sub-jected to endless tocks of training, reading manual after manual and poring over pictures, but sometimes you can learn about a thing only by experiencing it firsthand.

And sometimes you had to get those hands dirty.

No one had ever bothered to teach Ophelia that there was treasure to be had in trash cans (outside of broken turkey bones, of course). She wasn't trained to be a Scavenger. They certainly hadn't told her that it was possible to find *doughnuts* in the garbage. Such a ludicrous thought. Who would throw away doughnuts?

And yet, here they were. A whole box of them sitting near the top of the plastic bin, beckoning with sugary promises that made her mouth water. Granted, it hadn't been easy getting up there. Ophelia wasn't at all ready to risk flying and further injuring her wing, so instead she carefully perched on Sam's nose and he leapt up, putting his front paws as high as possible.

"Excuse me," Ophelia said to the circle of bees who were dutifully fulfilling their own mission: Operation Feed the Queen. "Do you mind sharing?"

The bees, perhaps noting some distant kinship with another winged creature, simply nodded. Not much for conversation, bees. Great dancers, though. Ophelia stared greedily at the box that had come open when it was dumped. Its contents appeared untouched, though she was certain the bees had put their hairy mitts all over them. Half of the doughnuts glistened with glaze, and the other half were coated in white frosting like a crust of hard-packed snow on a mountain's peak. Ophelia carefully lowered herself over the lip of the bin onto the box and took a deep breath. Garbage never smelled so good.

"Regular or frosted?" she called out to Sam.

"I don't know. Which one is better?" he barked, the tip of his nose just peeking out over the edge.

"You really can't go wrong."

In the end she tossed over one of each for him, getting sugar flakes all over the front of her uniform, which was annoying but would be worth it. Then she took another white frosted for herself, heaving it up over the side before climbing back onto Sam's snout and hanging on tight as he lowered her down. Both of the frosted doughnuts had hit the asphalt frosting side down and all three were covered in grit, but that didn't stop Sam, and it wouldn't stop her either.

"*Oh,*" he said, woofing down his first in three bites. "*Oh. Yes*. You were right. This is *so* much better than dead stuff."

"Told you so," Ophelia said, carefully picking out the tiny rocks and bits of dirt from the top of hers and then daintily tearing off handfuls with only her fingertips, already sticky. The doughnuts were stale—there had to be some reason they were thrown out—but even an old doughnut with enough frosting is better than most other things she could imagine. Ophelia broke off another piece and let it slowly dissolve on her tongue, the glaze going straight to her head, making her dizzy. "How did you know these would even be back here?" she asked.

Sam had moved on to his second now and was devouring it with as little chewing as possible. Ophelia wondered why nature bothered giving dogs so many teeth when they didn't seem at all interested in using them. "Trash is sometimes all there is to eat," Sam replied.

Ophelia paused mid-bite and looked hard at the mutt, wondering just how long he'd been out here on his own. Long enough to learn to check behind the backs of restaurants and bakeries for food. Ophelia had been beyond the borders of the Haven for only less than a day, and it had nearly killed her. Twice. The dog might not be the brightest star in the sky, but he was a survivor.

"What happened to you, Sam?" Ophelia asked. "Where's your master? The one you told me about?"

"Master? Oh. Yes. That is a sad story. Do you want to hear

163

it?" Ophelia nodded. Sam licked his chops. "It was many days ago. We were going Out in Truck. We'd gone Out lots of times before. Master always let me stick my head through Truck's window. This time was different though. He kept Truck all closed up. And I could tell we were going someplace really far away. Then Truck stopped and Master told me, 'Get out,' so I did. Then Truck went away and I lost him," he concluded. "Or he lost me."

Ophelia nodded. So that was it. He *had* been abandoned. She reached out and stroked behind his ear with her sticky hand. "I'm sorry," she said.

"Oh, don't be sorry," Sam barked brightly. "If I hadn't lost Master, I might not have found you. And we might not have found doughnuts."

Ophelia looked down at the last half of doughnut in her lap. "I think I'm full," she said. "You want the rest?"

The tongue eagerly flopping out of Sam's mouth was answer enough.

While he scarfed down her other half, Ophelia twisted to inspect her busted wing. The pain had subsided somewhat—provided she didn't try to move it too much—but it was still a mess. Fairies were notoriously quick healers, but not that quick. Not *matter-of-hours* quick. She needed to bandage it and brace it, make a splint of some sort to make sure it healed right. She didn't want to go through the rest of her life with a bent wing. She'd fly sideways or do barrel rolls the whole time she was skybound.

Sam must have noticed her looking, because he whimpered and nuzzled her torn wing gently. For a second she worried he was going to try to lick her again, but he'd learned his lesson the first time. "You are sad," he said.

Ophelia sighed. "I'm not sad. I'm worried. There's a difference."

"You are worried about your wing."

"I'm worried about my wish. I've got to find it, Sam. I'm a Granter. It's my job. If I don't find it, then I might not be able to stay a Granter any longer." *And that is only the half of it,* she thought. The whole Haven was counting on her, but she didn't feel like explaining it all.

"Oh," Sam said. He seemed to consider this a moment, then swished his tail along the ground. "What's a wish again?"

"A wish is something you want really badly but is often too difficult for you to get yourself," she explained. "It's a magical thing. A rare thing. And somehow I lost one." *My first one, no less.*

Sam looked confused. "What does it look like?"

Ophelia shook her head. "You can't see it. Besides, it's not *really* the wish we are looking for. The wish is embedded."

"It's sleeping?"

"Not *in bed. Embedded.* It's attached to something. An object. This particular wish was made on a coin," she explained. "I need the coin if I'm going to make the wish come true. That's just how it works. Unfortunately the coin was taken before I could finish the granting."

Sam nodded as if he understood completely. "Like the bone," he said.

"The bone?"

"Oh yes. It was a *big* bone. Master's friend gave it to me. Master's friend was nice. I chewed and I chewed and I chewed, but I couldn't finish it, so I buried it by a tree. But when I went back the next day the hole was empty and the bone was gone. Like your wish."

"Yeah, something like that," Ophelia said.

"Empty holes are the worst," Sam added. He licked his jowls, making sure he got every last flake of hardened glaze. "So what is it for?"

"What?"

"The wish. Is it yours? Did you make it?"

"Fairies can't make wishes," Ophelia said. "We're not allowed." *And what could we possibly want?* Everything she needed, the Haven provided—minus an unlimited supply of magic, of course. But you can't use magic to produce more magic; no such thing as wishing for more wishes. "It's for a girl. Her name is Kasarah. She wants a bike. A purple one."

"Oh. I see." Sam nodded. "What's a bike?"

Ophelia shrugged. "It's like Truck, I guess," she said. "Except with only two wheels. You ride it." *Sort of like what I've been doing with you*, she thought, picturing what she must look like astride Sam's back, arms flung around his neck, though thankfully she didn't have to pedal to make him move. Just scratch behind his ears.

"Is she your friend?" Sam asked.

He meant Kasarah. Ophelia shook her head. "No. She's just a name picked at random out of a tree."

"Oh," Sam said, sounding even more confused and uncertain than before. She could guess what he was thinking: *This is a long way to go for a name picked out of a tree.* Or maybe that was just her. So much trouble already for someone she didn't even know, had never even met and probably never would.

It will be worth it, she reminded herself. And it's not as if she had a choice. She thought of the sign in the lobby of Grant Tower. Every wish granted. Every promise fulfilled. The leaves fall, the Granters fulfill, the magic keeps flowing, and the Haven endures. That's how it had been for over a hundred years, and she would rather break *both* her wings than be the first fairy to let her people down.

Ophelia stood up and looked around, trying to get her bearings again. She had a sense of what direction the wish had been traveling when she and Sam took their detour, but the whisper was weak—impossible to get a proper fix on. There were too many other noises down here. The buzz of the swarm of bees by the trash can, the hum of the metal box by the building, the sound of the cars driving by, the steady *thwap thwap thwap* of Sam's tail against the pavement. She couldn't concentrate.

She spotted a line of trees not too far from where they sat, a small woods that had somehow resisted being chopped down to make room for banks and coffee shops. One in particular, an old white oak that topped out over the others, looked promising. If she could get to the top of it, maybe she could focus and pick up on the wish's trace. Up among the trees, the magic might speak stronger.

Except what would normally be an easy flight, barely a jump to the top, now looked like an arduous task. She pointed it out to Sam. "I'm going to climb to the top of that big tree and see what I can see," she said.

"Then I will pee on a different one," Sam declared, which was more information than she needed. He bent down so she could saddle up again, then carried her toward the little woods, dropping her off by the old oak before finding another one for his business.

Ophelia looked up. She had never climbed a tree before— why climb when you can fly—but how hard could it be? Cats could do it. And monkeys. Ants. Spiders. Even snails could make it up—albeit slowly, and only because they were so repulsively sticky.

Sticky.

Ophelia glanced down at her still slightly sugary fingers— not nearly tacky enough for gripping tree bark. But she knew what might be. She opened her mostly empty pack and found her roll of Super Silver Sticky Strips, peeling them off and attaching them, one by one, sticky side out, to her boots. She secured them along the side with even more strips until the she had used up the whole roll, but by the end her boots had practically changed color, shining bright in the sunlight.

"What are you doing?" Sam asked, returning after having found three or four different trees that suited him.

"Believe it or not, I'm making something," she said. "It's not really a talent of mine. I'm no Builder. But I think this might just work." She finished attaching the tape to her second boot, then tested them out by standing up. She wouldn't be able to hang upside down from a branch by her feet or anything, but the newly modded boots should provide some additional traction. "Just wait here and watch over my bag," she said, setting her satchel by Sam's paw. Then she started up.

It really wasn't as hard as she expected—the advantage of small hands and nimble fingers, capable of digging into the fissures of the tree's thick bark. Her sticky feet found more purchase than they would have otherwise, but she still found that most of her progress came from pulling herself up, finding twigs and branches that she could use as ladder rungs. Once she got high enough, the branches became much more plentiful. Her left shoulder was starting to throb again, and she wondered if this would even be worth it. What did she expect to find up there? Did she really think she was close enough to spot the coin? That she could catch the glimmer of its halo or even hear Kasarah's wistful voice from this far away? But she had to try. Branch by branch, hand over hand, she scrabbled her way up to the top of the white oak, finally breaking free of its tufted top growth, crawling on her hands and knees along one of its flimsy upper branches to get the best possible view.

Ophelia sighed.

There wasn't much to see. Mostly grays and beiges and blacks. Houses and towers and roads. Far off she could make out a line of rectangles that was probably an even bigger city.

Back in the Haven, in the Tree Tops where she lived, you could look out and see the mountains. Endless, undulating waves of green and the wispy smoke of fog settled over everything like cotton stretched thin. In the fall you could see the sunset captured by the tree leaves, rust-colored oranges blending with lemony yellows and crackling reds. It was a breath-hitching moment, every time.

This was mostly buildings and streets. Nowhere did she catch the sparkle, the faint glow of Kasarah's nickel pulsing with promised magic. But maybe, just maybe, she could hear it.

She closed her eyes and let the wind whip around her, rifling through the leaves whose stems she held on to, feeling the branch sway and bend. What she wanted, what she wanted more than anything right now? Just a sign. Anything. She bit down hard on her lip again, tasting coppery blood, probably from the same spot as before.

Then she heard it. Coming from far off to her right.

I wish.

Her heart leapt. That was it. She'd found it. It was still within reach.

I wish.

And then another sound.

A piercing *caw*.

Followed by the beat of wings.

And Ophelia felt her breath squeezed out of her.

27

Had she been a robust sort of fairy, the size of a muskrat or a groundhog, she would have been killed instantly. The talon would have neatly pierced her soft middle, punctured a lung perhaps, or plunged straight into her heart.

But the red-tailed hawk that spotted Ophelia dangling from the oak's branches was full grown and large for its kind, and Ophelia was small for hers, despite the doughnut cravings, and so the bird's clawed feet wrapped clear around her instead, squeezing the very breath out of her, but not, at least, impaling her on the spot.

Small consolation, Ophelia thought as she hovered eight hundred feet above the ground, turned faceup so that she could see the patch of gray on the hawk's broad chest, the burnt-orange spray of feathers from its fanned tail. For a fleeting moment, Ophelia was jealous—such beautiful, unmarred wings—and then her predicament hit her: she was clutched in the talons of a beast that saw Ophelia as nothing more than food.

Ophelia's chest burned with each breath, her arms struggled to get free, her legs kicked out, but it was no use—the raptor had her locked tight. She couldn't reach for her spray or her knife or even give the bird a heart-stopping, Fayitsu-palm-heel strike to its breast. Her only hope, she realized, was to get the hawk to let her go. To talk the beast down.

Unfortunately she hadn't had a great deal of luck conversing with birds lately.

"Excuse me," Ophelia croaked out, shifting as much as she could to breathe better. "Excuse me. I think there's been some kind of mistake. See. I'm not what you think I am."

The hawk bent its head, eyeballing her for one moment and then ignoring her, renewing its flight with another beat of its perfect wings. It wasn't interested in conversation. Just lunch.

"Hey! Hawk! Seriously! Listen! I know what you're thinking, and it's not going to work."

The hawk bent her sleek head again. This time she cawed out, a long, piercing screech that confirmed everything Ophelia'd been taught about their kind: they were ruthless hunters with a singular purpose and almost no sense of humor. "I'm *thinking*," the hawk said, "that I've caught mice with more meat than you. You look wiry and gamy. But I bet your insides are soft and warm and will make a passable meal for my hatchlings—after I've minced you a bit, that is." The hawk resumed its slow and steady flapping.

Minced me? Ophelia knew she wasn't in the position to argue, but she did anyways. "Yeah, but that's where you're wrong. I'm no mouse. I'm a fairy. And not just any fairy. I am a Granter from the Haven, and I'm trained in multiple disciplines of hand-to-hand combat. I'm heavily armed, potentially lethal, and on a bit of a sugar high, so the moment you set me down in your nest I'm going to get completely mythical on you. And you do *not* want that. Trust me."

The bird squawked at her again. "The moment I set you down in my nest you'll be dead, because I fully intend to squeeze the life out of you before landing. I just thought I'd keep you as fresh as possible until I got there."

As if to back up the threat, the hawk's talons clenched even tighter. Ophelia felt something snap, part of her already broken wing breaking even further, causing her to cry out in pain. Hawks were incapable of smiling—a lack of lips will do that—but Ophelia thought she could see the equivalent of a satisfied grin in its eyes. She had to find some way to get free before they reached the bird's nest. Something that didn't involve the use of her pinned arms or weapons she couldn't reach.

Which left only one option.

She would have to sing her way out of this.

Human lore is rich with tall tales and superstitions regarding the mystical power of song. Supposedly humans once believed in fantastic creatures who had nothing better to do than to sit

174

half naked on rocky beaches and lure simple-minded sailors to their deaths with enchanting music. Myths abound of people with fish tails for legs who could convince those same sailors to jump overboard with their boots on, sinking to their briny deaths, simply by singing to them. Nymphs and sorceresses whose haunting music could walk you straight off cliffs or nightingales who could warble you into an eternal sleep.

None of it's true. But it might have all come from the same original source. Because there is one creature whose song holds a bewitching effect.

Anyone who has ever heard it could tell you that fairy song is a powerful thing, except they wouldn't know to call it by name and would be too befuddled by the song itself to remember. It was often songs that the Whisperers sang when they coaxed the trees to grow or the flowers to unfold. It was sometimes a fairy song that could be heard by hikers near the Haven that filled their bellies and brains with a fear and made them turn around and go back the way they came. In truth, those sailors from long ago—the ones who supposedly heard "mermaids" and "sirens"—went insane because life on board a ship is maddening, but it's highly possible that a *fairy's* ditty hastened the process.

A fairy's song was its own special kind of magic, not beholden to the Great Tree or the wellsprings of fairy dust, but it didn't have quite the potency that human myth imagined. A fairy couldn't cause a man to pitch himself off a cliff just by sing-ing to him. The effects weren't that strong, and they differed by the fairy and the listener both. Each fairy had just one song with potentially magic effect. Many were ancient, passed down through generations, with lyrics and melodies seemingly as old as the trees they lived in. Many were in the human tongue, appropriated by the creatures of the fay for their own mischievous ends. "Greensleeves" or "Carraigdhoun." Several fairies Ophelia knew were fond of "Rolling in the Dew." They believed the older songs and chants had a more haunting appeal. Some of the younger fairies had rebelled against this notion and started going with Frank Sinatra ballads. "Come Fly with Me" was all the rage three seasons ago.

For Ophelia, however, it was Ozzy Osbourne.

More specifically, "Crazy Train."

It was one of the songs her Founder taught her, and it wheedled its way inside her and stuck, becoming the magical tune that she kept tucked away in case of emergencies.

For many fairies, singing had an enchanting effect, capable of making the listener dreamy eyed and woozy and warm, as if they'd polished off the last of the wine. For others it was the opposite. Ophelia knew of several fairies whose songs simply made you irritable or drove you absolutely batty.

That was the effect of "Crazy Train."

And to make matters worse, she wasn't a very good singer, which tended to lessen its potency. But when you are in the clutches of a coldhearted bird of prey determined to serve you to her brood with no way to reach your knife or your spray, your options are limited, and only Oz can save you.

"Okay, bird," Ophelia huffed. "You asked for it. *All aboard!*"

Ophelia started to hum at first, summoning the opening riff. She even did the little *aye-aye-aye*s, but the hawk ignored her, just kept its slow rhythmic beat and glide until Ophelia kicked in with the lyrics, singing as loud as she could with all the pressure on her chest.

"Crazy, but that's how it goes. Millions of people living as fo-o-o-o-oes."

The hawk gave Ophelia an eyeball, the cockeyed look of any creature who's not sure what's going on but is certain they don't like it. She felt the claws hug her tighter, but the bird was afraid of ruining her family's dinner too soon before arrival. Instead the hawk shook her head again and tried to press on. Ophelia gathered enough air to belt out the next line.

"Maybe it's not too late," Ophelia continued. *"To learn how to love, and forget how to ha-ee-ay-ee-ate . . ."*

The hawk's whole body started to quiver. She felt it dip in altitude suddenly. Ophelia's song was working. Her captor cawed down to her. "Stop that confounded racket or I will tear you in half!"

But Ophelia closed her eyes and channeled her Founder, Paolo, a fairy who was seldom inclined to speak but never afraid to sing.

"I'm goin' off the rails on a crazy train . . ."

"Stop it!" the hawk cawed. She swooped and twisted, but didn't let go.

Ophelia started to bang her head, repeating the same verse over and over again. The hawk let out a prolonged screech of annoyance or madness or both. Then, to Ophelia's relief, those pinching talons sprung open and Ophelia was free.

And free-falling.

28

Ophelia Fidgets prided herself on her forethought. Charlie often mocked her for setting her clothes out the night before or sharpening all six pencils at her desk even though she never used more than one. The only way to stay one step ahead is to think two ahead.

Had she been thinking two steps ahead at that moment, she might have reconsidered her plan, since it probably would have looked like this:

Step 1: Sing to the bird until it lets go of you.

Step 2: Fall to your death.

There was little time for reflecting on it now, however, as she plummeted, headfirst, hundreds of feet down. She acted on instinct instead, unfolding her one good wing to its full span, concerned that the other was too busted to do her any good. Even an accomplished flier can do only so much with one wing, however, and the best Ophelia did was slow her descent, catching what little wind she could to start spinning, making a vortex toward the surface, which, she noticed with a mixture of hope and despair, held an oval of green water.

A softer landing, at least. Ophelia angled as much as possible, aiming her body toward the scum-dappled surface of the pond, ignoring (not forgetting—just choosing not to acknowledge) the fact that she couldn't swim.

Ophelia hit the surface sideways, out of control, her good wing barely folding in in time. She went under, blue hair pillowing out above her, the bracing chill stealing what breath she had left. The water was dark and murky and she couldn't see the mud-covered bottom, though she knew she was sinking quickly toward it. She could hear nothing.

She twisted to get upright, kicking out with her arms and legs, but her uniform grew heavy and weighed her down. Her sticky-strip-covered boots felt like blocks cemented to her feet. She pushed harder, sensing the light playing on the surface above her, her lungs prickling, then burning, then begging. Her arms windmilled. Even her one good wing trembled, aching to fly her to the surface. *A deep breath*, she thought. *That's all I want.*

Her vision started to fog over, the murky green of the water giving way to gray and black.

She thought of the Femoriae. Back in the Haven. The names etched into the wall. *No. Not like this. This can't be how it happens.*

She kicked her legs one last time like a frog's, willing herself back to the surface, breaking free just long enough to take a breath, except she took water with it, choked once, and then felt herself sinking again. The last thing she saw before going back under was something huge moving toward her.

Underneath it was quiet again. And Ophelia closed her eyes and wondered if somewhere there weren't magical creatures who granted wishes for fairies the same way fairies granted them for people. And if there were rules about which wishes you could grant and which you couldn't. And if there was a limit to the number of wishes. And how lucky would you have to be to get yours. She felt an ache deep inside, blossoming outward. She thought of Charlie and Paolo and even Barnabus Squint. She thought of Kasarah Quinn. And, oddly enough, of the boy at the diner, the one in the green jacket, with that look of longing in his eyes. She thought of all the wishes that she would never get to grant.

The tightness around her chest intensified. She felt something hard against her back.

She felt her body move. A rush in her ears. The burst of light against her eyes.

She took a first instinctive gulp of air, coughed up a spray of water, then choked down another breath and another. She could feel herself moving but was too delirious to do anything else but breathe.

Yet she knew someone had heard her.

29

Ophelia opened her eyes to reveal something warm and rough pressed against her face. The last thing she remembered was seeing the sky again, the burning in her lungs, and a feeling of weightlessness.

And now there was a pink scratchy thing leaving a trail of spit along her cheek.

Ophelia reached out with both hands, shoving it away, then pushed herself backward in the grass, out of reach, blinking against the sun and the profile of the giant beast hovering over her.

"Oh. You are awake. I can stop licking you now."

Ophelia looked up into a pair of giant brown eyes.

"Sam?"

"Yes!" Sam barked. His fur was dripping. He was soaked to the bone.

"You saved me?"

The dog nodded, then barked again. "Oh yes. That is exactly what I did. I saved you. You were up in that tree and you were taken by a very big bird and we played chase but it was not a good game because birds are very fast and don't come down and I can't jump high enough to get them. Plus the bird looked scary and—"

"Wait a minute!" Ophelia interrupted. "You came after me?" She wasn't certain how long she'd been airborne, how far the hawk had carried her, but it felt like a fair distance. "All that way?"

Sam nodded. "I had to run my fastest to follow that bird, so I did. I got hold of your bag and I followed it. And then I saw you fall into the water and try to swim, but you are not a very good swimmer, and I *am* a very good swimmer, so I came to get you and I got you but you were sleepy so I woke you up and then you said my name and now I am telling you *all* about it."

Ophelia could barely believe it. This mongrel who she'd just met in an alleyway only a couple of tocks ago, who owed her nothing really, except maybe half a doughnut, had tracked her all that way and swum out to the middle of the pond to rescue her. Ophelia stood up, her uniform sopping, one hand shooting to her neck to make sure the vial was still there. She pulled it from under her wet shirt and inspected it—the dust still swirled and danced inside, not a drop of water had gotten in. She carefully tucked it back in and then brushed back the damp blue locks hanging in her face. She shivered where she stood, her skin clammy, the cold reaching down to her bones. But she was alive and in one piece.

The dog looked at her and whimpered. "Are you okay?"

Ophelia opened both of her arms and took a step toward him. Sam flinched. Something he'd undoubtedly learned from his master.

"It's all right, Sam," she said. She moved close and wrapped both arms around his neck, burying her face into the patch of wet fur where a name tag on a collar would sit, feeling his skin, much warmer than hers, on her cheek. "My hero."

"Oh," Sam said.

Ophelia squeezed him even tighter.

"Um . . . while you're there . . . if you could just . . . ?"

Ophelia reached up and started to scratch behind Sam's ear, and when Sam let out a long, low grunt of satisfaction she smiled, even as his butt rose up into the air, his tail swishing about, flicking pond water everywhere. "Oh yes. That is it exactly."

But Ophelia tuned him out; her scratching slowed and then stopped altogether. She stood there, pressed tight to Sam's chest, her hands clutching clumps of wet fur, listening to the voice in the wind.

Kasarah's voice.

And make it purple.

The sound was stronger than it had been since she'd lost track of it at the diner. The hawk must have taken her in the same direction as the man in the white car. Judging by how clear Kasarah's voice was ringing, they had to be close.

"Do you hear that?" Ophelia asked. But of course Sam couldn't, though it didn't stop him from perking his ears. "It's the wish," she explained. "It's nearby. We need to hurry." She stepped back and took Sam's muzzle in both hands, his wiry whiskers shooting between her fingers. "Do you still want to play chase?"

"Do I have to chase any more birds?" he asked.

Ophelia shook her head. "I certainly hope not," she said.

"Will there be more doughnuts?"

Ophelia shrugged. "I can't make any promises. But I do know that I can't possibly do it without you."

Sam looked at her hopefully, expectantly. "Does this mean we're friends?"

Ophelia reached up and gave him another hug, pressing her face close to his perpetually itchy ear.

She told him that was exactly what it meant.

30

erendipity.

Serendipity was the name of the coffee shop on the 147th floor of Grant Tower. Fairies were fond of giving their shops such names. The tailor's shop was called Sew It Goes. The bakery near Ophelia's cottage was called Fortune's Cookies. The vendor four doors down was called Destiny's Market—though *that* was because Destiny Daffodil Pincher ran the place, not because one was *destined* to eat her candied fruits and nuts (though they *were* pretty good). It was cleverness, mostly. Fairies being ironic about the fact that they could shape the fortunes and fates of others but most of the time preferred to just sit around in the woods, drink coffee, eat cookies, and shoot the breeze. The Haven was a truly magical place.

As she sat up on Sam's back, hoping the wind might dry her

uniform faster (though her behind, planted on Sam's wet fur, was never going to get dry), Ophelia couldn't help but wonder if a little serendipity hadn't come her way, lifting her up out of that tree and depositing her so much closer to Kasarah's coin. Except there was nothing serendipitous about a hawk hoping to have you for dinner. And she wasn't saved by fortune, fate, or good luck.

She was saved by a stray dog. One who now trotted pompously along, prancing like a show pony with his head high, grr-ing softly to himself the whole time in a kind of singsong voice.

"Oh, I am Sam. And I'm a hero. I saved Ophelia from the pond. She can't swim. So I saved her. That makes me very very very very awesome. Oh . . . I am Sam. And I'm a hero. I saved Ophelia from the pond. She can't swim. So I saved her. That makes me very very very very very . . ."

"Sam," Ophelia said.

". . . very very very very very . . ."

"Sam," Ophelia said again, leaning closer to his ears.

". . . very very very VERY VERY very very . . ."

"SAM!" Ophelia shouted and tugged hard on a fistful of fur.

Sam yelped and twisted his head to give her a look. "What was that for?"

Part of it, admittedly, was to get him to shut up. But most of it was because they were back on the streets again. They'd crossed through a meadow beside the pond where she fell, then circled around a fence that skirted a neighborhood of identical-looking houses, and here they were back on cement, looking at a paved road and a string of shops directly across from it.

And oh so close. There was no doubt in Ophelia's mind now. The wish spoke loud enough that she no longer had to concentrate to hear it, even over Sam's singing. She pointed to the row of buildings across the way. "There," she said. Maybe the man in the striped shirt was in one of them. Or maybe he'd handed the nickel off to someone else. Either way, she had traced it here. "We need to cross the street."

But Sam was already one step ahead of her, running down the grassy embankment and right out into the road, heedless of the cars that barreled toward them. Ophelia gripped hard with her legs and tried to dig her way under his fur for fear of falling, but they made it across with only two volleys of honks and one car slamming on its brakes. "Get out of the road, you mangy mutt!" the man who had to stop shouted from his window, but Sam paid little attention, leaping across a ditch and galloping into the parking lot.

Ophelia scanned the rows of cars until she found exactly what she was looking for: the boxy white turtle with the rusty doors. The same one that had sprayed her with the blue stuff and then catapulted her into that oncoming truck. It was parked right outside the biggest building in the strip.

"Super Pets," Ophelia muttered, reading the red-lettered sign with the black paw print beside it.

"Super pets," Sam echoed. "Wow. That sounds terrific. I

want to be super-petted."

"I don't think that's what it means," Ophelia said, squinting, trying to spy through the tinted windows of the storefront. "I think it means the animals are super."

"Oh yes! Me too! I am super!" He began to sing again. *"I am Sam, and I'm a hero. I saved—"*

"No. It's just the name of the store," Ophelia interrupted. "They probably sell food and supplies for dogs and cats and things."

"Doughnuts?" Sam wondered.

"Not doughnuts," Ophelia guessed. "And I don't think it would be a good idea if you went in." She was actually certain of it. The humans inside would take one look at Sam and immediately recognize him as a stray. No collar, no tags, scratched up and dopey eyed and in sore need of a bath. She wasn't sure what would happen then, but she guessed they would be separated. "Besides," she added, "this part requires stealth and subterfuge. And while you *are* an excellent chaser *and* swimmer, I'm not sure you can be subtle."

"Oh. I am very subtle," Sam barked. "What's subtle?"

"Subtle is not darting out into the street without looking for cars. Subtle is not growling at everything that moves. Subtle is definitely not sniffing other creatures' butts."

Sam looked disappointed. His big eyes seemed to sag.

Ophelia got an idea. "But that's all right, because you have an even more important job to do. I need *you* to *stand guard*."

"Oh yes," Sam said eagerly, tail suddenly wagging again. "I

am a very good guard dog. Do you want me to bark if someone goes in?"

"No. That won't be necessary," Ophelia said.

"Oh. Okay. Do you want me to bark when somebody comes
out?"

"No. You don't need to do that either."

"Oh. Okay," Sam said. He seemed confused. "So what am
I doing again?"

"I need you to wait close to the door, maybe by those bushes
over there," Ophelia said, pointing. "And if you see a man
with blue pants and a striped shirt come out and I'm right
behind him doing this—" Ophelia started jumping up and
down, pointing dramatically and mouthing the words *Get
him*. "*That* means I need you to keep the man from getting
into his car."

"Oh. I see," Sam said. "Should I bite him?"

"No. Just . . . you know . . . scare him a little."

"But what if he scares me back?" Sam asked.

Ophelia could see it in his eyes: Sam had some memories
that ran long and deep. She reached over and put a hand on
his muzzle. "I know how brave you are," she said. "But if anybody ever tries to hurt you, you run." She stroked the scruff of
Sam's chin. "I won't be long at all. Promise."

Get in. Get the nickel. Get out. She could perform the ritual
after when she met back up with Sam. Generally you weren't
supposed to invite an audience, even if that audience was a

190

dog, but it wouldn't hurt Sam to see that sometimes wishes could come true.

"Okay," Sam started barking. "I will be brave. Because I am Sam. And I'm a hero. I saved Ophelia from the—"

"Sam?"

"Yes?"

"Not subtle," she said.

"Oh. Okay."

Following her pointing finger, Sam trotted over and slunk down among the bushes, while Ophelia furtively made her way across the parking lot, hiding behind tires and crouching beside curbs. When she was certain there was nobody around, she stood in front of the sliding glass doors leading to the pet supply store. She'd seen these kinds of doors before: humans simply walked toward them and they opened. Magic, but not really.

Except they didn't open for her. She jumped up and down and waved her arms, even called the doors a few choice names, but nothing happened. Humans and their stupid contraptions! If they were designed to make life easier, how come they were all so fernfaddled complicated? She was about to give up and whistle for Sam's help, when the doors dinged and slid open, revealing a lumbering white furry monster with giant teeth. Ophelia barely dodged out of the way, pressing herself into the thin recess that the door vanished into as the Saint Bernard and his owner passed by. As soon as they'd gone she felt the door on her back, pushing closed again, and spun side-ways, into the store.

That's one way to do it, she thought.

She turned and gave Sam a salute through the glass, then quickly took cover behind a box of Crunchables dog biscuits on a bottom shelf.

Stealth and subterfuge. Ophelia hoped she'd do a better job of it than she had at the diner. This time she knew to stay calm and focused. She scanned what she could see of the store, marking every potential danger. The place was huge—almost the size of the Glade, though there were no magic wish-picking trees growing out of the center of it. There were lots of cages, however, and those cages contained animals of all different kinds. Hamsters and rabbits and turtles and mice. Along one side she could see a half dozen cats prowling and rubbing their flanks against their wire walls. The air gave off a musty funk that Ophelia likened to riding on Sam's back. If she wanted to, she could probably hear what all these crea-tures were saying with their mewls and squeaks and hisses, but instead she tried to focus only on Kasarah's voice.

I wish.

The coin was here. Ophelia couldn't see the man in the striped shirt, but she could sense the coin's presence. She noticed one cashier at the front of the store ringing up a cus-tomer, her money-eating drawer opening and shutting with a clang. The whisper wasn't coming from in there. A couple more employees appeared to be wandering up and down the aisles, stocking shelves. She would do her best to avoid them; they all wore bright red shirts, so they were easy to spot. No doubt one of them could easily get his hands on a broom if he wanted.

Ophelia circled around the aisle, staying close to the shelves, ready to sneak back behind stacked cans of Meaty Morsels or giant bags of Puppy Grub, keeping her eyes peeled for her target and trying to ignore the strange noises and smells that surrounded her. At the sound of footsteps coming from behind she leapt onto the lowest shelf and hid behind the first thing she found, realizing too late it was just a glass bowl and that anyone who cared could see right through it. But she was low enough that the woman passing by didn't notice. Ophelia dropped in behind her and crept to the next aisle.

No man. No nickel. She went to the next. Not there either. She found herself standing near an aquarium housing a black rat snake thick as a tree branch. He looked at her with interest, flicking his tongue against the glass of his enclosure. "Don't even think about it, mister," she said, and ducked behind a bin advertising chew toys near the center aisle. She could still hear the wish calling for her, but she couldn't tell what direction it was coming from. There was too much interference. Cats crying. Hamster wheels squeaking. Birds squawking. The *ding* of the door. The *ching* of the cash register. The *clop* of feet. And all the time, the bright lights above made her squint. As big as this store was, Ophelia still felt claustrophobic, imagining herself trapped inside one of these glass boxes, sleeping on a bed of cedar chips, being fed pellets out of a bag. She closed her eyes and tried to concentrate. *Where are you, you stupid coin?*

When she opened them, there he was.

Five aisles over, toward the front of the store. He had one of those huge green bags of dog food cradled in one arm and was picking out a box of biscuits to go with it. It was definitely him, the one who had spritzed her. Striped shirt and blue denim. And he still had Kasarah's wish. She could see it glowing faintly through his pocket.

Ophelia reached down and unhooked her last can of spray and quickly devised a plan. Circle back around the shelves and approach from the side. Use the rack to climb up to the register since she could no longer fly. Spray him right as he was paying. With any luck he would put the nickel on the counter, making it an easy grab. Ophelia would shoot him and the red-shirted cashier both and then be out the door before anyone else in the place knew what was happening. It wasn't ideal, and Squint certainly wouldn't approve of her knocking *two* humans unconscious. But Squint wasn't here, was he? This was still her mission, and it was her call. And besides, the girl standing behind the cash register was yawning already. She could probably use a nap.

Ophelia took a deep breath and a step into the aisle but paused when she heard barking coming from the back of the store.

It was a pet store. She'd heard barking from the moment she came in.

Except she knew this bark.

"I am Sam. I'm a hero," the bark said.

"Do you need to be saved?"

31

"Fishtickles!" Ophelia cursed.

What was he doing here? Why didn't he stay outside like she asked him to? Ophelia had passed several empty crates and cages. Suddenly all she could picture was Sam's pathetic face peering out from behind wire bars. She glanced back at the man in the striped shirt, now standing in the checkout lane behind one other person. So close—the wish was so close it was practically *shouting* at her. *C'mon! What are you waiting for? Grant me, for Haven's sake!*

She heard Sam bark again behind her.

"I am a very good rescuer. I am very subtle."

"Arghhh!" Ophelia groaned, probably too loud, and then turned her back on the man in the striped shirt. She skittered to the back of the store, rounding the corner to find Sam staring at a row of steel cages and the three dogs he found inside, each of them whining and pawing at their doors. "Sam," she hissed. "I told you to wait outside!"

Sam turned to her, tail thumping. "Oh, I did," he panted. "But then I got worried because you said you wouldn't be long and you were long and I thought you were in danger so I came in to look for you. And then I heard talking and came back here to see what was going on and that's when I saw them." Sam turned back to the row of kennels. "They are trapped! We need to rescue them!"

That was exactly what Ophelia was afraid of. She looked around. None of the Red Shirts had come back here yet, but she could hear footsteps. And the man with her nickel was already checking out, was probably digging it out of his pocket right at this moment. She didn't have much time.

"No. Listen to me, Sam. They aren't trapped. They're fine. Look at them."

She looked at them. They looked pathetic. Well, two of them looked pathetic. The littlest one, whose sign said his name was Fritz, looked ecstatic, bouncing up and down like he was about to explode. They were all barking, though, and all saying basically the same thing.

Let us out. Let us out.

Ophelia shook her head. "No, Sam. Please. We need to get my wish and get out of here before somebody spots us." She grabbed Sam's tail and gave it a tug, but he didn't budge.

"We can't," he growled. "We have to help. They want us to set them free. That's *their* wish."

Dogs don't get to make wishes, Ophelia was about to say when another voice echoed above her. A human voice calling out over her shoulder loud enough for the whole store to hear.

"Whosever dog this is needs to come get him. Pets have to be on leashes at all times."

It was a young woman, one of the Red Shirts. She was holding an aquarium with a giant tarantula in it. She looked down and spotted Ophelia.

"And did somebody accidentally let one of the canaries out of its cage?"

Clearly the camo was still working, but it hardly mattered if this human thought she was an escaped bird. She and Sam were both only seconds away from being locked behind bars. She needed a distraction.

"Sam," Ophelia whispered, knowing that even if the woman heard anything it would probably just sound like chirping. "Spider on the loose." She looked up at the aquarium in the girl's hands.

Sam gave her a funny look. "What?"

"Spider. On. The. Loose," she repeated, gesturing toward the tarantula, who looked almost as eager to get out as the three dogs. She saw a sudden spark in Sam's eyes.

"Oh," he said. "Right."

Sam jumped. Not high enough to pull a hawk out of the sky, but plenty high enough to get both paws on the aquarium in the Red Shirt's hands. It probably surprised her more than anything, this strange dog jumping at her, and the glass aquarium slipped and tumbled out of her grip, crashing shatteringly to the floor. Ophelia shielded herself behind Sam's legs and then watched as the aquarium's hairy brown inhabitant quickly recovered from the destruction of his home and scuttled across the tiles as fast as his eight legs could carry him.

Right out into the center aisle, where he was spotted by another human.

There came a spine-rattling scream.

And, just as Ophelia expected, chaos.

The Red Shirt girl looked from the broken glass to the stray dog to the fleeing spider to Ophelia (the freed bird, presumably), obviously trying to figure out what her first priority should be. But the scream couldn't be ignored. The girl chased after the spider, giving Ophelia a few precious seconds.

She quickly went to the cages and unfastened the locks, pulling the doors open, one after another. All three dogs came bolting out, two of them heading straight for the front door and one of them, Fritz, simply running around in circles. Ophelia pulled herself onto Sam's back. "Go!" she said.

Sam scrabbled across the slippery floor, following the other two dogs toward the front of the store, where a line of Red Shirts was waiting to intercept them. Ophelia could see past them, the doors just starting to close. She caught a glimpse of the man in the striped shirt, his purchases in hand. She saw the faint glow pulsing in his pocket, could hear the whisper. He still had it. And it was getting away. Again.

"Giddyup!" Ophelia said, urging Sam on, but one of the

Red Shirts stepped in their way and Sam had to skid to a stop and change direction, shooting down an aisle full of hamsters. One working frantically on his wheel squeaked at Ophelia as she passed: "Run run run run run run run run!" It was advice she really didn't need.

Sam circled around the aisle, saw another Red Shirt blocking his path, and reversed direction, heading back toward the center of the store. Ophelia watched as one of the dogs—a big black Labrador—was corralled and quickly strung up on a leash. The other big dog was cornered and collared as well. Fritz, on the other hand, had simply run straight to the first human he saw and jumped up into her arms.

With so many Red Shirts occupied, it left a gap in the line. Ophelia steered Sam toward the front of the store again and dug in her heels. They bolted for the closed doors, a lone Red Shirt—the cashier—right behind them with a leash in her hand, like a cowgirl hoping to lasso a wild stallion.

"Stop!" Ophelia shouted, and Sam skidded to a halt ten feet from the door, a move so sudden that the young woman behind didn't have time to slow, tripping and tumbling over Sam and sprawling, starfish style, right in front of the entrance.

Ding.

The doors slid open and Sam leapt over the poor Super Pets employee and tore outside, sliding to a stop at the edge of the parking lot.

Just in time to see the boxy white turtle pulling away.

"Chase?" Sam barked. And Ophelia almost said yes, but she

knew there was no way he could keep up with the car once it was on the road. The escape from the Super Pets had winded him—she could feel his heart hammering against his sides. Plus, the Red Shirt who had unwittingly opened the door for them was slowly picking herself up off the floor, leash in hand, ready to pursue.

"No," Ophelia said. "Let's just get out of here."

Sam licked his chops and started running while Ophelia watched her wish speed away.

32

Ophelia collapsed, crestfallen, burying her face in the back of Sam's neck.

Gone again. She was starting to think this wish didn't *want* to be granted. And frankly, she was ready to let it have its way. Not that a wish could want such a thing, of course. A wish *is* want. It's longing and bellyache and fantasy and desire. It's late nights spent wondering *what if* and passing fancies for new dresses spotted in store windows. A wish is "Why not me?" and "Just this once" and "I swear I will never, *ever* do that again." A wish could be any of these things, but above all it was hope. But like everything else Ophelia had brought with her on her mission, her hope was in dangerously short supply.

She'd been *so* close. Within inches. And yet the more she chased after it, the farther away it got. It was almost as if it was mocking her, the magic itself preventing her from carrying out her mission, leading her on this wild-goose chase (complete with wild geese), knocking her out of the sky and dragging her back up into it, bringing her right to the cusp of making a girl's dream come true and then yanking it away at the last possible moment.

Maybe the Great Tree had made a great big mistake, she thought. Maybe Kasarah Quinn's wish wasn't meant to be granted at all. Or maybe Barnabus Squint had made the mistake, and Ophelia just wasn't the right fairy to grant it. That, at least, was possible. The Tree didn't make mistakes; the wishes were chosen at random. But Ophelia felt as if she'd made ten too many.

Maybe starting with becoming a Granter to begin with.

They traveled in the same direction as the white car, just not at near the same speed, and Ophelia could feel the wish getting farther away. After several blocks of billboards advertising to cash your check or change your oil, the signs of advanced human civilization petered out. The buildings grew sparse again, giving way to ragged patches of grass and weeds and a winding road punctuated by the occasional cluster of houses or corner gas station. Ophelia could feel Sam's steady panting, his skin hot beneath her hands. She pointed to a spot under the pink-and-white explosion of a cherry blossom, a sight that normally would have made her smile. At least it offered a promise of shade. "Time for a rest," she said.

Sam didn't argue. He collapsed on his side beneath the boughs, tongue loose, his flank rising and falling like a bellows.

The late spring day had grown warm, at least for a fairy who was used to the mountain chill of the Haven, and she was grateful to at least be out of her flight suit, though thinking of it served only as another reminder that she couldn't fly. Ophelia leaned up against Sam, gently pressing her sore back against his still-damp fur. The smell of the cherry blossom tree nearly canceled out the odor of wet dog. Nearly.

"I'm sorry, Sam," she said. "About what happened back there. I know you were only trying to help."

They hadn't said a word to each other since leaving the pet store, save for the directions Ophelia gave and Sam's questioning growl every time a car zoomed by. She judged the long stretch of silence to mean that he was disappointed. Maybe in her. Maybe in himself. Probably her.

"I am sorry your wish got away," Sam replied.

Ophelia stared at the sun, already calling it quits for the day and slinking toward the edge of the world. Soon the sky would ripen, blushing pink and purple. Then it would be evening. That might make the wish easier to track, at least. Humans often shut down in the evenings, scurried home, holed away like hermit crabs. Maybe the man in the striped shirt was headed home now. Once it was dark out it would be easier for her to sneak around. Even Sam could probably be stealthy in the pitch black of night.

Except she couldn't wait *too* long. Squint had given her enough protection to last only until the end of the day. She wondered just how many tocks she had left. *Should have been enough to grant one stupid wish. Should have been on my way home by now. Should have just sprayed the old man when I had the chance. So many should haves.*

"What happens to them?"

Ophelia shook her head, her thoughts interrupted by the sound of Sam's voice. "The wishes?"

"The dogs. How long are they in those cages? They don't *live* there, do they?"

Ophelia wasn't sure. The answer to Sam's question was probably down in the Archives somewhere—most things were—but it wasn't something she'd studied in depth. The dogs were for sale; she'd seen prices by the cages. Sort of strange to know how much a living thing was worth, down to the nickel. "Somebody comes and buys them and takes them home," she said.

"A master?"

Ophelia caught the wariness in Sam's voice. "A master, yes, but someone nice. A whole family probably. With kids to play fetch and chase. And a big backyard with plenty of places to bury a bone." For herself, she couldn't quite imagine wanting to eat a dug-up, dirty bone, but the family part sounded nice.

"Oh," Sam said, impressed. "Home."

"Home," Ophelia repeated. She pictured the Haven. The frothy waterfalls. The emerald crowns of trees, pools of light peeking through their branches. Charlie waiting for her outside her cottage, sitting on her porch, whistling to himself. She probably would have been back by now, if everything had gone according to plan. Sitting beside him, splitting that bottle of wine and watching the sunset with satisfaction rather than worry.

"Where is your home?" Sam asked.

Ophelia started to say something, then stopped. That was confidential information. Of course this was only Sam, and Sam was harmless. She reached for a cherry blossom petal that had been knocked loose. It was just starting to curl, but it still felt like velvet against her fingertips.

"It's called the Haven and it's very far away." *Too far for a fairy who can't even fly*, she thought, her heart aching as much as her back. "Where I live is called the Tree Tops. High up in the mountains. We have a whole city up there with everything you could imagine. Clothes menders and cheese makers and coffee shops. And lots of nuts."

"Dough-nuts?" Sam asked hopefully.

Ophelia shook her head. "No. Not usually. Sometimes, though. We get those from the Scavengers, who come to collect human things for us to study and learn from. We have to know as much as we can about them so that we are prepared when we come out here to grant wishes."

Prepared. She thought she had been, but now she realized there was still so much about humans she didn't understand. They were all strangers. Pictures in a book. Names on a leaf. Voices in her head that she was tired of listening to. "To be honest, I'm not even sure they're worth it," she muttered, as much to herself as to Sam.

"Humans are bad," he agreed.

Ophelia stopped fidgeting with her petal and looked over at Sam. Of course he would think so. And she couldn't blame him. Not after how he'd been treated. She leaned back into him, nestling in his fur.

"Maybe they're not *all* bad," she amended. "They just lose sight of what's important sometimes, worrying so much about what they don't have that they forget what they've already got."

"Like home," Sam said.

Ophelia grew quiet, feeling Sam's heartbeat pounding beneath her. She had absolutely no idea how she was going to get back to the Haven. It seemed an impossible distance now. She knew Squint would send somebody after her eventually, but by then there was no telling what shape she'd be in. She pictured her name scratched into the walls of the Femoriae: *Ophelia Delphinium Fidgets. Went out into the world and never returned. Total wishes granted: zero.* Just yesterday she'd imagined herself granting hundreds of them. Now she just wanted to be done. More than anything, she just wanted to feel safe again. Back in the Haven.

She closed her eyes again and picked up Kasarah's voice, a barely traceable whisper. They'd rested for only a few ticks, and Sam was still panting. She couldn't ask any more of him. Ophelia stood up and placed a hand gently on his muzzle.

"I've got to keep going, Sam. I've got to try to find this wish, even if it kills me. But you don't have to. I know you're tired. I honestly don't even know why you've come this far."

The dog licked his front paws a few times each. His tail gave one halfhearted thump. Then slowly he stood up, shaking out his fur.

"Because you are my friend," he said. "And empty holes are the worst."

He lowered his front half so that she could climb onto his back. "Let's find your wish so that you can go home."

33

The whisper seemed to follow a straight path, at least. And so did they, Ophelia pointing and Sam doing his best to keep up a steady pace as they tromped through the wildflowers on the side of the road. The houses aged the farther they went, paint-peeled fences and long, gravel driveways and yards full of trees thick enough for a huddle of fairies to live in. They were heading south, judging by the setting sun, in the general direction of the Haven at least.

She could hardly feel her left wing anymore—it had gone numb—but she could still sense it there, practically useless. It made her feel lopsided, even just sitting here, bouncing on Sam's back. A broken, filthy fairy riding a homeless, smelly dog chasing after a wish they would probably never catch for a girl she didn't even know.

It couldn't possibly get any worse.

And yet Sam still wagged his tail as he walked, as if he sensed something that Ophelia with her magically attuned fairy brain could only guess at, and before long she realized they were actually *gaining* on the wish. Kasarah's whisper seemed to grow stronger with every step, and Ophelia began to hope that it was no longer on the move. Perhaps the man in the striped shirt had stopped somewhere for good. She imagined him standing in the bedroom of one of these creaking old houses, emptying the contents of his pockets onto his dresser, perhaps giving Kasarah's nickel a lucky spin before leaving it there for some sneaky creature to filch. She peered down every driveway, hoping to spot the white turtle at rest, trotting for another mile or more, passing house after house. *C'mon, coin, where are you hiding now?*

Suddenly Ophelia's ears rattled with a volley of barking. She had to hold on even tighter as Sam began to cavort in circles. "I see it. I see it. I see it."

She looked up the road at the car just cresting a hill.

"Is that it?" Sam asked excitedly. "I think that's it. Is that it?"

The white box, rolling quickly toward them. It certainly looked like the right car. The driver had one hand on the wheel and another wrapped around a blue cup, but she recognized the striped shirt. It was him, the paper-club-wielding nickel hoarder. Coming straight at them.

Ophelia knew she had to stop that car, but how? She couldn't risk riding Sam into the middle of the road, straight into its path. What if the man didn't see them? The car was going much too fast for her to grab hold of, not without flying to keep pace. Should she pull out her knife and lunge for a tire as it passed? What if the car veered out of control and ran off the road? She sat upright on Sam's back, paralyzed, desperately trying to come up with a plan.

The car shot past, the man in the striped shirt not even giving the dog by the side of the road a second glance.

Sam continued to bark. "Was that it? I think that was it!"

"That was it," Ophelia croaked, blinking in the dust kicked up by the car's tires.

"Oh. Oh. Okay. So do we go after it? What do we do? Ophelia?"

Ophelia didn't answer. She was staring after the car, head cocked, eyes asquint, listening.

"Chase?" Sam nudged again.

"Quiet," she told him.

The car was speeding away, now just a white speck on the black road.

Except the whisper of the wish wasn't fading. In fact, it was just as strong as before. The same steady pining for a purple bike, coming from the other direction.

"He doesn't have it," Ophelia whispered. She smiled and leaned close to Sam's ear. "The coin. He doesn't have it anymore."

"Oh, good." Sam sighed. "Because I do not think I could have chased that car. It looked even faster than the bird."

The man in the striped shirt had obviously passed the coin on to someone else. Someone nearby. Ophelia felt a surge of excitement. "That way," she ordered, pointing again. "We are close now, Sam. I can feel it."

Sam took off, his feet scrabbling on the loose gravel along the roadside, Ophelia holding on as tight as she could.

It was only a matter of ticks before they saw the sign that told her she'd come to the right place.

34

The sign told Ophelia everything she needed to know about how Kasarah's nickel had ended up here.

Lemonade $1.

Beside it was a drawing of a lumpy yellow potato with freckles. The poster leaned up against a red wagon as rusted as the white car that just passed. In the wagon's bed stood an orange cooler named Igloo and a bag full of supplies. Two bikes, neither of them purple, were piled beside it.

Behind all this, two kids sat cross-legged in the grass, pulling it up, blade by blade.

"Go slow," Ophelia whispered. "Try not to let them see you."

Sam slunk through a swath of chest-high weeds, taking his sneakiest steps and keeping his snout shut for once. Ophelia didn't want to scare the children off, or even alert them to her presence. Not before she'd thoroughly assessed the situation.

One thing was certain. The wish was here. She could hear it loud and clear.

"Get down," Ophelia said when she felt like they were close enough. Sam pressed his belly to the ground. Ophelia slipped off and peered through the curtain of thistle and tall grass at the makeshift stand on the other side of the road and the children manning it. A boy and a girl. The girl was clearly the younger of the two. She wore a jacket, a green one with lots of pockets. Ophelia had seen that jacket before. She recognized the yellow sundress underneath as well, with the ribbons to match. She took a long look at the boy's face.

She'd seen them both before.

Anna. Her name is Anna. And his is Gabe.

The boy had obviously given his jacket to his sister—it was much too big for her—and now wore a black T-shirt that had *US Marines* printed across the chest. He also wore boots not too different from Ophelia's. A clear plastic bag full of money, most of it change, sat at his feet.

The bag was glowing.

She couldn't tell what the kids were saying from this far away, but the girl lunged for the bag and the boy pulled it just out of reach. When the girl pouted, the boy said something else and her face brightened instantly, stretching into a smile as long as the road. She wrapped both arms around him and he playfully pushed her away, then looked up at the sky and frowned.

Ophelia never expected to see that frown again, yet there it was.

Kismet. That's what the Mystics would say. Magic flows in circles. Follow its path long enough and you'll come back to where you started. *Perhaps*, Ophelia thought. *Maybe*. She'd seen magic do some pretty wondrous things, after all.

Or maybe the man in the striped shirt was just thirsty and wanted some lemonade.

The boy stood up, tucking the bag of coins and bills down the front of his shirt, presumably to keep it safe. Instinctively Ophelia's own hand reached to the vial of dust hanging around her neck.

"Do they have your wish?" Sam growled softly from behind her.

Ophelia nodded.

"So what do we do now?"

She didn't like her options. They were just kids. If Sam ran up to them barking his head off, it could scare them to death. She could spray them, of course, but then what? Leave two children unconscious by the side of the road where just any-body could find them? Could she trust humans to do the right thing, to stop and get help?

She couldn't. She didn't want to frighten the children, either, and Kasarah's coin was tricky to get to at the moment. She needed to think of something quickly, though. The kids were packing up. The little girl was already getting on her bicycle, and her brother was busy securing the handle of the wagon to the back of his own bike with a length of rope. Children were unpredictable. Some of them saw what they weren't supposed to. It would be better if she could get the nickel without them knowing. Take it while they weren't even looking. The boy mounted his bicycle now and was already starting back up the road, away from town, his sister pedaling behind him. Sam looked up at Ophelia expectantly.

"Okay," she said. "*Now* we chase—but *quietly*. We keep our distance and wait for a better opportunity." Ophelia looked at the sun off to her right, starting to paint the sky.

There was still time, she told herself.

Besides, there was something else that gave her pause, even beyond the fact that Kasarah's coin had found its way here (though that still nagged her too). It was something about the boy. Ophelia was no Mystic; most of the time she couldn't read a creature's aura if it was spelled out for her in flashing neon letters blinking above their heads. But even from far away she could sense this. A dark spot. A longing that seemed to follow the boy like a gray cloud.

That didn't make him dangerous. No more dangerous than the lady with her broom or the Red Shirts with their leashes. But it did make her curious about him, and *that* made her wary. Because she couldn't afford any more distractions. He was an obstacle. Just one more thing standing in her way.

But not for long. She waited until they had a far enough lead.

"C'mon," she told Sam. "And don't let that wagon out of your sight."

35

Sam had no trouble keeping up this time ("No. Nothing like the bird," he said). The boy towed the Igloo in the wagon, and the girl dutifully rode behind her brother, often bumping up against the back of him and then slowing down again, afraid, it seemed, to take the lead. Sam kept his distance as commanded, padding softly in the grass on the opposite side of the road, past a corn field and branching dirt roads, to a big yellow farmhouse with white-gray windows and a wraparound porch. The boy and girl pulled their bikes up along the winding driveway and parked them by the side of the house.

The mailbox by the road said *4462* in yellow script, and underneath in smaller print, the name *Morales*. Sam stopped behind a row of boxwoods, his head poking out over the top, Ophelia's head poking out over his like two groundhogs peeking out of a burrow.

"That is a big yard," Sam said.

It was a giant yard, Ophelia admitted. And full of trees, almost as if a hunk of the Haven had been carved from the mountaintop and transplanted here. A grizzly old oak held court from the center of the yard, a tire hanging from one thick branch, spinning slowly, first one way and then the other. There was one car in the driveway—a red van with a dented backside and a sticker that said *Support Our Troops*. A few toys were scattered about. A baseball hoop—it was called baseball, wasn't it?—towered by the garage. A flag by the front door snapped crisply in the wind. There were boxed flowers everywhere you looked—someone in the house took pride in having green thumbs.

This, Ophelia thought, *is what home looks like.* She wondered if Sam was thinking the same thing.

The boy and his sister unpacked their wagon, him hefting the cooler and her carrying the stack of cups. She heard him holler, "We're back!" as they went through front door, taking Kasarah's wish with them.

"Now what?" Sam asked.

"Reconnaissance," Ophelia said.

Sam looked at her dumbly.

"Spying," she clarified.

He still looked confused.

"We sit and watch."

Sam panted happily. "Oh. That is good. I am very good at sitting. It is the first thing I learned how to do." To prove his point, Sam dropped back onto his rump. Ophelia patted his nose.

"That's terrific—but I need to get somewhere I can see. Come on."

She led him up to the house, careful to keep by the trees and bushes and out of direct view of the windows. The closer she got, the more clearly she saw the shape the house was in. The gutters sagged. Several shingles had been ripped from the roof. The yellow siding was more of a greenish gray in spots, almost black in others. Some of the wooden trim was rotting. She and Sam crept past the bicycles and pressed against the side of the house.

Ophelia paused. The sound of Kasarah's wish carried through the walls, and her heart fluttered. The day had been a total disaster. Absolutely nothing had gone as planned. But compared to planes and hawks and brooms, breaking into this house seemed . . . if not *easy*, then at least *doable*. She had the coin cornered.

She could hear muffled voices coming from one of the windows above. A planter with the tulip sprouts struggling upward hung below it. "Give me a lift, will you?"

Ophelia perched precariously on the end of Sam's cold nose again, just as she had at the bakery, and he jumped up, planting his paws against the siding, giving her just enough height to pull herself over the edge. She rolled over one of the flowers, getting dirt all over her uniform, but after being slobbered on, spritzed, foamed, and dropped into a pond, she hardly cared. Ophelia apologized to the pansy and then crawled to the window ledge and lifted her head just enough to see through the crevice where the curtains didn't quite meet.

A small kitchen. Apricot-colored walls. A circular wooden table sat at one end, covered in newspapers like the one Ophelia had been swatted with back at the diner. Several glass jars were lined up along one counter with all kinds of rocks and leaves inside, each one chosen, it seemed, for their odd shape, rich color, or sparkling glint. Someone in the house was a collector. A sign above one entry asked anyone who read it to *Bless This Mess.*

The children's mother—the one who insisted they come home and play outside back at the diner—stood by a stove, stirring something in a large black pot, her back to the window. Ophelia couldn't smell through the glass, of course, but she could see the steam drifting up, and her stomach grumbled at the thought that it might be something good inside. Rhubarb soup, perhaps? Or maybe a giant pot of strawberry jam. As Ophelia watched and the woman stirred, the children came in and took turns washing their hands at the sink. The boy then reached into his shirt and set the bag of money on the table. Less than twenty feet away, but separated by a pane of glass and the bigger pain of three humans and their spying eyes. Crouched close to the window, Ophelia could make out their voices at last.

"How did it go?" the mother asked, and Ophelia got a good look at her face, pale and weathered and bracketed by strands of coppery hair. She had the same long sloping nose as her son. Her eyes were hazel, like her daughter's, though puffy gray crescents hung underneath. Her voice was sweet and soft, and Ophelia had to press a little closer to the glass to hear what she said. "Did you make a lot?"

"I wasn't allowed to count," Anna complained, drying her hands on her mom's apron. "But Gabe says we sold fourteen cups."

"We *sold* twelve," the boy corrected, drying his own hands on the legs of his jeans. "But that guy at the end gave us extra because he felt sorry for us."

Ophelia wondered if that wasn't the man in the striped shirt—the one she'd been cursing all day long—tipping these kids an extra couple of bucks, or maybe just forking over all the change he had in his pocket without even counting it. She felt a little bad for wanting to knock him unconscious earlier. Just a little.

"Seven each isn't bad," the mother said, cracking open the oven and peeking inside.

"Are you kidding?" the boy snapped. "It's not even minimum wage. We stood out there for three freaking hours!"

"Gabriel Morales, you watch your language!" the mother

snapped, her voice suddenly plenty loud enough for Ophelia to hear. She pointed the wooden spoon at him. He rolled his eyes.

"Whatever," he said. "That's not even a bad word." He slumped down at the table, chin digging into his crossed arms. It sure sounded like a bad word to Ophelia. At least the way he said it.

"Anna, did you have fun at least?"

The girl shrugged. "I'd rather have gone fishing."

"I'm sure your brother would have taken you fishing."

Brother and sister glanced at each other.

"I'd rather have gone fishing with Dad," the girl amended, then slumped in a chair next to her brother. "No offense," she murmured.

The boy didn't seem offended. In fact he gave his sister a sympathetic look and then proceeded to draw an imaginary picture on the table with his fingertip. The mother sighed and went back to stirring. "We didn't miss him, did we?" Gabe asked tentatively.

Their mother didn't stop, just stared into the pot as if it held the answer to her son's question and she had to keep mixing to bring it to the surface. "He said he would *try* to call. But you know how it is. It's, like, two o'clock in the morning over there. And if he's out on patrol or off base for any reason . . ." She paused, spoon in hand. "He could still call," she finished.

"Sure," Gabe said.

"We can stay up late tonight, just in case."

"Right," he sighed. He pushed his chair back, the ear-scraping screech of wood on wood, and looked at his sister. "You want to go upstairs and divvy up all this hard-earned cash?"

She nodded. "But I get the bills."

"You can have *some* of the bills," he said.

The boy grabbed the bag and raced out of the kitchen, his sister close on his heels. Ophelia watched them leave, a little vexed to have Kasarah's wish out of her sight again. When she looked back, the mother was leaning over the kitchen counter, head cradled in both hands. Clearly Ophelia wasn't the only one having a rough day.

She motioned for Sam to help her climb back down, walking over his nose like a bridge and then sliding down his back to the grass below. "Did you recon the sense?" he asked, keeping his voice to a soft growl.

Ophelia nodded. "Three people in the house. No pets, as far as I can tell." Though there could easily be some beast lurking somewhere. "The wish is upstairs now. Probably in one of the kids' rooms." She started tugging on a loose strand of hair, twisting it round and round, a tiny blue hair tornado. "We need an entry point. Preferably something secretive. An open window. A hole in the wall. Something big enough for me to squeeze through. You go look around back. I'll check the front again."

"I am a very good hole finder," Sam boasted.

"But quietly," she reminded him, putting a finger to her lips.

"Oh yes. Of course. Subtle and healthy."

"Stealthy."

"Yes. That too."

Sam trotted off and Ophelia stood with her hands on her hips and surveyed this side of the house. The windows were all shut. She could break the glass easy enough—provided she could scrounge up a good-size rock—but that wasn't exactly subtle *or* stealthy. Besides, judging by the look of her, Mrs. Morales didn't need a rock through her window. Ophelia could pry one open, maybe, provided they weren't locked. But a woman living alone with two kids wasn't likely to leave her windows unfastened.

If only there was a chimney. Of course, that would require her to get on the roof, and Ophelia wasn't sure she could even do that, what with her broken wing. She thought back to the incident at the diner. A dryer vent maybe? It was possible there was a cellar or some other way she could sneak in from underground. Or something she missed around front. Houses this old were bound to have a crack or two. With her wings folded Ophelia could squeeze through a hole the size of a plum.

At least she'd soon be operating under cover of darkness. The sun had nearly vanished now, leaving the sky swollen pink. In half a tock dusk would settle in, giving her plenty of shadows for slinking around in. She ran her hand along the side of the house, headed back toward the front, but just as she was about to turn the corner she froze.

Somebody was watching her. She could sense it.

Some*body* or some*thing*.

It wasn't Sam. Him she would have smelled. And besides, he would never sneak up on her (as if he could). Ophelia's right hand crept down to the handle of her knife, drawing it slowly from its sheath. She wouldn't need Ozzy Osbourne to save her this time.

She spun around just as her stalker attacked.

36

"*Reyowrrar! Fifftt!*"

A streak of fur leapt high into the air and landed three feet away, back hunched, hissing and spitting. A cat—and not a small one either—smoky gray with white spots like patches of snow, including one over his left eye. His hair was afrizz, like a poofy dustball with whiskers. His yellow eyes flashed surprise.

Ophelia gestured with her knife, a little lunge to get him to take another step back. Full-grown cats were not to be trifled with, she knew. She'd heard stories of fairies getting caught in their claws, mangled and mauled, causing the creatures to rank high on the Granter's list of common dangers. The walls of the Femoriae spoke of a few fairies who never escaped a feline's pounce, though judging from his prodigious paunch, it looked like this particular cat couldn't pounce if he wanted to. He'd certainly done a poor job of sneaking up on her, and he was already trying to take it back.

"Whoa! Whoa-ho-ho! Watch where you're waving that thing!" the cat said, tail standing straight up, fur spiked. "Clearly there's been some kind of misunderstanding."

Ophelia kept the tip of her blade pointed at the dustball's pink nose. The hairs on her neck bristled as well. "A misunderstanding? You were just about to try to have me for dinner." As she spoke she calculated her chances of winning this fight. The cat was nearly twice her size. And she was wounded and exhausted. But she did have a knife.

"*Dinner?*" the cat mewed in disbelief. "Wait. You think I want to *eat* you? Please. Do I *look* like I'm hurting for food?" The enormous feline turned sideways, his stomach swinging like a pendulum. "I get my dinner from a can, man. Besides, I couldn't catch you if I wanted to. See?" He held up one paw. Ophelia wasn't sure what she was supposed to be looking at. "No claws. At least you've still got the one."

He meant her knife, she realized. Ophelia raised an eyebrow, but she didn't bother to put the blade away. Not yet. "So why were you sneaking up on me, then?"

"Honestly? I thought you were a bird. You know . . ." The cat made an awkward flapping motion with one paw. "I like to get 'em all startled and fluttery, squawking off at the mouth and losing feathers as they take off. It's a hobby," he said with an air of satisfaction.

Ophelia thought about the hawk that had snatched her out

of the tree earlier today. Not all birds were so easily flustered, especially by a cat without claws. "You should maybe think twice about how you spend your free time," she said. "Besides. I'm no bird."

"Yes. Well. Obviously I see that *now*. You've got, like, arms. And no feathers. And your beak's way too short. And you're not ugly. I mean, you're not pretty, but you're not *bird*-ugly. Not to mention your voice is kind of annoying and not musical at all. Nah, you're more of a"—the cat circled the air with one clawless, white-gloved paw—"of a . . . you know . . . one of those . . . with the pouch hanging down . . . and the strange smooth fur . . . like . . . maybe a weird, deformed sort of . . ." The cat finally gave up. "What the heck *are* you?"

"Someone not to be trifled with," Ophelia said coolly. She looked around for Sam, but he was nowhere to be found. It was all right, though. She had come to the conclusion that this creature was no match for her. She slipped her knife back into its sheath but kept one hand on the hilt for good measure.

"Funny place to keep it," the cat remarked, then gave his paw a lick and smoothed his whiskers. "I'm Patch, by the way. At least that's what my Old Lady calls me."

"Your old lady?"

"You know. My poop scooper? My feeder, petter, groomer, and all-around servant? Crazy as catnip and snores that'll shake the floor, but who's gonna complain as long as the pâté keeps coming, you know what I'm saying?"

Ophelia shook her head. She had no idea what he was saying.

She didn't know what pâté was and couldn't possibly imagine why one creature would stoop to scooping up another's business. She looked through the trees opposite the driveway to the house next door: a white two-story in even worse shape than the Morales residence, though at least it had a crumbling chimney you could crawl down. "You live over there?"

Patch arched his back and nodded. "Yep. Land of milk and tuna. Though don't get any funny ideas. I'm pretty sure the Old Lady's not going to take in some mutant, miniature bird person—or whatever you are. The litter pan isn't big enough for the both of us."

Ophelia made no attempt to hide her disgust. "I have a home already," she said. And she needed to hurry up and get back to it. Which meant she needed to find a way inside the house behind her. "Do you know the people who live next door?" she asked, pointing.

"The neighbors? Of course I know 'em," Patch said. "They're decent folks. The woman puts cream out for me every now and then. The sweet stuff, goes down nice and smooth." Patch licked one paw appreciatively. "The girl's a sweetheart, too, always good for a belly rub, though the cuddling can get intense. She once squeezed me so tight I thought my ribs would break."

Ophelia wondered how you could even *find* ribs buried under so much cat, or how little Anna Morales could lift the beast to begin with. "And the boy?" she asked.

"Eh . . . he's been kinda moody lately," the cat remarked,

collapsing to his side as if he couldn't bear to hold up his own weight any longer. "He used to be good for a scruff-scratch at least, but not anymore. Not since their old man took off. Now the boy just hisses and tells me to go away. As if he's the boss of me. Puh-lease. Nobody's the boss of *this* cat."

Their old man. Gabe's father. The one who still could call tonight, though the mother didn't sound too sure. It wasn't any of Ophelia's business, of course, but she couldn't stem her curiosity. "How long has he been gone?" she asked. "The father?"

"What do I look like? Somebody who gives a sniff? The dad's all right, but the mom's the one you've got to impress. Got *that one* wrapped around my back paw." The cat struggled back to his feet and began to strut. "Sometimes if I just stand outside the door and yeowl, they'll open up. Then I hit 'em with the heavy purr and a little leg rub, and it's leftovers on the porch. Of course there *was* that time she caught me peeing on her flowers," Patch mused. "Who knew she could throw her shoe so fast?"

Patch the cat continued to drone on about the shoe and a few other things that had been thrown at him over the years, but Ophelia had stopped listening. She'd gotten the inklings of a plan, though she would need this chatty, chubby, puffed-up cat to pull it off.

"Hold on," she interrupted. "You say they sometimes open the door for you? If you meow annoyingly?"

"I prefer to think of it as *serenading*," Patch said. "I actually

231

have a gorgeous falsetto. I can hit most of the high notes. In fact . . ."

But Ophelia had already tuned him out again. If she could just get the door to open, she could sneak inside while they were distracted. First she had to figure out how to convince this cat to help her. Maybe she could interest him in her ball of twine? She was starting to fish it out of her bag when she noticed a rustle in the bushes by the back corner of the house. Followed by a snout, just poking out through the leaves.

Followed by sixty pounds of Sam barreling through the grass at top speed.

Ready to play his favorite game.

37

"Chase!" Sam growled.

"Sam!" Ophelia shouted.

"Hacking hairballs!" Patch exclaimed, his body exploding in a firework of frazzled gray fur as he leapt backward once and then took off, moving much faster than Ophelia would have thought possible. His clawless feet scrambled beneath him as he tore across the Moraleses' yard and through one of the gaps in the neighbor's fence with Sam in hot pursuit, a bundle of tongue-flopping, tail-wagging joy.

Patch disappeared. The dog pulled up and peered through the slats, then paced back and forth before sitting again, staring, as if he actually expected the cat to come back and finish the game.

"Sam!" Ophelia said again, quieter this time. "What are you *doing*?"

"*That* was a cat," Sam said, as if it was the only explanation necessary. He continued to stare at the fence, tail thumping.

"I know it was a cat," Ophelia replied. "That *cat* and I were having a conversation. I was working on a way inside the house."

Sam's head sank, and he finally turned to her, his eyes droopy. "But it was a *cat*."

"Yes, Sam. I realize that. But he was actually being helpful. Sort of," she admitted. "You didn't have to chase him off."

"But it was a *fat* cat."

Clearly she wasn't going to win this argument. Ophelia craned her neck to see if she could catch a glimpse of Patch through the fence, but the Moraleses' feline neighbor was long gone, no doubt bolting back into the safety of his house with its poop-scooping Old Lady. She turned back to Sam and noticed his paws were crusted in a new layer of dirt. "Did you find something, at least?"

"Oh, I found something, yes," Sam barked enthusiastically. "I found a hole."

Ophelia's eyes lit up. At last, a way in. "In the house? Is it big enough for me to fit through?" She imagined a crack in the siding, a mouse's escape route perhaps. She could become as skinny as a mouse if need be.

Sam shook his head. "Oh no. Not in the house. In the yard," he clarified. "Though it really wasn't much of a hole. More of a bare spot. By a tree. But now it is *definitely* a hole."

That explained the dirty paws. While she was busy trying

to negotiate her way inside, Sam was digging random holes in the Moraleses' backyard. Ophelia collapsed, cross-legged, in the grass, head in her hands. "Well, unless you dug the hole all the way underneath the house and back up through the floor, I'm not sure how that helps me," she snipped.

Sam flinched at her tone. He nestled down beside her, chin on his forepaws, wet nose nestled against her leg. He gave her those eyes. Those pitiful eyes. Dolefully dark with just that sliver of white underneath. Every time she saw them her heart melted, just a little. "I'm sorry," he said. "I should not have dug the hole. And I should not have chased the cat. I'm a bad dog."

Ophelia looked back at the house. At Sam. Back at the house. She rubbed her hands together. "No, you're not. You're brilliant!" she said. "That look. It's perfect. I mean, if the cat can do it just by meowing . . ."

Sam abandoned his sorrowful pout and now just looked at Ophelia with his head cocked. "Do what?"

Ophelia put her hands beneath each of his scratched-up ears and drew her face close to his.

"Sam. I need you to put on a show."

38

He would have to be pathetic.

Pathetic and needy and but also sweet and harmless. He could be those things, she knew, but she wasn't the one he had to convince.

She had to get the family to open the door, but that wasn't enough. She also had to get them to come outside. At least far enough that she could slip past them while they weren't looking. Even with the camo, they would likely take offense at some small creature darting into their house. She had to get them outside and *keep* them there as long as possible. Which is why she needed a distraction.

A lovable, furry, somewhat distraction.

"People adore dogs," she insisted as she led Sam around the front of the house. She wasn't sure if the Moraleses liked dogs or not, but if they fell for Patch's purportedly gorgeous falsetto, surely they'd fall for Sam's big brown peepers.

"What if they kick me?" he whimpered.

"They won't kick you. I promise. They're nice. The girl even gives belly rubs. The cat said so."

"Oh, the *cat* said so," Sam growled, letting Ophelia know exactly what he thought of Patch's credibility.

"And you saw them yourself. Did they look mean?" Gabe looked a little *down*, maybe, but that wasn't the same.

"Master didn't look mean," Sam retorted. "Not always."

Ophelia sighed. She was asking a lot. All day she'd instructed him to avoid people, to skirt around the pockets of humans they passed, and he'd seemed happy to do so. And now this.

"Why can't we try digging the hole under the house like you said?" he asked.

"Because this at least has a *chance* of working." Fifty-fifty, Ophelia thought. But she couldn't do it without him. He couldn't run off the moment they opened the door. This whole enterprise rested on his performance, on them taking the bait. "I need you, Sam."

"You do?"

Ophelia nodded. "But you have to look the part. Deprived, but not desperate. Hungry, but not sickly. Loving, but you can't go licking faces. Hang on—you've got some goop in your eye." Ophelia reached over and brushed some white glop from the corner, wiping it on her already filthy pants. If Charlie could see her now, he'd hardly recognize her. "Besides, do you know what they are probably doing, as we speak?"

"Sitting on Couch, watching TV, and passing gas?"

Clearly Sam had a limited notion of how humans spent their free time.

"No, Sam. They're probably eating dinner." She remembered the woman checking whatever was in the oven. Sam's tail gave a triple thump. "And if you do this right, maybe you can get in on some of it. But you have to be charming. Can you be charming?"

Sam sat up straight. "Oh yes. I am very charming," he yipped. "What's charming?"

Ophelia shook her head. "Forget it. Just be yourself. And whatever you do, don't get too close to anyone's face." His breath still smelled like garbage. Doughnuty-sweet garbage, but garbage just the same. "The important thing is to keep them outside for as long as you can."

She didn't know how long she'd need. She'd never actually been inside a human house before. They had a couple of model rooms set up in Grant Tower for training purposes, and she'd seen plenty of pictures. But she'd never stepped foot in one for real. "And don't come looking for me. I'll come find you when I'm done." The last thing she needed was a repeat of the incident at the pet store.

Of course, a plan for getting in wasn't the same as a plan for getting out. She would have to improvise that part. *Just wing it*, Charlie would say.

With only one wing.

She and Sam tiptoed up the front yard and Ophelia pulled

herself up to the two cement steps of the porch to stand right by the door. She turned and gave Sam a thumbs-up. *Here goes.*

The barking that followed broke the stillness of the evening, drowning out a chorus of crickets that had just warmed up their legs. He wasn't saying anything in particular. Just shouting whatever came to mind.

"I am Sam."

"I am charming."

"Come be distracted."

"Bring me food."

To the mother and two children inside, of course, it would simply sound like *wroof, wroof, wroof,* but Ophelia understood, and she couldn't help but smile.

Sam stood in the grass by the first step of the porch as instructed, far enough away to draw them out but close enough that they could see those big brown eyes of his. Ophelia pressed flat against the door frame so tight it made her broken wing throb again. She thought maybe she could hear voices. She nodded at Sam to keep going, and he started barking even louder.

"I am Sam. And I'm hungry. Cats are stupid. La la la."

The front door opened and Ophelia chanced a sideward glance up to see the boy standing there, holding half a biscuit and staring at Sam. Ophelia hoped she was out of view.

"Mom. There's a dog on our front porch," Gabe called over his shoulder.

There were more footsteps. Sam slowed his barking, but his

tail swept the ground enthusiastically. Anna and her mother appeared, all three of them gathered there, just as Ophelia'd hoped. Unfortunately they filled up the doorway, blocking it completely. Nowhere for her to squeeze through without brushing up against a leg and getting noticed.

"Must be a stray. I've never seen that dog before. Have you?" the mother asked.

"I think I saw him earlier. On our way home," Gabe said.

So much for keeping their distance and staying out of sight.

"Is he friendly?" Anna asked. "Can I pet him?" She started to step out.

Yes!

But the mother stopped her, placing a hand on her shoulder. *Drat!*

"We don't know this dog," Mrs. Morales said. "He's not wearing a collar."

"He looks skinny. I bet he's hungry."

That was a word Sam recognized.

"Oh yes. Oh yes. I am hungry," he barked. Ophelia flashed Sam a look. *Even more charming*, it said. Sam understood. He took evasive maneuvers.

Like a falling tree, the dog flopped lazily down on his side, then rolled onto his back, front paws bent, tongue hanging out, eyes still fixed on the family of three standing in the doorway. *There was talk of belly rubs*, his look seemed to say. *And I've come to see if it's true.*

It was a clutch performance, impossible to resist. At least for

Anna, who somehow wiggled free of her mother's grip and came out onto the porch, cautious steps, one hand out. Sam rolled back onto his feet and gave the hand a tentative sniff. Then he took a step forward and nudged it with his head, as if flashing a sign that said *Scratch here*. Gabe was right behind his sister, holding out his own hand.

"Kids," the mother admonished, but they ignored her. At last she sighed in exasperation and stepped through the door onto the porch after them.

Clearing the path.

With an unspoken *thank you* to the most charming creature she'd ever shared a doughnut with, Ophelia Fidgets slipped into the Morales house to get her coin.

39

Ophelia's cottage in the Tree Tops held all of two rooms. Two rooms that, combined, were only half the size of the entryway she stood in now, with its skinny, leafless tree for hanging coats and its pile of muddy shoes in the corner. The rest of the house appeared enormous. In actuality, it was probably only average as far as human dwellings went, but when you are only a foot tall and looking to burgle a place, a house with even a half dozen rooms can seem impossibly large and fraught with dangers.

Ophelia walked on tiptoe, mindful of everywhere those toe tips tapped. She'd studied human habitats extensively and had some idea of what to expect, but she wasn't prepared for the sheer amount of *stuff* that surrounded her. Humming lights and buzzing boxes and at least twenty different places to sit. Humans must be very good sitters as well. She passed a set of bookshelves. One contained a row of miniature humans trapped in porcelain and painted exquisite colors, standing on gold pedestals, their hands clasped above their heads in a frozen pirouette. Another shelf held rows of books, hundreds of them. (Though the only one familiar to her, *Grimm's Fairy Tales*, was a total rip-off. Most of those stories had no fairies at all.) She thought of the many long afternoons she'd spent in the Archives, nose pressed to some page, and then imagined Gabe and Anna, stretched out across the floor with books in hand, feet kicking the air, getting lost in some fantastic adventure. She smiled despite herself.

Ophelia crept across the thick carpet that reached to her boot tops, following the sound of Kasarah's voice. She glanced in the kitchen, not because she expected the wish to be there, but because the smells were intoxicating. Fresh bread. Sliced strawberries. Roasted corn. The food had mostly been devoured, but the aromas lingered. Of course there was also the half-carved carcass of a dead bird in the middle of the table. Chicken or turkey—she really couldn't tell with half the flesh picked off its bones. Ophelia counted her blessings that Kasarah's wish rested on a coin.

She turned away from the kitchen and headed toward the staircase, certain that the wish was calling from the second floor, but paused again when her eye caught on a picture on the wall. It was the entire family: mother, father, and two kids. Gabe and Anna were noticeably younger. They all looked nice, tucked in and standing straight, but the father was the most striking of the bunch, dressed in a sharp navy blue uniform with red stripes and exquisite brass buttons that Ophelia's fingers just trembled at the thought of fidgeting with. He wore a white hat with a brim like a black-billed goose and a serious expression that contrasted with the smiles of the other three. *Here* was a man after Ophelia's own heart. Uniform sharp. Brass bits polished. The only things she didn't understand were the colorful strips and baubles he had pinned to him, all clumped together like extra buttons that had been sewn in the wrong place. Those she could do without.

Clomp. Clomp. Clomp. The sound of footsteps bursting through the front door broke Ophelia's trance, and she scrambled for cover behind the leg of a chair as Anna ran into the kitchen, quickly grabbed something, and rushed with it back outside. She heard Sam barking at the sight of whatever the girl had brought him—no doubt what was left of the bird. "Oh yes, oh yes, oh yes, it looks delicious!" The door slammed shut again.

"Eat up, Sam," Ophelia whispered to herself. "You earned it." *And buy me as much time as you can.*

She looked up at the flight of stairs. *Flight.* Stupid word for something you had to *climb* up. Each step was nearly as tall as her. Fairies don't believe in stairs. There were no stairs in Grant Tower or anywhere in the Haven for that matter. Of course, just because you don't believe in something doesn't mean it doesn't exist. If anything, that just makes it harder when you're suddenly face-to-face with it.

244

She glanced behind to make sure nobody else was coming through the door, then she started her ascent. It felt like she was climbing one of the pine-covered peaks of home. The effort of lifting her body up and over each step was excruciating, causing her shoulder to burn as she pulled and scrabbled and scraped her way to the top. She stopped halfway to catch her breath, hoping the humans were still preoccupied. If they came in now they would surely spot her; there was nowhere on the stairway to hide.

"Come on, Fidgets," she huffed. "You didn't survive an airplane, a disgruntled goose, a broom attack, and a hawk-snatching just to be beaten by a handful of steps, did you?" With a series of grunts and a few more curses, she struggled up the last six stairs, then lay on her back, chest heaving, staring at a ceiling seemingly miles away. She took a deep breath to steady herself, then got to her feet.

She found herself in a hallway with branching rooms. The voice in her heart told her the wish was at the far end, but she thought it best to peek in each, just in case. There were more pictures lining the walls here, mostly of the children. The boy looked happy in all of them, cradling his baby sister, standing with his parents at the edge of a beach, laughing as he sat atop his father's shoulders—that last picture especially, a smile brighter than sunshine. A far cry from the glum expression she'd seen him wear today. Ophelia suddenly found herself wondering about the father—where he'd gone to and why, and when he was planning to return.

Not my problem, she reminded herself. *Kasarah Quinn is my problem*. The mission. The wish. She passed the first room with its huge square bed, unmade on one side, and the piles of dirty clothes on the floor. So sloppy. Maybe if Mrs. Morales spent less time feeding the neighbor's cat and more time on the laundry she'd be able to see her floor, but that just made her think of Charlie, which, in turn, made her belly ache. Ophelia moved on.

The second room was much smaller, the walls a canary yellow with peeling pink flowers stuck around haphazardly in between pictures of dolphins and kittens and rabbits, some of them photographs, others obviously drawn by a child's hand. Ophelia's eyes darted directly to a collection of rocks crowding a set of bookshelves, so many that she was surprised the shelves didn't come crashing down under the weight. Quartz and gypsum and pyrite and obsidian. This had to be Anna's room. It was bursting with knickknacks, every surface covered with trinkets and hair ribbons and plastic dolls. Even her closet door bulged. It would have been a challenge to find Kasarah's coin in this dump, but thankfully the wish still whispered from down the hall.

As she turned to go, Ophelia glanced in the corner and her whole body froze.

There was a bear.

Just like Charlie warned, sitting less than three feet away, silently staring at her. It was nearly three times Ophelia's size, with thick brown fur, a big beige snout, and glassy black eyes.

It watched her and she watched it, neither daring to move. A grizzly bear, in Kettering, Ohio. At least, she thought that's what it was. It looked like all the pictures of bears Ophelia had seen in the Archives.

Except grizzly bears really should be even bigger than that. And they didn't normally have bright red bows clipped to their hair.

Or plastic teacups set between their feet.

The bear looked at her dumbly with its marble eyes, mocking her with its stitched-on grin.

"Real funny," she snorted. A stupid toy. What kind of girl wants a stuffed version of a vicious carnivore watching her while she sleeps? Humans were so strange.

Ophelia kicked the toy bear in its padded foot and moved to the last door on the left.

Gabe's door.

Where her wish was waiting.

40

The sign said *Keep Out!* in bright red letters.

It seemed like sensible advice, and at any other time, Ophelia probably would have heeded it, but she could hear Kasarah calling to her from behind the door, which, despite the sign, was open just a crack. Ophelia squeezed through.

And into Gabe's room. Which was, she noted with a sigh of appreciation, immaculate. Not a thing out of place. Nothing on the floor. Certainly no stuffed grizzlies standing guard. His bed was carefully made. The books on his nightstand stood in a perfect line, marching from shortest to tallest, accompanied by a couple of framed photos. One of Gabe and his sister standing beside a lopsided sand castle. Another of him and his father dangling by ropes from the side of a cliff. They were both smiling.

Oddly enough only the ceiling was cluttered; a collection

of plastic airplanes hung from hooks and string. Infernal contraptions. Seeing them made Ophelia shudder, but then her eyes fell on the small wooden desk by the window and the soft glow emanating from it.

The coin. And for once, not a single soul around to stop her. All she needed was a way up. Maybe shimmy up the bed and jump from there? She blocked out the sound of Kasarah's constant pining so that she could concentrate. Just get up, complete the ritual, and then find some way out of here and start what would no doubt be a very long journey back home.

She was halfway across the room when she heard a crash—a door below her slamming shut, followed by voices, loud enough to carry up the stairs. She froze, listening.

"But why not?"

It was Gabe. Angry or hurt. Challenging and defiant. It was followed by his mother's voice, stern and just as loud, but more controlled.

"I just don't think it's a good idea."

"You never think *anything's* a good idea!"

"A dog? Really, Gabe? The last thing I need in this house with your father gone is another thing to take care of."

Ophelia cursed under her breath. They were fighting over Sam. Not exactly what she'd meant by *Keep them distracted*.

"Because taking care of us is already too much work," Gabe snipped.

"That's not what I meant."

"He obviously doesn't have anywhere to go. He was starving.

249

He practically swallowed that chicken whole."

That was definitely Sam. Ophelia wondered where the mutt was now. Still outside with Anna? Or had he scampered off and found some place to hide? She couldn't hear him barking anymore. She couldn't hear anything save for the wish in her head and the sound of mother and son arguing at the bottom of the stairs.

"Lord knows we have enough going on without taking in some stray animal. What has gotten *into* you lately?"

Ophelia counted five heartbeats before the boy spoke again, his voice softer but his tone no less defiant. "Dad would let us keep him."

"Maybe. If he was here. But he's not. So that means you're stuck with me. And I say we can't. I'm sorry."

"Yeah, me too."

Gabe's last words were followed by the sound of footfalls stomping quickly up the stairs and down the hall. Heading for his room.

Heading for her.

Ophelia took a sharp breath and looked frantically for a place to hide. If it were either of the other two rooms, she could sneak behind a pile of toys or dive beneath a heap of dirty laundry, but here her only hope was to scurry underneath the bed. She dove and rolled just as the boy stepped through the door, slamming it shut with a wall-rattling shake, closing off her only escape route.

Gabe stood there for a moment, then strode over to the

window by his desk, unlatching it and pushing it open with a grunt, the earthy smells of outside immediately tickling Ophelia's nose. The boy collapsed into the desk chair with an exaggerated sigh.

Ophelia inched to the edge of the bed, lifting the blanket that draped down so she could get a better look, much the same way she had back at the diner. The boy's shoulders shook. She saw him wipe furiously at his eyes with the sleeve of his shirt. Sam must have really turned on the charm.

The nickel continued to glow from the desktop, the halo only she could see, the girl she'd never met refusing to shut up about the bike she didn't have yet. *Make it purple.*

I know. I know. I'm working on it, Ophelia thought.

She needed the boy out of the room, but his heaving sobs caused a knot to form in Ophelia's chest. What *was* it about this kid? He slumped over his desk now, staring out the open window. The sun had vanished completely, drawing dark curtains over the horizon. She couldn't tell from her angle, but she guessed out here—far from the haze of a hundred blazing streetlights—the sky was probably studded with stars. She wondered what the boy saw when he looked out there. An ocean of waiting promises? Or just emptiness, distant and cold? Through the open window Ophelia could hear the cricket symphony resume their overture, a screeching soundtrack to accompany the voice.

I wish. I wish. I wish.

She couldn't wait under this bed forever. Ophelia looked at

her belt, at the canister of weaponized fairy dust resting on her hip. He was a skinny kid. One shot would surely do it. She could sneak up behind him, catch him by surprise. His mother would find him curled up in a ball on the floor and lift him gently into bed and in the morning everything would be better for him. Somehow. Maybe.

Sorry about this, kid, she thought to herself, pulling into a crouch, ready to spring.

Gabe stiffened as if he'd actually heard her thoughts, suddenly sitting up straight, causing Ophelia to take a cautious step back, farther under the bed. He pushed up out of his chair and stared down at the clump of wrinkled bills and loose change on the desk. He seemed to be searching for something in particular.

When he found it, he stuffed it into the front pocket of his jeans and headed for the door.

No way. No flea-flicking way.

Ophelia shot out from underneath the bed, spray in hand, fumbling with the button as she ran, hoping to cut him off, but it was five of her steps for his one. The boy swung his bedroom door closed behind him, trapping her inside.

"Fignuts!"

Now what? Ophelia pressed her belly flat to the carpet, hoping she could squeeze through the thin crack underneath the door. She pushed an arm under, both arms, but her head wouldn't fit and knew she'd tear her wings off trying. As she lay there with her ear pressed to the door, she could hear the boy's voice, shouting again as he clomped down the stairs.

"I'm going down by the creek."

The sound of a door opening. Then the mother's voice from even farther away.

"What if your father calls?"

But the only answer was the sound of the door slamming shut.

Followed by a fairy's hysterical laughter.

41

Fairies love to laugh, though anyone who'd spent time with Mortimer Magnolia Pouts might have cause to doubt it. In fact, a fairy's laugh is one of her best features, rumored to sound like the tinkle of wind chimes, or the murmur of a mountain stream, or the rhythmic patter of rain against a windowpane.

Ophelia sounded like a lunatic.

The sound that erupted from her in that moment was more like a hundred nails scraped across a hundred chalkboards. Like glass shattering in a metal sink. Like ten thousand fat gray cats meowing all at once.

Twenty coins up there. At *least* twenty. And he grabs *that* one? *The* one?

She tried to choke it down, to stay quiet, but it was no use. It was too absurd. It was as if he *knew*. As if he took that stupid nickel on *purpose*. But how could he possibly? Did he somehow catch that glimmer of the light or that fragment of the whisper that supposedly only a fairy could hear? If so, it would be a first. Some humans were more in tune with the deeper synergies of nature's magic than others, but surely this boy couldn't see through the coin to the wish that was trapped inside.

Impossible. This was just the latest dead-end turn in a giant, stinking labyrinth of absolutely rotten luck, a muddled maze where Ophelia seemed to be irrevocably lost. So she did the only thing she could do at the moment: she exploded, muffling her face in the carpet so that her laughter wouldn't carry through the bedroom door.

A door that she couldn't open. Not without getting airborne. And even then it could be tricky.

Ophelia lay there, staring up at the doorknob so far above her, when she felt a cool breath of air on the back of her neck.

Gabe had left the window open.

Serendipitous.

Ophelia sprung into action, gripping the corner of the boy's blanket and pulling herself to the top of his bed. From there it was a clumsy jump over to the table beside it and an even longer, clumsier, knee-banging jump onto the desk with its edge pressed right up against the windowsill. Ophelia looked out.

It was a long way down.

She stood there for a moment looking over the Moraleses' front yard with its giant oak tree and its rows of budding rosebushes, her skin prickled by the breeze. No doubt if anyone had looked up, they would have seen her—or would have seen *something*—standing in the window, silhouetted against the light of the room. A sparrow or a starling, perhaps.

Certainly not a fairy trying to figure out how to make a twenty-foot drop.

She *could* jump. Use her one good wing to try to manage the descent. Except it was all sidewalk directly below—not a soft landing. She took a step back and her eyes found the photos again—the one of Gabe and his sandy sister sitting on the beach. And the other, of him and his dad, just hanging off the edge of a cliff, dangling at the end of a rope.

Okay, she thought. *Let's do it your way.*

Ophelia dug in her pack for the fishhook and the twine she had left, and in a matter of seconds she had a makeshift grappling hook, the twine triple-knotted like her bootlaces. In another tick she had the hook lodged securely in a crack in the windowsill and threw the ball of twine over the edge. It came up short, but a little drop was better than a giant one. Ophelia gave it a strong tug. "Here goes," she whispered, and stepped over the edge.

She nearly lost her grip at first but managed to hang on, her satchel swinging beneath her, her arms straining. The twine bit into her palms from gripping it so tight, and rappelling down the side of the house aggravated her sore left shoulder even further. Spiders made it look so easy, though Ophelia suspected that if she had a supply of sticky rope that shot straight out of her hindquarters, it would be easy for her too. She couldn't imagine what Gabe and his father were smiling about.

She grunted her way down, hand over hand. Finally, three feet from the bottom, the twine gave out and Ophelia let go, landing in a combat-ready crouch the way she'd been taught. She listened for Kasarah's voice, still close, coming from behind the house.

Ophelia turned and tugged at the twine, hoping somehow to dislodge the hook anchored to the boy's windowsill, but it held fast. She would just have to leave it. Squint wouldn't approve. Leave no trace—that was one of the big rules. Not a footprint. Not a mark. So far Ophelia had done a terrible job of it. Her bag was nearly empty. Everything she'd brought with her, including her pink flight suit, was lost or abandoned. Maybe after she completed her mission, she could come back and clean up her mess.

If she completed her mission.

Crouched there in the darkness, she called out for Sam as loud as she dared, listening for a bark or the sound of his feet galloping across the lawn. No answer. "Where are you, you stupid mutt?" She didn't need him to track the boy, at least. Not with what was tucked in his pocket.

What does a boy want with just one flipflapping nickel any-how? You can't buy anything with it, not where he said he was going.

Down to the creek.

257

Ophelia groaned.

It doesn't have to be a well or a fountain. Just about any body of water will do.

She had to hurry. She had to stop him. She followed the whisper, running along the front of the house and then around the corner, concentrating only on Kasarah's voice and the promise she had to keep. So intently focused that she didn't see the net come down.

42

Trapped!

The tightly meshed black ropes surrounded her, pinning her to the ground. Ophelia hadn't spied the girl standing in the shadows by the side of the house, holding her net—the kind a human might use to catch butterflies—tonight used to catch lightning bugs.

And fairies.

The webbing enveloped Ophelia, giving her hardly any room to move, though that didn't stop her from trying. A giant pickle jar sat on the ground beside the girl, three lightning bugs already flitting helplessly inside, intermittently casting their glow as if signaling for rescue. Their captor, a pigtailed Anna, bent close to the net, examining her prize with eyes suddenly wide with wonder.

"What the heck are *you*?"

Ophelia flinched. What did she see this time, this collector of rocks and leaves and bugs? A new kind of dragonfly or cicada? Some elaborately patterned moth? Clearly something different from what she'd spied in the alleyway earlier that afternoon. This girl was exactly the kind of human you had to worry about—too curious for her own good. Ophelia turned her back to the girl, hoping the camo would hold up better if Anna Morales saw mostly wings, broken or not.

"You're amazing," Anna whispered. "I've *got* to show Mom." Ophelia felt something brush softly against her back, a curious finger, a tentative prod. Ophelia winced, her good wing fluttering in agitation. "So cool," the girl added.

Let me poke and prod you *and see how cool it is*, Ophelia thought, just as angry at herself for being caught as at the girl for catching her. Ophelia thought of the rocks lining the shelves of Anna's room like museum artifacts. The girl already thought she'd caught something rare and beautiful. Just wait until the next day when the camo wore off, then imagine the look on her face. She looked over her shoulder to see the girl fumbling, one-handed, with her jar, trying to undo the top and set her other captives free to make room for her new discovery. Ophelia took advantage of the girl's momentary distraction to pull on the net, but the rope was much tougher than she expected. She glanced down at her remaining can of spray, knowing she was plenty close to get a good shot, but she might need that for the boy. Then she saw her knife clipped to the other side.

"You're beautiful," Anna said. "I'm going to keep you

forever, no matter what Mom says."

Anna bent down again, her face so close that Ophelia could see the flecks of green in her otherwise amber eyes. Ophelia let one hand slip down to the handle of her knife. The girl had left her no choice.

"Meyrrrourrr!"

The high-pitched caterwaul—a less-than-gorgeous falsetto—startled both of them, but only Anna twisted around, peering at the neighbor's fence.

"Patch, is that you?" the girl asked, her eyes flitting back and forth. "Where are you, kitty?" But there was no answer. With a shrug, Anna turned back to her catch, her jar empty.

She looked at her net and frowned.

Her beautiful new discovery was gone. Vanished. Leaving only a hole in her net the size of a plum.

43

Thank you, Patch, Ophelia thought as she slipped into the darkness, sheathing her knife and glancing back only once to catch the look of disappointment on Anna's face. *And may the saucers of cream be ever flowing.*

She stayed low, following the sound of Kasarah's voice, running as fast as her tired legs allowed, first through the long, cool grass that reached her knees, then down a slope spotted with trees and ivy toward a small woods that sat back behind the house. Up above her the silver moon struck through a wisp of dark clouds, a legion of stars grouped around it like sentries. So many wishes, but only one that counted.

As she ran, the trees seemed to whisper to Ophelia with their wind-rattled leaves.

Hurry, they said. *Hurry before it's too late.*

Because she knew what the boy was up to. Why he'd

stormed out of the house with only the one coin in his pocket. Why he'd come down to the creek.

Hurry.

Make it purple.

Don't screw up.

"Shut up, all of you!" Ophelia hissed at the chorus of voices inside her head. She broke through a wall of white oaks and stumbled into a clearing, a grassy expanse that led farther downward toward the water's edge. She came to an abrupt halt, a hand over her pounding heart.

There he stood, dressed again in his long green jacket, his feet at the edge of a creek swollen from spring rains, though he'd picked a shallower part strewn with rocks, where the water ran clear as glass. She could hear it babbling—like the laugh of a not-totally-insane fairy—and see it catch a glimmer of the moonlight from above. The large, rough-barked trees on the opposite bank stood like solemn giants, looking over the boy as he held up the nickel—Kasarah's nickel, Ophelia's nickel, certainly not *his* nickel—between finger and thumb.

The light from the wish was almost blinding now, and Ophelia sensed that this place, this particular spot, surrounded by reeds and mossy rock and old earth, was heavy with magic. Some places were like that. The Haven was like that. Places where the mystic energy hadn't yet been buried under steel and concrete and asphalt. Where ancient trees grew and shed, fell and rotted, and were reborn. This was one of those places, and it made Ophelia wonder again about the boy, if he knew way more than he should. This boy who was about to ruin everything.

Ophelia unhooked her canister from her belt, her finger poised above the button. She would need to get closer to get a good shot. She didn't bother to consider what would happen after that; she needed that nickel and she needed it *now*.

He didn't see her coming.

He held the coin up to the moonlight.

The trees still seemed to be begging, *Hurry, hurry,* though suddenly Ophelia wasn't so sure they were talking to her.

Gabe shut his eyes. Ophelia charged and pressed the button, and a blast of glittery spray shot out, forming a fine silvery mist that engulfed the boy's head. He breathed it in and coughed, opened his eyes, and looked at her, just for a moment, through sparkling tears.

He blinked twice and his body went limp, collapsing in a heap by the water's edge.

Falling, along with the coin—flipped from his fingers only a moment before.

44

A wish is many things. It is hope and desire and daydreams. It is impossibility and improbability and something in between. It is stardust and well water and spectrums of light in the sky. It is half-melted birthday candles and Christmas lists. It is broken turkey bones. It is the willing suspension of disbelief.

And sometimes it is desperation. It is a hole in your heart that wants filling. It is more-than-anything-in-the-world.

She was a second too late.

She saw the coin somersault from the boy's fingers the moment she shot him. End over end, tumbling in a wide arc out into the center of the stream. She heard it hit the water and knew what it meant, the woods around her letting out a creaking sigh, a breath that had been held too long.

Ophelia dropped her canister to the grass and went over to

the boy, kneeling by his head to make certain that the spray did what Rolleye said it would and only that. She hoped she hadn't hurt him. She hadn't meant to hurt him.

His eyes were closed. His chest rose and fell in a steady rhythm. She put a hand against his cheek: warm and wet. He was deep asleep. Nothing more. Thank the Havens.

She turned back to the creek, and the coin that still sparkled through the water, its light refracted, making the entire stream glimmer with an iridescent blue gloss, almost as if the creek were lined with topaz. She stood at the water's edge and contemplated taking off her boots and rolling up her pants—she'd finally dried out from her unplanned high dive into the pond—but there hardly seemed a point after everything she'd been through. She waded into the shallow stream all the way up to her waist, careful of her footing on the slick rocks, until she stood above the shining nickel, the face of some silvery old man staring up at her. She bent down and lifted it with both hands, surprised at how heavy it was.

Even before she touched it, she knew. She could hear it. Could hear *them*. Kasarah's voice, of course, just as loud as ever, but also what was underneath.

The second wish.

He hadn't said it out loud. He didn't need to. That's not one of the rules. In fact, it's better if you don't, just in case someone overhears, because wishes are not for sharing. But she didn't need a coin to know what was in the boy's heart.

I wish he would come home.

Ophelia Delphinium Fidgets stood in the shallows of the stream, holding the nickel to her chest, dumbstruck. Two wishes on the same coin, the second one applied while the first was still active. She wasn't sure if such a thing had ever happened before. If it had, no one ever taught her how to handle it. There was nothing in the Granter's Code of Conduct that she could recall. But she could hear them both, clear as a sparrow's song. Perhaps it was this place, heavy with magic, that caused Gabe's voice to ring out just as loud as Kasarah's. Or maybe it was because she was so close to the Wishmaker himself. Two voices suddenly clamoring in her head.

I wish I had . . .

I wish he would . . .

Ophelia waded back to the bank and set the nickel gently down in the grass next to the boy's feet. She dropped to her knees and untied the glass vial from around her neck, removing the stopper and swirling the dust it contained. It felt like everything inside her was spinning as well. She stared at the coin, blinking, bewildered, hesitant. What happens now?

I wish . . .

Ophelia shook her head. It didn't matter. It changed nothing. Kasarah's wish was still there, waiting, *wanting*. A leaf fallen. A promise made. Just think of how happy she will be when she wakes up and finds that new bicycle sitting on her doorstep. Think about how nice it will be to just finish this and finally get back to the Haven.

To get back home.

The word made her shiver.

She looked over at Gabe. The boy who had somehow picked this nickel out of a dozen coins, *that* coin picked out of a million possible wishes. This petulant, pouting boy whose father was half a world away. She thought of the pictures of them together, one laughing on the other's shoulders, the two of them hanging side by side. She could easily imagine them standing at the edge of a stream much like this one, Gabe's hands grasped firm around his fishing pole, his father's bigger hands clasped over his son's, ready to reel in their catch. Ophelia never had a father. Or a mother. Only her Founder. But she knew how it felt to want something desperately. To feel helpless and broken, and yet still harbor hope that, somehow, you'd find a way to get it. Even if it meant believing in the impossible.

I wish I had . . .

I wish he would . . .

But that wasn't how it worked.

"Please understand. It's nothing personal," she muttered to the sleeping boy. "I'm just doing my job."

Now she sounded like Squint. *There are rules.* A wish that had been chosen had never gone ungranted, not since the Great Tree was created. Not since the Haven was secured. The dust could be wasted, or worse, it could backfire somehow. It wasn't worth the risk. Yet there she stood at the edge of the creek, in this place that hummed with the deep-rooted promise of magic, the vial of dust poised above the coin in her trembling hand, hesitating, muttering to herself, *It's nothing personal.*

And wondering maybe, if that wasn't the problem.

I wish . . .

"Phee?"

Ophelia jumped to her feet and spun around, clasping the vial to her heart, looking toward the backdrop of trees to see a dark shape hovering in the night sky. She recognized the whistling wheeze of that voice. As he came closer there was no mistaking the spikes of pink hair sticking out on all sides.

"Charlie?" she croaked out. "What are *you* doing here?"

With a flutter of two working wings, Charlie Whistler alighted beside her, his arms crossed, his eyes narrow, concerned and questioning.

"Looking for you, obviously." He was out of breath. He had no supplies. He wasn't even wearing a flight suit, just his usual shabby uniform. His wings shivered from what must have been a cold journey through the clouds. Charlie nodded to Gabe and the empty canister on the ground beside him. "Your handiwork?"

Ophelia nodded. "I had no choice. He got . . . involved." It was as good a word as any. She glanced down at the coin lying at her feet, then back at her friend. "How did you even find me?"

"You activated your distress signal tocks ago. Squint assembled a rescue team, but I left just before them."

"I never—" Ophelia started to say. Then she remembered.

269

The truck. Somehow the locator must have been triggered when she was struck, all the way back at the diner. She'd thought she'd lost it, assumed it had been smashed to pieces. "Wait, you left without permission?"

Charlie shrugged. "I was worried about you. And I knew Squint wouldn't let me come along." Suddenly his face pinched as he pointed to her busted wing. "What in the Haven happened to you?" He took a step toward her, but she waved him off.

"It's all right. I mean—it's not, obviously. It's probably shot, but I'm all right."

He frowned at her. "You don't look all right. You look like something an owl hurked up."

Ophelia didn't argue. Her uniform was mud-streaked and torn in several places. She was soaked from the waist down. Her hair was a tangle of knots. Bruises, scratches, and scrapes covered what felt like every inch of her, though there weren't that many inches to account for. "It's been a long day."

"You're telling me. You wouldn't *believe* how difficult it was to track you down. Eventually I just gave up and followed the wish—you know, make it purrr . . ." Charlie's voice trailed off. He pointed to the nickel by Ophelia's feet. He could hear it calling, too. Could hear them both. "Am I wrong or has that thing got . . . ?" He held up two fingers. Ophelia nodded.

"And is one of them . . . ?" Charlie glanced at the boy lying on the ground beside them. She nodded again.

"Oh," Charlie said, his eyes getting big. "Oh, wow. I mean, that's kind of incredible, isn't it?" He cocked his head, no doubt listening carefully to this new wish. "Who's the *he*?"

"The boy's father," Ophelia said. "He's been away for a long time. I think Gabe's afraid he might never come back."

"Gabe?" Charlie repeated. "You know this kid?"

Ophelia nodded again.

I wish I had . . .

I wish he would . . .

Charlie eyed the vial of dust in Ophelia's hand, open but unused. He looked from Ophelia to Gabe and then back again. He took a step back. "Whoa, hold on. You're not thinking what I *think* you're thinking, are you?"

Ophelia didn't respond at first. The fact that she was thinking about it all was enough. Gabe's green army jacket was bunched up underneath him like a rumpled cape, his face awash in the moonlight. He looked peaceful for the first time all day. She looked into the vial of dust twinkling in her hand, brighter than the moonbeam. "He just wants his father back," she murmured.

"Sure. And the girl just wants a bike. Everybody wants something, Phee," Charlie sputtered. "It's not our place to judge."

But Ophelia could tell he wasn't so sure. She could hear it in his voice. "What would you do?" she asked.

"*Me?* I'm probably the *last* fairy you should ask. But it doesn't

271

matter what I would do. You're the Granter. It's your mission. It's your call."

Her mission. Her call.

I wish . . .

"But whatever you're going to do, you better hurry," Charlie said, "because we're about to have company."

The moment he said it, there was a low-pitched hum. Ophelia looked up to see the trees spit out a line of winged creatures all wearing the gray-and-black flight suits of the Haven's Emergency Response Team, the ones called into action when a mission turned sour. They crossed over the creak in formation, hovering above Ophelia and Charlie. One of them called to her through a conch shell that served as an amplifier.

"Ophelia Delphinium Fidgets," the voice said. "Put the vial down and step away from the coin."

She recognized that voice, too. It was one she heard in her own head only moments ago. Next to Kasarah's, it was a voice she'd been hearing all day.

Barnabus Oleander Squint had come to rescue her personally.

Or to do her job for her.

45

Ophelia took a step back, putting some space between her and Kasarah's coin, but she kept the glass vial clutched to her heart. The pool of moonlight in the small clearing was quickly filled with fairies, five of them in the ERT, including Squint.

They weren't here to protect her. They were here to clean up her mess.

"Form a perimeter and stay alert." Squint's goggles did nothing to make his eyes look any bigger. He pointed to Gabe, stretched out in the grass. "One threat neutralized, but there could be more." The other fairies fanned out, keeping their eyes on the woods. Squint grimaced at Charlie, who frowned right back. "We will discuss what you are doing here later, Agent Whistler. But I should tell you that your actions, while in keeping with your history of poor choices, are still disappointing, and will not go without punishment."

Charlie's chin dug into his chest, and the head of the Granters Guild turned his attention to Ophelia, who felt herself wilt as well under those shrewd, slivered eyes. "You are quite a ways from your distress signal, Agent Fidgets, and even farther from your original destination. I can only assume by what I'm hearing from that coin by your feet that you have yet to complete your mission."

It wasn't a question. He knew as well as she did what had happened; he could hear Gabe's wish overlapping with the one she was sent to grant. But if he was surprised, he didn't show it. She had never known Squint to be surprised by anything.

"I was just about to," Ophelia said hoarsely, still keeping a tight grip on the vial of dust he'd given her what seemed like ages ago.

Squint crouched down and ran his hand over the surface of the still-wet coin. "Isn't that something?" he grunted, shaking his head. "Two wishes. Uncanny." Then he stood up, wiping his hand against his suit. "It should never have come to this, of course. If you'd have done your job as you were supposed to, you wouldn't be in this position. *We* wouldn't be in this position," he said, indicating the other fairies. "Not that it matters. You know what you have to do."

What she *had* to do. She knew. Of course she knew. And yet her eyes flashed to the sleeping boy.

Squint caught her glance, and it told him everything he

needed to know. "Do I need to remind you that failure to grant a selected wish constitutes a violation of the code and presents a potential danger to all of us? There is no choice here."

But there was, wasn't there? He heard them just as well as she did.

I wish . . .

Ophelia shook her head. "It's not fair," she mumbled, though as soon as the words escaped her, she knew they were wrong. Fair wasn't the word, but Squint didn't give her the chance to take it back.

"It's perfectly fair!" he shouted. "There are millions of wishes out there, Fidgets. We don't have the luxury of debating each and every one. You don't know why Kasarah Quinn wants that bike. What it will mean to *her.*" Squint took another step so that he was straddling the coin, casting his shadow between the two of them, arms crossing his chest. "A leaf falls, a wish is chosen, and we grant it. That's how it is."

But it hadn't always been so. He knew it as well as she did. There was a time when fairies decided for themselves which wishes were worth granting. In the absence of rules, they followed their hearts. "That's how it is," she repeated. "But it's not how it has to be."

"Are you questioning my authority, Agent Fidgets? The system has been in place for over a hundred years. You have been a Granter for one." Squint shook his head. "Clearly I sent you out too soon. You weren't ready. This responsibility is too much for you to handle." He sighed. "And this wish is no longer yours to grant." He raised his hand, signaling to the surrounding fairies. "Response Team, please restrain Agent Whistler and Agent Fidgets and secure the vial."

The circle started to close.

Ophelia spun, taking in the faces of the fairies moving in. She caught Charlie's eye. *What's the plan?* his own eyes asked, but she didn't have one. They were outnumbered, and she didn't want to fight with her own kind. What she wouldn't give for some sort of distraction.

Two members of the Response Team grabbed Charlie by the arms, holding him back as the other two approached Ophelia from either side. She closed her fingers around the vial and stole another glance at Gabe. *I'm sorry*, she thought.

I wish, she heard him say.

The members of the ERT reached for her.

Squint bent down for the nickel but stopped with his hands over it, his head cocked, one ear angled toward the edge of the woods.

And the howl that filled the night.

46

There were few sounds Ophelia liked as much as the roar of wind in her ears during flight. The thunder of a ferociously pounding waterfall. The piccolo trill of a wood thrush greeting her in the morning. The familiar chirp of Charlie's whistle.

And now this. The eardrum-drubbing bay that caused the members of the ERT to freeze, including Squint, whose eyes opened so wide they *almost* looked normal.

That howl, and the barking that followed.

"I am Sam!"

He burst through the swath of white oak trees at a gallop, charging into the moonlight, scattering the ring of fairies like a swarm of gnats. Even Charlie took flight, jumping a full ten feet into the air as the dog came barreling through, shouting

277

furiously. Only Squint held his ground, unflinching, as Sam skidded to a halt next to Ophelia.

"I found you," Sam barked.

"Yes. You found me," Ophelia said, reaching out and curling the fingers of her empty hand into Sam's fur.

The fairies in the sky above circled cautiously, afraid to alight with the huge, hairy, rumbling monster down below. That left only her and Squint, face-to-face. She had the magic; he had the wish. The head of the Granters Guild stood with the coin cradled in his arms.

"This is preposterous. Just give me the vial, Fidgets, and we can all go home," he barked.

No. Not all of us, Ophelia thought. *Not unless the boy gets his wish.* She shook her head and tightened her grip. Beside her, Sam let out a low, menacing growl.

Squint looked at her incredulously. "You're being insensible. You would seriously risk all of this—your job, the safety of the Haven, the integrity of the system—for some human you don't even know?"

Ophelia felt a warmth spreading through her, working its way up to her cheeks. "His name is Gabriel," she muttered.

"Excuse me?"

"His name," she repeated, louder this time, "is Gabriel Morales. But his family calls him Gabe." She kept one hand on Sam, the other clenching a pinch of magic in a tight fist. Her voice grew stronger as the words tumbled out. "He lives at 4462 Wellspring Road, Kettering, Ohio. In a two-story house in sore need of new paint. He has a sister who looks up to him and a mother who worries over him and a father who makes him pancakes with chocolate chips and takes him fishing. He likes building sand castles and hanging from cliffs. He has a room full of model airplanes and—"

And a hole inside him, she was about to say, but Squint cut her off.

"Enough!" he shouted, raising a hand to stop her, then his voice grew softer. "I've heard enough. I understand. You aren't the first fairy to think this way, Fidgets." Squint's shoulders slumped, his head bowed. And for a moment, Ophelia thought he was going to hand her the coin and let her grant the wish she wanted.

Instead he clutched the nickel closer to his chest.

"But it's not worth the risk."

Squint unfurled his beautiful, shining wings, and before Ophelia could make a move to stop him, the head of the Granters Guild shot up into the sky, taking both wishes with him.

"Fizzlebutts!" Ophelia cursed. Then she quickly restoppered the vial of fairy dust and set it between Sam's front paws. "Guard this with your life."

In response Sam hunched low, settling his scruffy chin over the fairy dust, his teeth bared, daring any creature—fay or otherwise—to come near.

Ophelia looked up at Squint, already near the tops of

the trees, and snapped her own wings open—broken and unbroken—blinking back sudden, stinging tears. She shouldn't even try, she knew. Doing so could damage her already busted wing beyond repair. But some chances *were* worth taking.

Gritting her teeth, Ophelia pushed off, using both wings, grunting through every excruciating beat as she darted upward, striving to close the distance between her and the escaping coin.

It was a game of chase.

And it should have been impossible. She was exhausted. Bruised and battered. Her tattered wing felt as if it might shatter into a thousand pieces with every beat, the pain like a splinter digging deeper into her shoulder, forcing her to bite and bloody her lip again as she fought against it. Squint was a strong flier, also first in his class so many seasons ago. Years of being cooped up in his office had made him soft, and the weight of the nickel in his arms slowed him down, but he still had the edge.

Only Ophelia didn't know when to quit.

Some fairies called her stubborn.

She preferred the word *determined*.

They flew higher, well above the trees now, aiming for the clouds, Squint looking over his shoulder at Ophelia on his heels, somehow getting closer. Reaching out. Getting ahold of Squint's boot. Then his leg. Clawing her way up his suit toward the coin, his wings doing most of the work of keeping them alight. Had you been looking you might have seen something different: two lovebirds entwined in a courtship dance, two dragonflies chasing each other's tails. Certainly not two fairies wrestling in midair over which wish to grant. Ophelia got both hands on the nickel, the frantic beating of one good wing twisting her sideways, throwing both fairies off balance.

"Let go!" Squint grunted over the wind and the beating of their wings. "This magic wasn't meant for him! It's not your choice to make!"

Ophelia knew better. Somewhere along the way she'd done exactly what Charlie had warned her about: she'd lost sight of what was important.

But then she found it again.

"My mission," she said. "My call."

Ophelia gave one last, tremendous tug, prying the coin free from Squint's hands. The move sent her tumbling backward, out of control. She heard her already ragged wing snap once more, a final blow that rendered it completely useless and caused her to blink away spots of black and red as she spiraled downward, through the canopy of trees to the shimmering creek below. But she held on to the coin. She wasn't about to let go.

"Gotcha!"

Pink hair. Cockeyed smile. Arms under her shoulders, hugging her tight as he swooped underneath her. "Told you you needed a wingman," Charlie said.

He set her gently on the ground beside Sam, who tucked his tail and continued to flash the teeth he never bothered to chew with, keeping the other members of the ERT at bay. Ophelia collapsed to her knees, her left wing hanging completely limp beside her. She reached between Sam's paws for the dust. Gabe lay directly in front of her now, oblivious to the chaos that was happening around him, but she could still hear his voice inside her head.

With Sam guarding one side and Charlie on the other, Ophelia leaned over Kasarah's coin (the old man's coin, Striped Shirt's coin, Gabe's coin) and dumped the contents of the vial over its silvery surface. The dust flickered, floating just above, waiting for the words. The air around her hummed with magic. She could feel it, pulsing, in the ground beneath her knees, coursing through the roots of the trees, burning in the light of a million stars.

I wish . . .

So did she. She wished she could grant both of them, but there was only so much magic to go around.

"Think very hard about what you are about to do. The Haven—our entire way of life—may depend on it."

Squint stood across from her again, right by Gabe's feet, his wings outstretched, but no longer moving to stop her. The cloud of dust hovered between them. The coin shimmered in the grass.

"I have," she said.

Ophelia closed her eyes and whispered the words.

Your wish is granted.

The dust flared and disappeared like sparks from a fire, burning sun-bright before turning to ordinary ash. The trees around her sighed with rustling leaves.

And Ophelia realized, only then, what she'd done.

47

The ritual is the same.

The wish is found. The dust is sprinkled. The words are spoken.

And then, *boom*.

The magic happens.

But some wishes are harder to grant than others.

And everything comes at a cost.

48

Among their other numerous and remarkable attributes, fairies are naturally quick healers.

Cuts can close in a matter of minutes. Bruises often fade within the hour. Even a completely busted wing will mend itself naturally if given the chance to do so.

Provided you don't make it worse by trying to *fly* with it. Provided you be still and *allow* it to heal. But some fairies aren't very good at being still. They are twitchy and restless and fretful by nature, and though they may pride themselves on their rule-following, an inner voice often prods them to do otherwise, to press on, even if it means they may never fly again.

Ophelia Fidgets woke in a wooden bed, wearing a slick silk-woven robe and cocooned in a woolen blanket. Her eyes opened to the silver hair, half-toothed smile, and deep-lined skin of one Edna Echinacea Pudge, a pear-faced, squat-bodied fairy, and also the most gifted Healer in the Haven.

"Hello, dear. How are you feeling?"

Ophelia shook her head. She felt terrible. Groggy. Stiff. And her back still throbbed at the wing joint, though that was much preferable to the thorns of pain that she remembered. "Um, okay I guess," she lied. She tried to sit. It took a tremendous effort just to prop herself on her elbows. "What happened? Where am I?"

"You're in the recovery wing of the infirmary, love. Had a nasty break, among other things. A real nasty break. I'm afraid we had to knock you out."

"Knock me out?"

"Put you to sleep. It was the only way you'd let me properly set your wing. And you must have needed the rest, because you've been out for three full days."

Three days. Had it been that long? Ophelia thought about Rolleye and his knockout gas, wondering if that's what she'd been hit with. If so, it felt like they'd used a gallon of the stuff. She rubbed her eyes, then struggled to sit fully upright, looking over her shoulder to assess the damage. Whatever it was, she could handle it. At least that's what she tried to tell herself.

"Huh," is what she actually said.

Her left wing was no longer the torn-to-tatters catastrophe it had been. The delicate bones had already mended, and the membrane had regained some of its gossamer glow.

"See, not so bad after all," the old fairy purred.

Ophelia gave it a test flutter, just a little twitch, but stopped when she saw the reproachful look on Pudge's pinkish face.

"Now, don't push it. It still needs another day or so to finish healing. And even then you'll have to be careful. Though from what I've heard, that's not exactly your style, is it?"

Ophelia frowned. Careful. Yes. She usually *was* careful. At least she used to be. "Three days?" she repeated.

"You do remember coming back here, don't you, dear?"

No. Not exactly. She couldn't remember coming to the infirmary. She certainly didn't remember Pudge knocking her unconscious and setting her wing. She had some faint memory of seeing the mountains, however, and then the Tree Tops. The shiver that comes from crossing the magical barrier into the Haven, but even that was cloudy, mostly impressions, glimpses in between periods of blackness.

Everything before that, though, Ophelia remembered perfectly.

"To be honest, with the shape you were in, I'm surprised you made it back here alive."

Alive and in mostly one piece. She'd had to be carried back, actually. That she knew. After the words, the dust, and that *moment*, she'd actually walked over to Squint and handed him the empty vial. The next thing she knew she was hooked under her arms, caught between two members of the ERT, who pulled her up into the sky, kicking and screaming, looking down at Sam running in frantic circles beneath her.

She remembered him calling out to her. Baying. *Wait. Come*

back. You are my friend. And she called back to him, as loud as she could, *Don't follow me.* Because she was afraid he would try. And no matter how good at chase he was, he could never make it this far. Not all the way to the Haven.

She didn't get the chance to scratch him one last time behind the ears. To tell him thank you for everything he'd done. For helping her grant her wish.

For helping her make it home.

"I imagine you'll be out of here shortly," Pudge continued. "Of course, judging by the look on Barnabus Squint's face when he dropped you off, I wouldn't be too eager to leave."

Squint. Ophelia felt a stone sink in her gut, remembering her midair wrestling match with her boss. The orders she ignored. No—*deliberately disobeyed.* That's the phrase he would use. His warnings about what might happen if she ignored the promise of the Great Tree. If she made the wrong choice.

It took a moment for Ophelia to muster the courage to ask.

"Is everything all right? Here, I mean? Is the Haven . . ."

"You want to know if your foolishness out there caused the magic to dry up and the Haven to collapse and all fay life as we know it to disappear forever?" Pudge prompted. "No. As you can see, that didn't happen. Life goes on, my girl. But I'm guessing you're still in a heap of trouble regardless."

Ophelia fell back onto her bed, relieved. She hadn't brought about the end of the fairy world. That was something at least. Edna Pudge bent down, putting her ruddy cheek next to Ophelia's. The Healer smelled like lavender and lemons.

"Though between you and me," she whispered, "I probably would have done the same." She straightened up and nodded sideways. "Looks like you have a visitor. Again."

"Well, well, well. Look what the fairies dragged in. And I mean that in the most literal sense."

Ophelia grinned. Charlie stood in the doorway, dressed in uniform, and for once it actually looked decent—not craggy with wrinkles or covered in stains. He'd even bothered to tuck in his shirt. She wondered what kind of trouble *he* was in to bother buttoning his collar. He stepped aside to let Pudge squeeze past, leaving them alone. "You certainly look better," he said after giving Ophelia a once-over.

"Not like owl vomit, you mean?"

"*Less* like owl vomit," he admitted. "How's the wing?"

Ophelia sat up again and twisted so he could get a look at the nearly mended wing poking out of her robes. He let out a whistle. "That Pudge is a miracle worker."

"It still hurts," she told him. "But she says I should be able to fly in a day or so. What's up with this?" She pointed to her neck to indicate his unusual primness. "Trying to make a good impression for once?"

He pulled on the collar with a hooked finger. "I feel like I'm being slowly strangled to death. Whose idea was it to make these things so tight?" He came and sat at the edge of her bed. He looked exhausted, and Ophelia couldn't help but wonder how many times he'd already been here to visit her, if maybe he hadn't spent a night or two in the splintery-looking chair in the corner. "I'm trying to be on my best behavior," he admitted. "It's intolerable."

"Squint?" Ophelia guessed. Charlie nodded.

"Not exactly my biggest fan right now. Wasn't to begin with, really, but I didn't make things any better by showing up where I wasn't supposed to."

"You didn't have to come after me," Ophelia told him. "Don't get me wrong. I appreciate it—especially the keeping-me-from-crashing-to-the-ground part. But you didn't have to. Especially if it meant getting you into trouble."

"Eh. I was already in trouble," Charlie said.

Ophelia pressed him with a look, pinning him there on the corner of the bed with a raised eyebrow.

"Okay. If you really want to know," he began. "Nearly ten seasons ago, before you were even part of the guild, I was out on assignment. Birthday wish. Twelve-year-old boy wanted a new pair of shoes. Adidas. Black. Very specific, just like your purple bike."

"*Kasarah's* purple bike," Ophelia corrected him.

"Right. Sorry. *Kasarah's* purple bike. Anyways, it was a standard infiltration and retrieval. The candle he'd wished on was in a trash bin in the garage, but the only way I could get to it was by going through the house, so I took my time. Did some recon, waited for the right moment, and I got distracted."

"That happens," Ophelia said, remembering standing in the flower box outside the Moraleses' house, looking in their kitchen, watching the children tease each other, seeing their

290

mother sobbing by the sink. She understood.

"Yeah, but this was different. Dante was the boy's name," Charlie continued. "Lived in this huge house. Had everything. Toys, playground, swimming pool, you name it. Except this kid, he wasn't just *spoiled* rotten—he *was* rotten. Straight down to the core. I watched him torture his sisters, yell at his mother, refuse to do anything he was told. You should have seen him, Phee. Throwing tantrums. Destroying everything in his path. And I was supposed to waste our precious bit of dust on *him*? With all those other wishes out there?"

Millions of wishes, Ophelia knew. Far too many to grant.

And not all of them the same.

Charlie shook his head. "I couldn't do it. I aborted the mission. Came back to the Haven and handed my vial to Squint and told him to find someone out there who deserved it or find another Granter to go out and finish the job. Of course you know how Squint is."

She nodded. She knew. No wish goes ungranted. Not on his watch. She couldn't blame him. He did what he thought was best for the Haven.

They all did.

"So he sent someone else in my place. Dante got his shoes and I got benched. Ever since then I've been stuck at my desk, waiting to get back out in the field. But after what I did a few days ago . . ."

Ophelia pouted. He was right. After that, there was little chance Squint would let him back out there, whether he buttoned his collar or not. "How come you never told me?"

"Squint didn't want me putting ideas in anyone's head. There are rules, you know. Besides," he added, "there are some things you just have to find out on your own. The hard way."

"Yeah, well, I wish you would have told me *how* hard," Ophelia grumbled.

"I tried," he said. "But you don't ever listen to me. You're kind of obstinate that way."

"I am not obstinate," she said. "I just happen to be right all the time."

Charlie chuckled, then reached across the bed and took her hand. "So how was it? Back there by the creek. Did it *feel* right?"

She knew what he was asking.

Her first granting. How could she describe it? The sensation had been immediate, the instant she'd said the words. A sudden surge, lightning-struck, every part of her crackling, her body thrumming, in tune with the trees, the water, the earth. She felt light and full all at once. Like she was about to explode and yet hungry, aching for more. It was the most exquisite sensation she'd ever experienced.

Amaratio.

Ophelia smiled. "It felt like my heart would burst," she said.

Charlie nodded thoughtfully. "Hold on to it," he said. "You never know when you're going to feel it again."

After everything she'd done, the trouble she'd caused,

Ophelia figured she might have to hold on to that one beautiful moment forever.

Even so, it would still be worth it.

She and Charlie sat for a tick without another word, listening to the trill of a wood warbler that had nested in the infirmary's thatched roof, calling for its mate. Finally he let go of her hand and gave his brushed pink hair a vigorous scratching, messing it up thoroughly. "Well, it looks like you're going to pull through, and I've got a mound of paperwork to get back to, but I'll check up on you later. Try not to get into any trouble while I'm gone."

"I'm stuck in this bed for another day. I don't see how that's possible."

"Oh. I think you could find a way." He paused in the doorway and mumbled something else.

"What was that?"

"I said, 'I'm proud of you.'"

Ophelia blushed. She couldn't help it.

Then she pointed out that one of his boots had come untied.

Because she couldn't help that either.

49

The next morning, Ophelia was cleared to leave, her release forms signed in Edna Pudge's messy scrawl. She was given a minty-scented ointment to rub on her wing joint and told to *try* to limit her flying time over the next few days, though even that was said with a wink.

She was also told to report directly to Squint's office. She had already missed the morning lottery, she knew, the Great Tree shedding its golden leaves, the names called and echoed, gathered in the little basket, a handful of fortunate souls whose wishes would—almost definitely—come true. That was all right; she was sure *she* wouldn't be granting any of them.

She fluttered slowly, in no real hurry to get to Grant Tower. The Haven was bustling as if it were any other day. The Builders were busy repairing roofs, the Whisperers were coaxing flower bulbs to bloom, the Gatherers were stockpiling for the upcoming festival (still not enough nuts). The air was as intoxicating as ever. The fairies she passed greeted Ophelia with waves and wide grins. Nothing seemed amiss. If anything, there seemed to be a slight charge, an undercurrent of energy coursing through the Haven, and Ophelia returned the cheerful faces she met with a cautious smile. Maybe it wouldn't be so bad.

She arrived at the Tower and flew straight up to the 160th floor, taking some small delight in having two wings that worked, though her feelings of warmth faded the instant she knocked on Squint's door.

"Come in, Fidgets. And have a seat." His voice was gruff and growly as always.

Expect nothing. Anticipate everything. Ophelia took a deep breath. The chair looked even more uncomfortable than last time. She anticipated that. Her boss's face looked even more pinched. She anticipated that, too. This was going to be almost as much fun as being thwacked in the face with a broom.

"I see Pudge got you patched up nicely from your little run-in with the truck," Squint said, not bothering to look up from the sheaf of papers on his desk. She recognized the folder he was holding. It was her post-mission report, the one that she had completed yesterday afternoon as much out of boredom as a sense of responsibility. He'd obviously been reading it. "How's the wing?"

She told herself to be strong. To sit up straight. To hold her ground and take whatever the head of the guild dished out.

"Edna's very good at her job, sir."

"*Some* fairies are," Squint remarked shortly.

So much for confident. Ophelia felt herself shrink down in her seat. She began to fuss with the bottom button of her uniform, a clean one that Charlie had brought from her house and *said* he ironed himself, though she was certain he'd asked her neighbor to do it.

"Sir, I think I should exp—" she began, but Squint cut her off.

"First I talk. Then you talk," he commanded. "This is the Haven. Grant Tower. *My* office. And I am still your boss, even as you seem to think otherwise."

"Yes, sir," Ophelia murmured. She braced herself by gripping the arms of the chair while Squint scanned one of the sheets of paper before him.

"We had a lot of cleaning up to do, Fidgets. A *lot* of cleaning up. You left quite a trail. A discarded flight suit. An empty canister of sleeping gas. A grappling hook dangling from a window. Out of curiosity, were you *trying* to get caught, or are you really just that sloppy?"

That was a first. Ophelia Delphinium Fidgets: Guild's Sloppiest Fairy. "No, sir. Circumstances were such that I couldn't always clear the evidence."

"Circumstances. Yes. There were plenty of those, too, it seems," he said gruffly. Squint pulled a different sheet from the folder and began to read. "One human left unconscious by the side of the creek and another one telling anyone who would listen about some exotic, rare butterfly that chewed its way out of a net. Care to explain that?"

Ophelia pictured the look of disappointment on Anna's face. *Chewed her way out.* As if she were some kind of wild animal. That girl obviously had quite an imagination. "The mission turned out to be more difficult than I anticipated. I couldn't always follow protocol."

"Couldn't or chose not to?"

Ophelia squirmed in her seat, but she still managed to force a tiny smile. "A little of both, I guess?"

Squint pouted back at her. "Hmph. Well, the good news is the situation was contained without the need for additional expenditure of magic, and no serious harm was done to fay or humankind—outside your own injuries, of course. To the best of our knowledge, no one spotted you directly or otherwise acquired any tangible evidence of our existence."

Ophelia knew she shouldn't interrupt, that it wasn't her turn, and that the question she desperately wanted to ask would probably only make him angrier, but she couldn't help herself. "And what about Gabe?"

Squint put down her report and grunted again. "The boy? Per standard procedure in emergency situations, I posted a surveillance team outside the Morales residence, just to make sure the dust settled. Kept them there through the night and into the next day. The boy woke up not long after we left. Thinks he slipped and fell on the bank and knocked his head on a rock. Slept through the whole ordeal. His mother threatened to take him to the hospital, but he convinced her he was okay."

Ophelia let out a sigh of relief. Gabe was all right.

"*You*, on the other hand," Squint continued sharply, causing her to suck the breath back in. "You still have a great deal to account for." He began to make a list, counting off on his fingers. "Disregarding protocol. Willfully disobeying a direct order from a superior. Physically *assaulting* a superior."

Physically assaulting? Ophelia hardly thought snatching a nickel out of Squint's hands counted as *assault*, but she somehow managed to keep her mouth shut.

"All of this is troublesome enough," Squint continued, "and certainly cause for a severe reprimand, but violating the code? Purposefully choosing *not* to grant a chosen wish? Going against the will of the Great Tree and the entire Haven? It's hard enough keeping this place running without having rogue agents acting on their own agenda. Just think of all the things that *could* have happened."

"And exactly what *did* happen, sir?" Ophelia interrupted.

Squint stared her down across the desk, but she refused to flinch. She had to know, and Squint was the only one who could tell her. Grumbling, he rifled through the papers on his desk until he found what he was looking for. "This is the report from the surveillance team. Apparently the family got a phone call the day after the event."

The event. That was better than fiasco or disaster, she supposed. Ophelia shifted uncomfortably in her chair. "And?"

"*And* there was an incident. With the dad." Squint scanned the report. "Anthony Morales. Corporal in the United States Marine Corps. Stationed in Iraq. There was an explosion, apparently, and a piece of metal buried itself in his shoulder. Shrapnel, they call it. Terrible, the things these humans do to one another."

An accident? Ophelia shook her head. This couldn't be. She'd said the words. She'd completed the ritual. She'd *felt* it. *Amaratio.* This wasn't what was supposed to happen. "Is he . . . did he . . . ?" She couldn't bring herself to finish the thought.

Squint finished it for her.

"Magic works in mysterious ways, Agent Fidgets. It would seem that Corporal Morales was fortunate. The injury was not life threatening. They were able to remove the metal and close the wound. The phone call was to tell his family that he was okay. And that he was coming home.

"Looks like somebody got their wish," he added.

Ophelia slumped back into her chair, wings quivering, careful not to smile too broadly for fear of making Squint even angrier, but she could hardly help it. She could almost picture their faces when they heard the news. The phone shaking in Gabe's mother's hand. Anna's bright eyes as big as full moons. There would have been tears. Laughter. Promises for a celebration. Maybe a mad dash for markers and paper to start making a sign. *Welcome home.*

And Gabe? What would he think? Would he wonder if maybe, just maybe, this was his doing? Did he have any idea?

Squint seemed to be wondering the same thing.

"You know, Agent Fidgets, I've been around for two hundred seasons. I've seen thousands upon thousands of wishes granted, and even I don't understand how it all works sometimes. We can't always know the full consequences of our actions. What I *do* know is that we are granting more wishes today than we did the day before and the day before that. Maybe—just maybe—there's a little more magic out there than we realize, and we just have to find some way to tap into it. I'm not saying you granted the right wish or the wrong one, but there is definitely one boy out there who believes more than he used to."

Ophelia could tell there was something working behind those squinting eyes. "What are you getting at, sir?"

"That maybe it's time we rethink how we do things around here. Trust our own judgment as to what's worth granting. Maybe if we granted more wishes that *we* believed in, we could bring a little more wonder back to the world."

He must have seen the hopeful look in her eyes, because he quickly added, "This doesn't excuse what *you've* done, of course. You disobeyed me and put this entire Haven at risk, and I can't let that slide."

Here it was. Finally. Her punishment. What would it be? A demotion? Pushing papers for the rest of her days like Charlie? Or maybe Squint would just kick her straight out of the guild. She'd be transferred. But to where? They wouldn't let her be a Scavenger or a Scout, nothing that would let her out of the Haven. Maybe she could try her hand at becoming a Whisperer. She had a way with animals at least, provided they weren't geese. Or hawks. Or cats. She tensed up, readying herself for what came next.

"You were reckless and irresponsible, no question. Of course, on the other side of the coin, you also exhibited resourcefulness out there," Squint continued. "A lot of fairies would have called for backup at the first sign of trouble, but you gutted it out. You completed your mission and granted your wish. Just not the one you were supposed to. And because of *that*," Squint said, sitting stiff-spine-straight, "I've decided to put you on probation."

Ophelia shook her head. *Probation? That's it? For disobeying orders? For assaulting a superior?* "For how long?" she asked.

"The rest of the season," Squint replied. "After which you will be eligible for assignments again. Given how long you waited for your first one, the time should fly by. We'll make it effective starting tomorrow."

"Tomorrow?" she repeated. She assumed it would be *effective immediately*. Squint was an *effective immediately* kind of fairy.

"Yes. Well, you've still got some unfinished business to attend to," he said brusquely. "Here's the file with everything you need to know." He excavated a different folder from beneath the piles of paperwork on his desk and slid it across to her. On the top was one name: *Kasarah Quinn*.

Ophelia was confused. "But sir . . ."

"A promise is a promise, Fidgets," Squint reminded her.

"And the guild has a reputation to uphold. I don't have any magic to spare, of course. I've got thirty-three *new* wishes to grant today. But a resourceful and spirited fairy like you, well . . . I'm sure you'll think of something. Go talk to your friend Whistler. He has experience with this sort of thing."

"This sort of thing?"

"Making mistakes. And trying to fix them."

Ophelia took a deep breath before taking the folder. Then she stood up and moved uncertainly toward the door, afraid that if she said anything else, Squint would change his mind and have her booted from the guild anyway. She was nearly out of the office when he stopped her.

"Oh, and Fidgets?"

Ophelia turned slowly. "Yes, boss?"

"There are quite a few fairies out there who are going to hear about what you did and call you a hero. Rest assured, I am not one of them."

"I understand, sir."

"I know you do," Squint said. And then he winked at her. Or at least he might have.

With him it was impossible to tell.

50

The four-hour flight north was easier this time, in part because Ophelia wasn't almost run out of the sky by an airplane, but mostly because she had company.

The whistling helped pass the time.

She flew slower than usual (and at a guild-approved altitude of eight hundred feet) under the excuse that she didn't want to leave her companion behind, though truthfully she couldn't have gone any faster if she'd tried. Her left wing no longer hurt, but it wasn't quite as strong as it had been before, and Pudge had told her not to push it. Charlie kept telling her the same thing.

He *insisted* on coming along this time. That was no surprise; he'd wanted to the first time. The surprise was that, this time, Squint let him.

He'd been waiting for her the moment she came down from

303

Squint's office, sitting at her desk again, looking even more smug than usual. "Whatchya got there?" he asked, pointing at the folder in her hands, even though he already knew. It was his idea, in fact, pitched to Squint the day before. A way for Ophelia to make amends and for Squint to preserve his precious record. Zero ungranted wishes.

More or less.

The folder Squint gave her contained very little: Kasarah Quinn's home address. Some directions. A requisitions order for some supplies, including a full day's worth of camo. But no dust. The wish itself wasn't listed. It didn't matter, of course. She'd only heard Kasarah make it a million times already.

"It's impossible," she told Charlie, pushing his feet off her desk again. "You can't grant a wish without magic."

"Oh, you *can*," he said. "You just have to make some magic of your own."

That made no sense, of course. If fairies could just *make* magic whenever they wanted, they wouldn't be in this position to begin with. But Charlie told her not to worry. He had a plan.

Which of course only made her worry more.

They suited up—Ophelia going with sky blue this time and Charlie choosing something called hot-rod red, which clashed horribly with his hair—and packed their satchels. Charlie's was bursting with stuff (and he called *her* an overpacker), including a couple more M&Ms and a map he'd drawn himself. Squint didn't bother to see them off this time. Apparently his day was full of important meetings with Pouts and the other guild leaders about the current state of magic regulation in the Haven and the process by which wishes were fulfilled. *Maybe it's time we rethink how we do things around here.*

She secretly wished him the best of luck.

Four hours later she found herself hovering over ground that was much more familiar this time, passing the giant river and the ponds full of geese, swooping over the houses and fields that had marked her way before. "There's the mall." Ophelia pointed to the sprawling box of a building with its fountain full of coins. She wondered how many wishes had been added to it since she'd been there and if the old man had come and gathered them up again to buy another bowl of soup. She felt guilty for cursing him before. A dozen ungranted wishes transformed into a warm meal. There was another kind of alchemy at work there—one that fairies had no part in—but it weighed on her heart regardless.

She hoped that if the old man ever made a wish, she would get the chance to grant it.

They were just above the fountain when Charlie grabbed her arm and pulled her off course.

"Where are we going?" Ophelia asked, but Charlie said, "Trust me," and made her follow him for a change. She could tell he was happy to be out here, granting a wish for the first time in years; his whistling grew more boisterous than ever.

They touched down several ticks later in front of a sign that said *Big Al's Lot-O-Junk* and included a crude drawing of what

Ophelia assumed to be Big Al himself, complete with a big tummy, reminding her a little of a cat she'd met not too long ago. *We pay cash for your trash*, the sign said.

Big Al must have had a lot of cash to spare, because he had accumulated a whole world of rubbish. The place was a wasteland. Lopsided piles of metal and plastic as tall as houses, most of them just stacks of beat-up old cars, rolling turtles that had outlived their usefulness, their shells sent here for scrap. Dented dishwashers. Broken furniture. A rocking horse without a head. A pyramid of tires as tall as a tree. Even a mountain of old, cracked commodes. A huge chain-link fence ran around the perimeter, keeping out anything that couldn't fly or squeeze and scurry through the holes, like the mouse she noticed darting in and out of a toppled refrigerator. Otherwise the place looked deserted.

"Where are we?" Ophelia asked

"Junkyard," Charlie said. "Scavengers love these places. Easiest way to pick up artifacts without attracting too much attention. I mean, most of it's worthless. And filthy. And it smells bad. But occasionally you can find something valuable."

"Reminds me of your house," Ophelia told him, stepping over broken glass.

"Funny," he said. "Now close your eyes. I've got a surprise for you."

She rolled them first, but she shut them as ordered, then gave

Charlie her hand and let him lead her, afraid she would trip and impale herself on some jagged bit of scrap. She thought about Gabe's father, Corporal Morales. *Shrapnel, they call it.* But he was fortunate.

She wondered if *he* felt fortunate or not.

Charlie brought her to a halt. "All right. You can open them now."

Sitting in front of her was a bicycle. Sunflower yellow with a white wicker basket and tarnished silver fenders. The paint was chipped in places and the seat had a couple of small tears, but otherwise it seemed in good shape. She couldn't be sure, of course—she'd never rode one before. And recent events hadn't made her any fonder of things on wheels.

"The chain slipped, but that was easy enough to fix. The seat's a little worn, but otherwise it looks all right, don't you think?" Charlie beamed proudly.

"OMW," Ophelia said.

"I know, right?"

"I mean . . . it's terrific." And it was. She couldn't believe the effort he'd gone to find it, presumably while she was in the infirmary, on the mend. "Really, really terrific . . ."

"But . . ." Charlie goaded.

"But what?"

"But you trailed off, like, *Wow, it's terrific, Charlie, except for this one part that you completely screwed up and it ruined the whole thing,*" he said, doing a terrible, high-pitched imitation of her

307

voice. "So what's the problem?"

Ophelia shrugged. "Well. It's just . . . so . . . you know . . . *yellow*," she said at last.

"Ah," Charlie said.

"Which is *great*," she added quickly. "I love yellow. I *adore* yellow. But Kasarah, you know. She was kinda specific."

"Uh-huh," Charlie said.

"And if we're going to do this . . ."

"No. I gotcha. Enough said." He put two fingers in his mouth and startled her with a piercing whistle.

Ophelia heard feet scrabbling over gravel. Something large tearing around the corner. Something large and fast and probably a little bit smelly. Or a lot. Her throat clenched as a bundle of beige fur exploded from behind a smashed car, nearly bowling her over, paws kicking up tiny whirlwinds of dirt as he skidded to a halt beside her.

"Sam!"

Ophelia wrapped her arms around his neck and squeezed, burying her face in his fur. She fully expected to feel a warm tongue sliming her from head to toe, except Sam was holding something in his mouth, a canister much like the ones that contained Arnold Rolleye's knockout spray, only bigger. He dropped it at her feet and licked his chops.

The label on the front said *Quik-Dry EZ Paint*. The color of the lid was a rich, royal purple.

"I brought you a present," he said. He pawed at the can of paint, just in case there was any confusion.

"Oh, Sam. But how did you . . . *where* did you . . . ?" Ophelia stammered. She looked back and forth from fairy to dog.

"It wasn't easy," Charlie admitted. "Several blocks away a bunch of hardware store employees are probably still telling a story about a dog who snuck into their store and stole a can of purple spray paint. This mutt is a pretty good thief."

"I am a *very* good thief," Sam corrected.

Ophelia hugged him again, this time making sure to scratch behind the ears. His back leg thumped like a rabbit's as he let out a long groan of satisfaction.

"All right. Reunion's over," Charlie said, popping the lid off the can, which was nearly as tall as he was. "This bike isn't going to purple itself."

They set to work, Charlie holding the can while Ophelia pressed the button, Sam wandering around, sniffing everything (broken commodes included), looking for something worth burying in a hole. In between coats they savored Charlie's M&Ms and Ophelia told him all about her mission, from Olivier's insults to Anna's net, impressing him with her ability to find trouble at every turn. When they got to the part where Ophelia fell in the pond, Sam came over to sing his song.

She skipped the part about the stuffed bear. She knew she'd never hear the end of it.

Fortunately Big Al's didn't see a lot of business on weekdays, and the few people who wandered onto the lot just dropped off more garbage and left. It was easy for Ophelia and Charlie to stay hidden, and nobody thought twice about a scraggly-looking mutt hanging around a junkyard. But by the time the second coat was dry enough to touch it was already dark, and Big Al's front gate was shut and locked for the night.

"It's very purple," Sam said, squinting at it in the moonlight. Ophelia wasn't sure whether that meant he liked it or not. You couldn't eat it, but you *could* chase it, so it could go either way.

"Now we just need to find a way to get it to her," Ophelia said with a smirk. A locked gate posed little problem for two fairies, but neither the bike nor the dog came with wings. "Did you have a plan for that, too?"

"As a matter of fact, yes," Charlie replied, producing a set of wire cutters from his bag. "But it might require breaking a few rules. That is, if you think you're up for it?"

As if he even needed to ask.

51

They didn't break as many as she thought they would.

They *did* break Big Al's fence, leaving a gaping hole big enough to wheel a bicycle through, but it wasn't the first time Ophelia had been forced to make an alternative exit. And she supposed they owed the junkyard owner a replacement bike as well, but Charlie said not to worry, another one would come along. Humans are good at throwing out perfectly usable stuff.

The real difficulty came in the delivery. The path Charlie had drawn to Kasarah's house was long and convoluted, but it avoided large streets for smaller ones that were mostly empty by this time of night. A necessity, Ophelia soon realized, as anyone passing by might happen to catch a glimpse of something bordering on the inexplicable: a purple bicycle with no rider being towed by a stray dog and held up by two odd-looking, oversize dragonflies.

Of course a second glance would instead find that same bicycle lying on its side in the grass and the stray dog sniffing around some bushes or eyeing a fire hydrant with insidious intent. Not nearly as remarkable.

They'd had to perform the maneuver only twice. Both times, the passing cars slowed for a moment, the drivers shaking their heads, thinking they'd seen something too strange for words. But it was late. And dark. And it couldn't have been what they first thought, because *that* would be impossible.

By the time they reached the Quinn residence, the moon was beaming brightly, eyeballing them as if to say, *I know what you're up to.* Kasarah's house was small, pressed up tight against its neighbors, but the shutters were painted a robin's-egg blue, so Ophelia liked it already. The mat by the door said *Welcome* in a winding, leafy script that made her think of the Tree Tops. Most of the lights up and down the row of houses were off, but she thought she could see the silhouette of someone behind the curtain of an upstairs window and wondered if that might be the girl whose nickel had caused Ophelia so much trouble.

"Is that you, Kasarah Quinn?" she whispered. She looked again at the shadow in the window and then at the freshly painted bike. If the girl *knew* she would get her wish, would she make the same one? Would she wish for this? Or was there something she wanted even more but was afraid to ask for, thinking it impossible?

That was the trouble with wishes, Ophelia thought. They

were easy to make but hard to believe in. And even harder, sometimes, to grant.

Charlie helped her prop the bike up against the side of the house, then removed a pencil and a slip of paper from his satchel. He was full of surprises today.

"We should leave a note," he said. "It will be odd enough just finding it here. She will think somebody accidentally lost it."

Ophelia thought for a moment, and then quickly scrawled something down.

Kasarah,
Heard you lost your bike. Had one to spare. Hope you like the color.
Sincerely,
A well-wisher

"Clever," Charlie said.

"I thought so," she said, smirking.

They tucked the note into the spokes of the front wheel and stepped back to admire their work. Sam sniffed at the bike once and then wagged his tail in approval.

"I guess that's it, then," Charlie said with a stretch. "Mission *finally* accomplished. But as much as I'm enjoying being away from the Haven, our camo won't last forever. We should head home."

Ophelia nodded, thinking about the long flight back when

she felt something cold on the back of her neck. She turned to find Sam's snout in her face, staring at her with his saucer eyes. He nudged her again and then dropped to the ground, nose stuck between his feet. The little whimper that followed made him look perfectly pathetic.

Ophelia knelt down and scratched under his chin.

She turned to Charlie. "There's still one more thing we need to do."

52

A wish is many things. It is apprehension and anticipation. It is lucky coins and dandelion fluff and rainbows stretching to forever. It is *loves-me*s after *loves-me-not*s and a pile of plucked flower petals at your feet. It's purple bikes and getting picked first and a passing grade in math. It's the marvelous and the miraculous. It's hunger and heartache. A wish is something extraordinary that you never hoped to have.

Or something very ordinary that most people take for granted.

It took some time for her to find the right road, but eventually Sam picked up a familiar scent and led the way, offering both fairies a ride on his back. Ophelia taught Charlie how to hang on to his fur without pulling too tight. As Sam trotted along the side of the road, he and Charlie talked about food, namely doughnuts, Charlie describing something called a Bavarian crème–filled Bismarck that set Sam to salivating, drool actually dripping from his jowls.

"The inside is like vanilla pudding," Charlie said. "And it gushes out like gooey yellow lava when you take a bite. And the top is usually covered in chocolate, which gets all over your fingers and has to be licked off. It is, without a doubt, the pinnacle of human achievement."

Sam started to whimper. "Oh, I want one. I want one really, really bad."

Ophelia told them both to hush; she could see the house up ahead.

They stood by the yellow-and-black mailbox, at the edge of the gravel driveway leading past the crooked tree with its spinning tire to the red wagon waiting by the door. The kitchen light was the only one on. No doubt the kids were asleep. Perhaps everyone was. But it didn't matter. They wouldn't be for long.

Ophelia sat Sam down and told him what to do.

"Same as last time," she said. "Except even more charming."

"Oh. I am very charming," Sam insisted. Then to prove it he licked her from heel to scalp. His breath hadn't improved in the last few days, but she didn't mind so much anymore.

"Okay. That's just disgusting," Charlie muttered.

Ophelia wiped her face on her sleeve, then stood on her toes and kissed Sam's black, leathery nose. "Do you know what a haven is?" she asked him.

"Oh yes," Sam said. "Haven is where Ophelia is from. It is

up on the mountains and covered in trees and I am not supposed to go there because it's way too far and I will get lost."

"Yes. That's true. That's *my* Haven. But a haven is just a safe place. A place you can go to stay warm. Where nobody kicks you or calls you names. It's a place where people love you and take care of you, no matter what."

"Like home?"

"Exactly. Just like home."

Sam looked at the house, considering it, then back at Ophelia. "What if they won't take me?"

"Then we will find someone who will," she assured him. "But I happen to know a boy who really wants a dog and a girl who is purportedly an expert in belly rubs. Plus, if I'm not mistaken, you already have a hole around here somewhere."

"Oh yes. There *is* a hole," Sam said excitedly. "But there is nothing in it."

"Then I suggest you find some way to fill it, because empty holes are the worst." Ophelia scratched his chin and playfully tugged one whisker. "I'm going to miss you, Sam."

"You are a very good friend," Sam said.

He gave Ophelia one last nuzzle, then turned up the driveway to the front porch.

Ophelia fluttered up to the first branch of the big oak and Charlie sat next to her, watching and waiting as Sam started his routine, a volley of three barks to break the silence. She found herself crossing her fingers. It was pointless superstition, she knew—some ritual humans cooked up to give their hands something to do in tense moments—but she could appreciate that. Even superstitions had their purpose.

After several more barks the porch light blinked on and a man that Ophelia had seen only in pictures came to the front door. He was taller than she imagined and now had a thin beard that seemed like it could be wiped off with a napkin. Ophelia could see the bulge under his shirt where a bandage wrapped around his shoulder. His left arm was in a sling. *He has a broken wing*, she thought, *and he still found a way to fly home*. When the man saw Sam, he didn't holler or chase him away or turn and slam the door. He just stood there, watching.

And then he was joined by the boy and the girl, both of them rubbing their eyes, peering groggily around their father's legs. Until they spotted Sam; then it seemed they were instantly awake, blabbering, running outside straight up to the mutt without hesitation. Ophelia couldn't quite make out what they were shouting over each other, something about him being here before and practically eating a whole roast chicken and not having an owner or a place to live. The man joined them out on the porch, bending down and patting Sam gently on the head. Sam didn't flinch.

"C'mon, Sam. Turn on the charm," Ophelia whispered.

As if he could hear her, Sam licked the man's outstretched hand, barked once, and rolled over onto his back with his paws in the air again, exposing the soft white fur of his belly. Anna squealed with delight. The man shook his head and laughed.

Ophelia elbowed Charlie. "It's his signature move," she said.

"Yeah, it's pretty adorable," Charlie agreed. "For a dog."

The three humans huddled together, the man in the middle. Ophelia could see their earnest, pleading faces assailing him from either side, the word *please* on both their lips. If they'd been tugging on a turkey bone at that moment, it wouldn't matter who got the bigger half, the wish would be the same. The girl wrapped her arms around Sam's neck as if determined to hold on to him for an eternity. The boy tugged on his father's shirtsleeve.

The man peered out into the darkness, past the tree where Ophelia and Charlie were hidden, to a place that seemed far away. He looked again at the dog, then at his children. Then he turned and looked up at his wife, who was standing in the doorway now, dressed in a nightgown, a blanket draped around her shoulders. The man said something Ophelia— even with her fantastic ears—couldn't hear, and his wife replied with a shrug.

Suddenly the kids exploded in a chorus of incomprehensible shouts, dancing on the porch until their mother reminded them how late it was and hissed at them to get back inside. Corporal Morales stood up and whistled, pointing at the open door.

Sam scrambled to his feet and bounded up the stairs toward the house. He looked back once before disappearing. His tail waved good-bye.

"So long, Sam," Ophelia whispered. She smiled, then blushed when she noticed Charlie staring at her. "What?"

"Look at you. You're gloating."

"I'm not gloating."

"You're totally gloating," Charlie insisted. "It's all over your face. You're, like, the ultimate wish granter. Boy got his dad back. Girl got her bike. Dog got a home."

"And I got probation," she reminded him.

"Everything has a price," Charlie reminded her, channeling his own inner Squint.

She gave him a sharp elbow in his side. "But I did all right, didn't I?"

"For your first time out? Yeah. I'd say you did okay."

Ophelia stood up. It would nearly be morning by the time they got back. A new day. A whole new set of wishes to grant, hopefully even more than were granted today. Not for her, of course. Not yet. But that was all right. There was still that bottle of dandelion wine to break open, and she figured she could use a day or two, just sitting on her porch in her pajamas, watching the clouds slink by. She removed her goggles from her pack, rubbing them clean with her thumbs. Charlie stood beside her and shook out his wings. To a human watching, they probably would have looked like two birds preening. Probably.

Charlie took her hand, turning it palm up. "Let's say things are different, and there are no rules against fairies making wishes. Here's a penny—" He dropped an imaginary coin into her hand. "What do you wish for?"

"What? You mean right now?"

"Yeah, right at this very moment. What does Ophelia Delphinium Fidgets's heart desire, as we speak?"

Ophelia pursed her lips. What *would* she wish for?

She glanced back at the yellow house where three had become five—through alchemy or serendipity, luck or magic, or sheer force of fairy will, she wasn't sure anymore. The kitchen light was still on, and she thought she could hear laughter even though it was far away and she could just be imagining it.

She handed Charlie's pretend penny back to him.

"I think I'm good," she said.

She checked to make sure everything was tied down and buttoned up. She cracked her knuckles and rolled her shoulders, working out the kinks. She gave her left wing a flutter—almost as good as new. "Bet you can't beat me home."

"Bet you're right," Charlie replied. "But I guess anything's possible." He pulled his makeshift goggles down over his eyes and grinned.

Yes, she supposed it was.

Ophelia Delphinium Fidgets sprung from the branch and launched herself into the star-studded sky, her best friend whistling right behind her.

The last time you blew out your birthday candles, what did you wish for?

And did you get it?

If not, don't take it personally. There's only so much magic to go around, and fairies don't always do what they're told. But things are looking up and the odds are getting better. So the next time you see a rainbow or a fountain or a star, you might try again.

Just make it a good one.

A Brief Word about Fairies

Ophelia Fidgets is a fairly modern fairy. I write this because if this book happens to be your first and only exposure to her kind, you should know that she isn't emblematic of her species. She is much more the product of the last two centuries of fairy lore, of Victorian paintings and Hollywood animation, than of the many centuries of fairy myth and fantasy that came before. More Tinkerbell than Oberon, though there is still a hint of old mischief in her.

If you have any interest at all in fairies, I recommend you go to the library and gather some books about them. They are fascinating creatures—and not always the flighty, benevolent beings you'd imagine. Many don't even have wings; they aren't all the size of a hummingbird; and very few of them, if any, grant wishes.

Oh, and they are all just make-believe. I am 98 percent certain of this. Just as I am 98 percent certain that if you drop a penny in a well or a fountain and ask for something, you are probably just wasting a penny.

But I still do it. Every time.

Acknowledgments

When I was younger I wished on many coins and candles to be a published writer. Though I don't doubt that luck, serendipity, and perhaps even meddling fairies were factors in making that wish come true, fulfilling that dream has required the hard work and dedication of many gifted humans as well.

Thank the Havens for the team at Harper and Walden for their insight, encouragement, and publishing panache. To Jordan for his guiding hand, Deb for her endless support, and Danielle for her marketing savvy. To Katie, Amy, Renee, Christina, Daniel, Bethany, Viana, Alana, and Caroline for their creativity, contributions, and careful attention to detail. To Julie McLaughlin for capturing the whimsical nature of Ophelia's journey on the cover. To Kate Jackson and Donna Bray for running the show. To Josh and Tracy Adams, agents extraordinaire, for the magic they work on my behalf.

To my mother (who has painted fairies frolicking across one wall of her house): Thanks for nurturing my imaginative spirit. To my father: Thanks for making it home safe nearly fifty years ago.

To Alithea: Thanks for always being my own personal Haven. I couldn't have wished for a better companion.

And to Isabella and Nick: Fly high, follow your hearts, and make all your dreams come true.